DISCARD

Batter Off Dead

Batter Off Dead

A SOUTHERN CAKE BAKER MYSTERY

Maymee Bell

CROOKED
LANE

NEW YORK

Published in the United States by Crooked Lane Books, an imprint of The Quick Brown Fox & Company LLC.

Crooked Lane Books and its logo are trademarks of The Quick Brown Fox & Company LLC.

Library of Congress Catalog-in-Publication data available upon request.

ISBN (hardcover): 978-1-68331-878-1
ISBN (ePub): 978-1-68331-879-8
ISBN (ePDF): 978-1-68331-880-4

Cover illustration by Mary Ann Lasher
Cover design by Melanie Sun
Book design by Jennifer Canzone

Printed in the United States.

www.crookedlanebooks.com

Crooked Lane Books
34 West 27th St., 10th Floor
New York, NY 10001

First Edition: December 2018

10 9 8 7 6 5 4 3 2 1

To Eddy:
Odo nyera fie kwan.
Forever...

Chapter One

Six months ago, if you'd told me I'd be living in Rumford, Kentucky, my small-town childhood home, I'd have given you all sorts of funny looks. I would've denied any part of your statement and claimed that you were one rung shy of a full ladder.

After all, I'd been following my dream as a lead pastry chef in a swanky New York City restaurant for the last year. Little did I know, I'd been following the wrong dream.

One of my mama Bitsy's sayings was, *"Sophia Cummings, don't get above your raisins."* I didn't really take the time to understand it as a child, but I sure knew what she meant now. Life takes you in a direction you never saw coming, and if you're open to it, life can be pretty great. With the opening of For Goodness Cakes, my own bakery in the hometown I never figured I'd come back to, life couldn't be better.

"This beats anything I've ever seen before now." I

muttered to myself as I stood looking at the bakery display window in utter disbelief that this was my shop. My dream.

An audible sigh escaped me, and a smile stretched across my face as I read the bakery name printed across the glass. I stared at my reflection and into my dark brown eyes. My mouth began to water at the creations I'd displayed there, and I wondered how on earth I'd always managed to stay a normal-size body weight considering I made it a policy to taste-test.

"Are you lollygaggin'?" Charlotte Harrington, my best friend, asked as she pushed open the swinging door between the kitchen and the bakery. She tucked a piece of her long red hair behind her ear and stuck her palm on her hip. "We've got a lot of baking to do. Chop-chop." She clapped her hands.

"Quit your bellyaching—I'll get it done." I ran my hands down my white apron and pulled my shoulder-length brown hair up into a hairnet before I headed back to finish up some baking. "You'd think you were the boss," I teased her after I walked back into the kitchen.

"Someone's got to do it." She shook her head and went back to rolling out the red velvet dough that was just the perfect-color dessert for The Heart of the Town red carpet fundraiser we were catering for the new addition to the Rumford Library. I'd named the pastry Heart of Rumford and even used a heart cookie cutter to shape them.

"Orders aren't going to get made by you standing around all day," she joked.

Charlotte was my one and only employee at For Goodness Cakes. When I opened the bakery, there was no other person I could imagine being by my side. Charlotte and I had had each other's back since we were in preschool. When I'd made the decision in kindergarten that I wanted to be a baker, she played and made dirt pies on the playground with me, and had been my biggest cheerleader since.

She was a godsend because she was also a great baker. She was the type of person who could look around and know what to do without me even telling her what needed to be done. She'd even gone as far as doing some of her own baking and coming up with her own recipes when time allowed, and I loved that.

"The red velvet roll is going to pair nicely with the Pinot Noir, Shiraz, Syrah, or Zinfandel Rose," I said, mentioning a few of the wines Giles Dugan had sent over. The fundraiser was at Grape Valley Winery, his winery.

I thought Heart of the Town was a very clever name for the fund-raiser because it was true. Almost everything took place at the Rumford Library. It was the only building that had a couple of bigger conference rooms to accommodate town meetings. All the local business held their monthly meetings there; all the clubs helped keep the rooms booked; and even the Chamber of Commerce rented out a room each month. It was time we got a renovation and addition.

"I know. I'm so excited for the new addition to be revealed." Charlotte leaned on the counter. "Can't you just give me a little hint of what it looks like?"

"Mmmhhh," I hummed with my lips pinched together. "It's a big secret."

I'd seen the new library addition in person a couple of times because I needed to see the venue. Catherine Fraxman, the librarian, had booked For Goodness Cakes for the ribbon-cutting ceremony. It wasn't going to be nearly as posh as Grape Valley Winery since the ribbon-cutting ceremony also included children. The Winery fund-raiser was hosting all the big donors and spenders in Rumford. The ones that belonged to the Rumford Country Club—RCC for short. There was going to be plenty of wine, whiskey, and other booze to help get residents loosey-goosey and open up their wallets.

I was really excited Cat had asked me to do the desserts for the ceremony because it opened up my creative side, allowing me to make fun pastries with book and library-card themes. But it was Grape Valley Winery that'd help me pay the bills for a couple of months. Giles had ordered large quantities of expensive desserts.

I'd yet to get a good system down for how my clients paid. It was always a hard thing for me to decide whether they should put down a deposit or pay in full. With the winery, I knew they were good for the money, so they paid ten percent down. Ingredients I didn't keep in the bakery and had to order I put on my credit card, but I knew I'd be able to pay that off once Giles Dugan paid me for the event. So I wasn't too worried. Plus, the exposure to all the wealthy people the fund-raiser would give For Goodness Cakes and my creations a considerable boost. I could see it now: I'd be booked for weddings, holiday parties, birthdays, and any special occasion that required a dessert. I was in a win–win situation all the way around.

"You're going to love the green roof space. It'll be so nice to sit up there and read. Plus, Cat has lots of fun events planned," I said, referring to Catherine Fraxman by her nickname. I scooped butter into the electric mixer and switched out the attachment to the paddle so it would beat the butter into a light and fluffy mix while I prepared to make the batter. I flipped the switch to medium and grabbed a few metal cookie sheets to line them with parchment paper. "She said they need at least half a million in donations to pay the renovation loan off completely."

Charlotte's jaw dropped. "Half a million?"

"Yeah. I thought it was a little steep too." I didn't know a thing about fundraising or how long it took to raise that sort of money, but I did know Grape Valley Winery was going all out for the big event, including bands, catering, and wine tasting. Plus, some of the wine sale proceeds would go toward the library. "If I know Giles Dugan, I'm sure he'll do all he can to make sure he gets the money raised."

"Standing here gabbing isn't going to get the pastries baked for the upcoming orders." Charlotte nodded to our dry-erase board with the days of the weeks on it. It was perfect for writing down orders.

"We have the Heart of the Town Fund-raiser tonight, which we'll mainly focus on today. Then I know Bitsy will volunteer us to do something for the Garden Club meeting this week." My brow twitched at the thought of how Bitsy volunteered me for anything and everything she was involved in. "I've got a meeting with Perry Dugan this week about doing an employee cake for Reba Carol. And we have a couple of kids' birthday cakes."

A few minutes later, I started to wash the dishes and utensils we'd already dirtied up from the Heart of Rumford cookies. It was one of those times when you looked at something and didn't even remember all the steps. I was on automatic pilot. Charlotte got the Heart of Rumford red velvet hearts in the oven. The bell over the shop door dinged, and I walked into the bakery to find Bitsy standing there.

"Speak of the devil," I muttered under my breath. Not that my mama was the devil; Bitsy Cummings—she just had some very Southern roots. That meant she wanted me to go to college, get an education that I'd shelve because I met a good Southern boy with solid roots, have babies, be a homemaker, and join all the clubs she's in.

"What on earth is all over your face?" I asked her after I noticed there was something on it.

"For goodness sakes, is that any way to properly greet me?" she asked, using her favorite saying. It was how I came up with the bakery name.

"I just saw you last night at the Junior League meeting," I reminded her. "It was like ten hours ago."

"It's the next day." Bitsy was sassy and raring to go. "Good early afternoon. Now, get over here, and give me some sugar," she said in her Southern voice, her arms outstretched. She was covered in dirt for no discernible reason.

Trust me when I said Bitsy was the epitome of a Southern woman who never got her hands dirty, much less her face.

"Oh, Sophia." There was displeasure in her voice. "Must you look so"—her eyes ran up and down my body—"*drab* when you work?" She patted the hairnet and forced a smile. "Do you have to wear that?"

"I'm baking," I gently reminded her. "Working."

"Being well-dressed is a beautiful form of politeness, and you could stand to be a whole lot politer." Bitsy had a way with words.

It was no big secret Bitsy wasn't the least bit happy that I'd decided to leave Rumford when I was eighteen years old and fresh out of high school. I set off to pursue my love of baking by enrolling in pastry classes instead of becoming a debutante. Not for a second did I believe she wasn't proud of me. She was, and many Rumford residents and customers told me so when they'd come into the bakery.

I could hear her now.

"You're not going to college?" She held her hand up to her chest like she was going to faint. Then she moved the back of her hand to her forehead. She cried, "You need an education. No one can take away your education." Needless to say, it was a trying time, but we all muddled through it.

"What have you been doing?" I asked her. Most of the things Bitsy said I had to let roll off my shoulders, or we'd never get along.

"A little of this and that." Her head tilted side to side.

"What's on your face?" I pulled the edge of my apron up and attempted to brush whatever it was off her face. "A new mud mask?" I joked. "I'm not sure, but I think you're supposed to wash it off before you go out in public."

"Gardening." She lifted her chin in the air.

"You've been gardening?" I asked. You could've blown me over with a feather. The only "gardening" I'd ever seen Bitsy do was to open a bag of carrots from the refrigerator or pick through a salad when we went out to supper.

"At this time of the day? After church?" There was something not adding up.

"The Garden Club plant and flower exchange is coming up. We've got to bring in a few samples this week to the meeting. You're bringing the sweet treats. Or have you already forgotten?" she asked, spacing her words evenly apart.

She was a master at turning a bad spotlight away from her onto somebody else. In this instance, it was bad. Bitsy never gardened.

She moseyed over to the glass counter that showcased some of my favorite cake designs, and eyeballed them.

"Nope. I've not forgotten." The Garden Club president, Dolores Masters, had contacted For Goodness Cakes and placed an order for the big event.

I pointed to one of the apple scones, and she shook her head.

"I've been planting," she said as if she were offended. "And digging up so I can take the plants I've grown."

"You? Planting? Digging? Growing?" I burst out in shock.

"What? I can plant a seed or two." She glanced up at me as if she wanted to see if I'd fallen for the clear lie she was trying to feed me.

"I know. You better be nice to me. You're gonna miss me when I'm dead and gone. Now, give me some of your father's favorite." She huffed and took a look around the bakery. "I'm assuming we'll see you tonight at the Heart of the Town fund-raiser?"

"Yes, you will." I turned around and took one of the white to-go boxes that had a logo with a domed cake stand in pink, and "For Goodness Cakes" written in teal where the cake was supposed to go. It was an adorable logo I was really proud of. "These were made this morning, so Dad will love them," I said, referring to the Nanner mini pies my dad adored. I put them into the box and drew a heart on the top with a black marker.

"Isn't that so cute?" Bitsy tapped the heart after I handed the box to her. "We raised over two thousand dollars from the girls at the Junior League. I can't wait to give the donation check to Cat tonight."

"That's great." Because I was an only child, when I moved away ten years ago, there was a little bit of guilt for leaving Bitsy here, though she still had my dad. I loved that she'd stayed in all of her groups and committees. "The new addition to the library is going to be so beautiful."

"Speaking of beautiful, you've got everything looking so nice in here." Bitsy looked around.

"I can't believe that I own the old Ford's Bakery." It was a dream come true. "Remember all the times you would bring me in here?"

"Do I?" Bitsy's brows lifted. "I couldn't get you out of that display window for anything."

"Oh, I'd get out with the bribe of one of the famous Ford's Maple Long Johns," I said.

Both of us stared at the display window, remembering through different eyes. Fond memories for us. Well, for me at least.

"You did love those Long Johns." Bitsy licked her lips. "There was a line out the door with people waiting to buy them. I remember Dixie Ford always saying she felt like she was herding cattle, but with customers." She laughed and looked around. "You could use some customers."

"We aren't open today." I pointed to the sign on the door, with the Heart of the Town flyer covering the bakery hours. "Remember, closed on Sundays?"

"Oh, I might've remembered if you were sitting in the pew next to your father and me at church," she said mockingly.

"I had to get all the yummies made for the fund-raiser. The fresher the better." Another thing Bitsy loved was going to church. She especially loved going to church with the whole family because she was a very proud Southern woman who loved to show off what she'd brought up. Daddy and me.

I put the box of Dad's treats on top of the glass case.

"Speaking of Ford's Bakery . . ." I motioned for her to stay put while I headed to the office space, through the door on the right when you came into the bakery. I didn't use it as an office and figured it'd be a good storage room. "You aren't going to believe what I found." I wiped my hands down my apron and opened the door.

"A stash of cash?" she asked, upbeat.

"I found something much better than cash." I flipped the light on, ignoring her questions, and picked up the old leather-bound journal on the desk. "The Fords' journal."

I walked back into the bakery and handed the journal to her. She flipped through and barely looked up at Reba Gunther when she came through the front door.

"Hi, Reba." I gave a half smile. "I'm sorry. We're closed on Sundays."

"I know you're not open today, but I was wondering, since I saw you in here when I was walking past, if I could just go ahead and buy some pastries for tomorrow. After all, you know how cranky Giles gets if I don't bring in a couple of those Cherry Flip-Flops." She put her hands in prayer position. "Please? I've got something to do in the morning, and I'll barely be able to make it to work on time."

"No problem," I said. "But I do hope those Dugans

know how hard you work for the winery. Even on your off day." Reba was the secretary for the winery.

I grabbed a box from behind the counter and filled it up with Cherry Flip-Flops. I'd intended to put them out the following morning, but my customer was here now. Besides, I had more in the freezer that I could easily pop in the oven, and voilà—perfection.

"I'll see you two at the fund-raiser tonight." Reba handed me the cash. Her soft red hair was cut in the cutest pixie cut that only she could pull off. Though she was about to turn forty, she sure did look a lot younger.

"You don't want me to put it on the winery tab you have open?" I asked. She came in every weekday to pick up some donuts and paid the bill once a month.

"Not today." She waved off and was on her way.

I went back to my conversation with Bitsy. "It's all of their recipes."

I couldn't believe my luck. When I'd been cleaning out the office to make it my own, I came across the journal. I put the cash in the drawer and walked back over to Bitsy.

"I made a phone call to see if I could buy the some of the recipes from them." Saying this reminded me to call again since I'd yet to hear back.

"Why can't you?" she asked. "You bought the place, and that includes everything in it."

"It's not so simple." I loved how Bitsy thought, and wished I could do as she said, but it was the Fords' intellectual property. There had to be some sort of law against it. "Maybe I can check with Dad."

Dad was a lawyer and had taken over his father's law firm, which made a great living for our family. So much so that Bitsy never worked outside the home. As in work for a paycheck, because she'd tell you she'd been working all day. Dad adored her nonetheless. He stayed busy but still came home every night to eat supper with her.

"He would know." She ran her hand down a page. "Their Long Johns. I wondered how they made them so perfectly."

When she gave me back the journal, I looked at the page. They did make the best Long Johns, and it was so tempting to recreate them, but it didn't seem right. When I'd read the recipe after finding the journal, I hadn't noticed anything special about the donut that wasn't already common knowledge. But their Long Johns didn't taste like the common recipe.

"I still want to check with Dad. Are you both coming to the fund-raiser tonight?" If they were, I was sure I'd have time to ask him then.

"We are. Your father pledged a nice donation to Cat, and she insists he give it at the fund-raiser along with Ray Peel's donation." She shivered with excitement. Bitsy loved a good fund-raiser, especially where a lot of money was to be given.

"Ray Peel?" I asked.

"Yes. The Friends of the Library are all aflutter with his pledge. It's about time he gives his share for this town." Her fine silky eyebrows rose a trifle. She leaned in to whisper a little gossip: "Half a million dollars."

"Half a million?" My jaw dropped.

"Cat is beyond excited. She was shaking when she told us. This means we don't have to hold any more fund-raisers after the addition is built. The loan they took out with the bank will be free and clear. I can't wait to see Bob Bellman's wife tonight. I heard he got a big, fat check for landing the loan from the bank."

"I bet." I still couldn't get past the fact that Ray Peel had donated half a million dollars.

"The Friends of the Library can continue to bring the library to the public and not worry about things like a silly little mortgage on the expansion." Bitsy had been a member of the Friends of the Library since before I was born.

Bitsy was a member of practically every club, society, and gossip circle in Rumford.

She lifted the edge of her sleeve and checked her watch. "I've got to run. And your father will be so happy to see you at the fund-raiser." She held the box in the air and played the guilt card. "You've been so busy here, we've missed you for supper or even just a drop by."

"I know. I'll be over soon." I smiled and hugged her.

"Then I'll see you tonight," she said. "Your father is going to love these."

"I'll see you tonight." I gave her one last hug before I walked her to the door and made sure she got into her car and didn't come back.

The old Ford's Bakery sure didn't look the same. I couldn't stop the smile from curling up on the edges of my lips when I turned around and saw all the changes I'd made. The old lights had been replaced with some hanging jeweled chandeliers. The glass display counter had been replaced with a long antique credenza I'd painted with white milk paint. A three-shelf glass display case sat on top of the credenza. The crisp lighting in the case really showed off the beautiful cookies, hand pies, donuts, and other sweet pastries. On the top, I placed domed cake plates holding delicious to-go cakes. All the old walls had been covered with white shiplap, and the floors had been replaced with white tiles. It was a sea of white with colorful treats to give it the perfect pop to make it cozy and inviting.

It was the display windows that were the most fun. Kentucky was a beautiful state in all four seasons. Each season required a different level of comfort in our food. It was no different with desserts. A heavy winter chess pie wasn't a big seller in the spring, so when I opened For Goodness Cakes, I knew I was going to cater to the seasons. The display window showed off the amazing spring season we were having.

There were two trees on each side of the window with white bud flowers and a mossy floor. Each tree trunk had a garland of magnolia leaves wrapped around it. I'd taken an old park bench I'd found in the antique store, painted it in white, and set four cake plates on top, each with a different spring cake.

"Are you okay?" Charlotte stuck her head out of the kitchen. "I heard Bitsy carrying on out here. Was she giving you some grief?"

"I'm good." I released a happy sigh. "No, I'm great. Let's get this all finished up before we run out of time."

As we headed back to the kitchen, the front bell dinged again.

"Mother, I'm busy." I twirled around on the ball of my foot, expecting to see Bitsy standing there to tell me one more thing she'd forgotten, but it wasn't her. A very chic blonde, who was obviously an out-of-towner, was standing in the door, carrying a very expensive handbag. Like the one I had wanted when I lived in the city.

"Oh." I was embarrassed. "I'm sorry. I thought you were someone else. I'm sorry, but we are closed until Monday. We aren't open on Sundays."

"Not even for catered orders?" The lady didn't look like she was going to take no for an answer, as she stepped right up to the counter in her black sky-high heels and very stylish blue cotton-sheeting jumpsuit. Her hair, though I could tell it was dyed, was the perfect shade of blonde, with the right number of highlights that no hairdresser around here could do. In fact, I only knew of one whose work was this perfect, and that was when I lived in Manhattan.

"I heard this was the absolute best place to come for

some fabulous pies and cakes." She snapped her purse open and took out a business card.

"Seeing as how your only other option is the grocery store, I'm going to have to agree with whoever told you that," I said.

"And she's being too modest," Charlotte chimed in, "For Goodness Cakes is the best Southern bakery in all of Kentucky." Charlotte was a little too overprotective. "If you don't believe me, you can walk right on out that door and see for yourself."

"Thanks, Charlotte," I said through my teeth like a ventriloquist, smiling. "I've got it covered."

Charlotte moved her head slightly to the right to see the woman over my shoulder before she focused back on me. I waited until she went back into the kitchen before I turned again to the woman.

"I'm sorry. We've got a big event," I started yammering, and once I get started it's hard for me to stop. "I mean, biggest we've ever done, and we keep getting interrupted. What is it I can do for you?"

"If you're the best in *all* of Kentucky, then you must cater my lunch event on Monday. I'm the president of the National Wine Tasters of America, and we're holding our annual shareholders' meeting at the Grape Valley Winery in a couple of days. I know it seems like short notice, but this is how I operate every year. I come into town and pick the best place for dessert, even though we've already got a food caterer. It's hard to get the caterers to realize I don't want their desserts, just the food." She swept her hand with the business card up in the air and held it out to me. Even her manicure was perfect. "Lanie Truvinski."

"You're going to love the winery. In fact, that's the big catering gig I've got tonight." I pointed to the flyer on the door. "The Heart of the Town fund-raiser. It's going toward the new addition to our library." I had high expectations of this event since the socialites were going to be there, and they loved to host parties, which meant referrals for me. "You should come. The more, the merrier." I stuck her card next to the register.

"Then you have to take my job. I'll pay you double your going rate." She ignored my invite and gave me an offer I couldn't refuse. It was money I needed to help pay off the debt from the updates to Ford's Bakery. "Besides, I'm getting a great deal on the place from Ray Peel. A longtime friend."

"Deal." Even though her event was a day away. "I only make pies and cakes for the season. For the spring I have some wonderful crumble cakes and Sunshine Lemon Pie. Every day I serve donuts, cookies, and other usual pastries."

Not that she was looking for everyday treats/pastries/ sweet. There I went again, yammering on.

"What is the light pink one in the front window with the cute macarons on top?" She pointed over her shoulder.

"That's Macaron Delight. A delicious three-layer cake. Fluffy chocolate, vanilla, and strawberry layers with some buttercream and strawberry jam filling." A very satisfied sigh escaped me. "I love using jams this time of the year from our local farmers' market. I try to use all ingredients made locally."

"I definitely want one of those. How do you think it'd pair with wine?" she asked.

"I'd pair it with a nice Moscato." I nodded with confidence. "It works well with strawberry."

"I'm going to have to agree with your employee. You do know what you're talking about." She plunked her purse on the counter and pulled out a wad of cash. "You are worth your weight in gold. How much?"

A few decisions later, Lanie Truvinski was walking out the door a very happy customer.

"Not too shabby for a day we aren't open," I said after I told Charlotte about the whole Lanie Truvinski conversation. "She said she got a great deal from Ray Peel to hold her convention there."

"Maybe there'll be more events held at Grape Valley, since wineries are becoming so popular in Kentucky." Charlotte stood next to me, and we watched Lanie get into her fancy silver car.

"Let's hope so." I turned and smiled at her. "It's proving to be good for business. But I thought Ray Peel only owned the land the winery was on, not the actual winery."

"Who cares?" Charlotte pulled the Heart of Rumford pastries out of the oven. "As long as we are getting paid, I don't care who owns what."

Chapter Two

"This is much better than the little Corolla." Madison Ridge greeted me at the Grape Valley Winery's barn they'd converted into the offices.

Charlotte, Madison, and I were always together as children, and as adults it wasn't any different.

"There was no way I could carry all my catered items in that little four-door." I patted the old RV that Poochie Honeycutt had found for me from the only used car lot in Rumford. "This way I can take the items straight from the oven and put them on the baking racks inside the bakery bus."

"Bakery bus?" Madison laughed and shook her head.

"Yes. And the passenger side opens up like a food truck, so I can take it to children's events or even business events that are set up outside." It really was a neat vehicle, and I was pretty pleased how it had turned out; another expense I was going to help pay off. "But I still have the Corolla for personal use."

When I'd moved back to Rumford, I'd had to use

Bitsy's car, but rather quickly realized I needed my own. Poochie also owned the gas station in town. He'd been so nice helping me get a car, I gave him free pastries for life—and he did come in on a regular basis for a sweet treat.

"What are you doing here?" I asked Madison, trying not to lose focus from the amazing landscape.

The vineyard was nestled to the right of the offices and appeared to be rolling for miles along the nooks and crannies of the holler. The grapes were round and fat. They'd be perfect for picking in a few months.

"I'm here to see Ray Peel." Her brows drew up. Ray was a very wealthy bachelor in Rumford who had been a couple of years ahead of Madison and me in school

"Seems like a lot of people are looking for Ray Peel." I laughed. "I heard he's giving Friends of the Library half a mil. That's all they need to pay off the new renovation." It was gossip and I probably shouldn't've said anything, but it was juicy gossip. Not many people around these parts saw half a million dollars, much less gave it away.

Madison's gaze narrowed.

"And his generosity doesn't stop there." I was talking to my best friend, so it just felt like girl talk. "He donated the use of the winery to the National Wine Tasters of America convention that's here in a couple of days. The president of the convention paid me rather nicely to make some desserts."

"That's odd. He's thinking about selling the land." Slowly she nodded when she saw my shocked reaction.

"This land?"

"Yes." She leaned in. "But it's hush-hush. He's getting an estimate from me on what I could list it for." She rubbed her fingers and thumb together in a big-payday gesture. "It would really help me out with getting that new car. I've been up since the crack of dawn working on numbers and crunching comps to see what we can ask for it."

"What about the winery?" I asked. A knot formed in my gut. I should've gotten my check for this event up front. "Is it going to stay?"

"I have no idea. I'm assuming the Dugans will still lease the land from the new owners." She shrugged.

Her words made me feel somewhat better, but still something just felt off. First off, I'd never known Ray Peel to give anything to anyone. That's how he'd gotten to be a millionaire. He'd been a shrewd businessman and taken after his own father. One standout memory I had that probably shaped my image of Ray was a story I'd overheard Bitsy and my dad talking about when I was a little girl. Dad mentioned how Ray's mama had left a note on the kitchen table to Ray's dad telling him she was leaving. They never heard hide nor hair from her afterward. Ray's dad died right after Ray got out of high school, and it was then Ray had taken over his dad's properties. After that I lost track of him and hadn't kept up with him the last ten years.

The office door opened, catching our attention.

"Shh." Madison flipped around, her eyes big. "Don't say anything."

She turned back to face the doors with a big smile on her face and a different tone in her voice.

"Ray." Madison rushed forward with her hand stuck out for him to shake. "I'm thrilled you've given me this time to talk to you."

"Madison," Ray said, nodding. "I expected to see you here, but not little Sophia Cummings." He strolled over to us. "I've got to get down to your new bakery. It's been the talk of the town. Plus, your Cherry Flip-Flops are delicious."

He stood six feet tall with a hint of gray in his coal-black hair. He had a slim, muscular build and nicely rounded biceps snuck out from under the short-sleeved shirt. You could tell he was a man who took very good care of himself.

"Oh," I said, smiling. "You've eaten my Flip-Flops?"

"Reba Gunther brought me some today and they were divine. Better than the ones you can get at fast-food restaurants." He rocked back on his heels.

I wasn't sure if that was a compliment or not, but I decided to roll with it.

"You'll get to sample some more at the fund-raiser," I said. "Which reminds me, I need to get in there and see Reba about my set up." I smiled at them. Really, I wanted to get in there and see her about my payment. I couldn't help but wonder why she'd given Ray the Flip-Flops when she said they were for Giles Dugan in the morning.

I reached in the van and took out a box I'd filled with some of my original peanut butter and jam sandwiches. It wasn't enough for me to spread locally made strawberry jam between two homemade peanut butter cookies; it was the buttercream mixed in with the strawberry jam that made this sweet treat a customer favorite.

*   *   *

I could've made more small talk, but I could tell Madison was really excited about the possible listing for her real estate office. She'd been waiting to bag a big fish so she could get a new car. She was hauling her two little kids all over Rumford in her parents' old wood-paneled station wagon.

"I've been thinking about your property," Madison tucked her hand in the crook of Ray's arm and led him off in the direction of the vines.

I headed on into the converted barn. The dirt floor had long been replaced by hardwood, and the haylofts had been taken out, making way for some industrial lighting. They'd kept the big open area in the front and built two offices in the back: one for Ray and the other for Giles. Made sense for Giles to have one since he did lease and harvest the vineyard.

Reba's desk was the first big desk in the middle as soon as you came in the door. Beyond her there were a couple of desks on each side. Tammy Dugan's name was printed on the wooden nameplate on one. Tammy was Giles's daughter, and word around town was she was really the one running the winery and was the money behind it.

"Do not tell me those are peanut butter and jelly sandwiches?" Reba's eyes light up.

Perry Dugan had contacted me about doing a special birthday cake for her, which was the only reason I knew her age. He asked me to keep it hush-hush because it was a surprise. Perry had made an appointment for later in the week to come pick something out.

"Okay." I ho-hummed. "I'll go put them back in the van."

"Don't you dare," she gasped with a big grin and outstretched arms, fingers doing the *gimme here*.

"I don't know. You didn't seem like you wanted them," I teased, and I handed her the box before she could pounce on me.

"Seriously, Dad." Giles Dugan and Tammy walked in the front door. They hurried past Reba and me.

When Giles Dugan looked at me, I said, "I'm glad you enjoyed the Cherry Flip-Flops. I'll be sure to bring some out again."

"Cherry what?" He looked at me.

"The pastries from Sophia's new bakery." Reba bit her lip nervously.

"Oh, yeah." He nodded, but I could tell by the blank look on his face that he had no clue what Reba was talking about.

It was odd, to say the least, but I wasn't going to waste any time on trying to figure out what Reba Gunther had going on. I just wanted to get paid, since I hadn't had them make a deposit. Lesson learned. Tammy didn't even notice me standing there.

"You can't just lie down and not fight Ray on this. This

is not right. This will impact not only the rest of your life and retirement, but mine and your grandchild's future. Paul is planning on going Ivy League, and if I'd known I was going to be out of a job, I'd have been saving for it. Are you going to tell him that he can't go because you couldn't stand up to Ray Peel? Well, by gosh, I will stand up to the jerk." Tammy continued to talk into her father's ear as they walked to the back of the building and into the office.

"I'm going to eat all of these before the day's over." Reba took a bite and nervously chewed.

"What's going on?" I asked.

"Giles just doesn't remember all the food he's had today. He really wants to make a good impression on the community with the fund-raiser since it's the first one they've hosted for the town," Reba said.

"I'm glad he likes the Flip-Flops," I said, knowing she hadn't even given them to him and had lied to me. "What's Tammy talking about? Why would she be out of a job?"

"Ray Peel wants to sell the land and not renew the winery lease that's coming due." She stuffed a full cookie in her mouth. "This week."

"This week?" That's why he wanted to see Madison.

Her chin drew an imaginary line up toward the ceiling and back down toward the floor in a dramatic nod.

"Can't they open a new winery somewhere?" I asked. I had no knowledge of how to make wine or even how the grapes were grown.

She shook her head and swallowed. "Grape Valley is

known for their sweet grape, which comes from the amazing limestone found here on this land. When the Dugans decided to make wine, they did a lot of research. That's when Giles made the lease agreement with Ray."

"There's plenty of limestone all over Rumford." It wasn't a secret that Kentucky's nickname, the Bluegrass State, was because the grass had a slightly blue tint from the rich limestone soil.

"Apparently not for growing the grapes for the wine that's made here. Giles even paid for some soil tests around Rumford to see if any matched the quality they have here, and there's nothing else like it." She glanced over her shoulder.

"So they're just going to close up if Ray sells?" I asked.

"I'm afraid it's their only choice. At least that's the way Giles sees it." The stress had found its way into the creases between her eyes. "It's a shame too. He's been doing so well since his wife died. He put all he had into this company, and with one swoop it's gone." Her lips turned down. She reached for another cookie, and her face relaxed. She bit into it. "This is so good."

"And the Cherry Flip-Flops didn't change his mind?" I joked, but Reba didn't laugh. I tapped the box of peanut butter and jam sandwiches. "I'm glad I could bring some comfort to you today." I was going to ask for the money they owed me for the catering, but right now didn't seem like the right time. "Where do you want me to set up?"

"You can go on down to the visitor's center where we do the wine tastings and selling. They've got a nice big tent for you to set up there. I drove by there this morning to make sure they had your tables set up." The phone rang. "Let me know if you need anything. Thank you for the cookies." She grabbed the phone receiver. "Good afternoon, Grape Valley Winery."

When Reba paused to listen to the phone, Tammy's voice echoed off the old barn walls and into the air as she stomped by: "Where is that low-down dirty dog? He's going to hear what I have to say, even if it's the last thing he ever hears!"

I quietly made my way out of the offices. This was my first big job, and I was already out a lot of money; I sure hoped they had enough to pay me.

At least the sun was shining, and it was turning out to be an unusually warm day for spring. Mother Nature had decided to grace us with an early budding, and the trees were nice, full of vibrant leaves that could be seen across the rolling hills of the vineyard, as were the swaying sea of colors from the wildflowers.

As I drove the van toward the visitors' area of the winery, I saw some employees already out in the vines and picking the grapes. It was a big operation to run a vineyard. It made me sad to realize just how many families would be impacted by Ray's decision to sell the land. Especially since there weren't any other vineyards in Rumford.

For now, I had to put all that in the back of my head. I needed to stick with the commitment at hand. The fundraiser for the library needed to be at the forefront, and since the wealthiest of Rumford were going to be in attendance,

I just knew they'd taste my delicious treats and hire me to cater more of their events. There was a rainbow in every dark cloud, I thought as I parked the van.

The winery was also a renovated barn, with a café that sat along the bank of a small lake with an amazing view of the vineyards. They had a gift shop inside of the winery, carrying the Grape Valley Winery logo on everything you could possibly imagine: shirts, cups, glasses, plates, napkins, purses, and their own signature bottles. There were three bars where customers could purchase drinks as well as taste the wine. One bar was inside and two bars were outside under a covered patio that included a dance floor, where the band was setting up. There were at least twenty round banquet tables with ten white folding chairs circling each. Empty bourbon barrels had been made into tabletops, and empty bottles with the winery label served as centerpieces with the most beautiful array of Kentucky wildflowers that I was sure came from the land right here on the winery.

There were so many people running around getting ready for the fund-raiser, I wasn't sure whom I needed to check in with, so I just started to pull the trays of pastries off the baking racks and put them on the tables before I retrieved the mobile display cases.

"Let me help you." Madison ran up to the van. Her face was as red as a tomato. Her jaw was set, and she huffed a couple of times.

I pushed the display case to the edge of the van, and she jerked it.

"Be careful. These were expensive, and they can break. I really need this job to help pay them off." I peered around the case and looked at her when she didn't respond with her typical positive words about how much Rumford needed the bakery and how I was going to be a huge success. "Uh-oh, you look really mad."

"That Ray Peel—he's a jerk." She tugged a little more and grabbed one side while I grabbed the other. We placed it on the ground. "If I weren't a good Southern girl, I'd strangle him with one of the grapevines out there."

"Lucky for us"—Catherine Fraxman, the librarian, had snuck up behind us—"that you're a good Southern gal. And no one is touching him until I get the money he's donated for the new addition to the library." She winked and pulled her long black hair behind her shoulders. She pushed her red glasses up on her nose and reached to help Madison with the end of the display case. "Let me help y'all."

"Thanks." I was glad to see her since she was the one in charge and it meant the fund-raiser was in full swing. I could go get the winery payment before the night was over. "Are you getting excited?" I asked after we set the case on the ground.

"I am. I don't know what Ray did to you, but I'm excited to see his big donation push us over the goal." She pursed her lips in satisfaction. "You have no idea how much the library needs his donation. A true lifesaver."

Lifesaver was a bit over the top, but like I said, no one in Rumford had ever just given away half a million dollars.

"I can tell you . . ." Madison started to grumble, but Cat's phone rang, and she quickly answered it.

"Over there," Cat whispered and pointed to the area where she wanted me to set up. "Hi, Ray. I just got here."

Madison rolled her eyes and took a deep sigh. She reached down and unlocked the wheels. She shoved the moveable case faster than the wheels could go.

"I'm not sure what's going on with you, but you're going to have to push slower on this gravel." I tried to steady the case so it wouldn't tip as she shoved it toward me, pushing it across the gravel parking lot and into the grass. We ended by the gazebo that had a perfect view of the lake and the entire vineyard.

Madison stopped; her eyes grazed my right shoulder. I turned around to see what she was glaring at.

I instantly recognized Lanie Truvinski, the president of the wine convention. "I know that lady." Ray Peel was walking up to Lanie, and he appeared to be on his cell phone. The big smile on Lanie's face didn't go unnoticed. "She's the woman that placed the big order this morning."

"What order?" Madison's voice was harsh with frustration. "Who is she?"

"She's the one I told you about that's in town for a wine convention." I shrugged. "Why do you ask?"

"I thought she might be some high-falutin' real estate agent." She brought her attention back to me and pushed a little gentler this time, helping me get the case in place safely.

"Are you sure you're okay?" I asked, trying not to pry.

"I'm fine." She gave me a quick hug, but the glare she gave Ray when he and Lanie walked closer to the winery didn't go unnoticed. "I'll see you here tonight."

We gave each other another quick hug, and I decided to give her space. She'd tell me when she was ready.

After I'd come back from retrieving the For Goodness Cakes banner from the van, Lanie and Ray were standing in the gazebo, looking out at the lake.

"I need the right buyer," I overheard Ray say to Lanie. He scoffed, "That agent you just met—she's what I'd consider low on the real estate scale. She can only handle the cheap properties with cheap buyers. More of the income type of seller, if you know what I mean."

"It takes a special person to be able to buy a winery." Lanie spoke with an air of confidence that made my stomach turn. Neither of them knew just how hard Madison would work to find the right buyer. She just needed a chance. "When are you going to shut down production?"

"Tonight." His words made me gasp.

Out of the corner of my eye, as I hung up my sign, I could see them look at me. I busied myself, acting as if I'd not heard them.

"You can't do that tonight." Lanie's voice held a hoarse frustration. "I've got over one hundred of the best wine connoisseurs coming here tomorrow."

"Too bad." There wasn't a sad tone to his words. "I'm losing money quicker than a speeding ticket."

"Ray." I could tell by her body language she was trying

to keep her cool, but there was a deep frustration in her voice. "Maybe one of the wine members will want to purchase the land if we still have the convention here. I'll be able to promote the land and the winery for you. Don't pull the plug on me now. You promised me."

"Well, honey," he snickered, "promises were meant to be broken."

"I should've known you'd do this. This isn't the first time you've disappointed me." Her words seethed out of her mouth.

The sound of her hand slapping Ray across the face caught my attention. I quickly looked away as he responded with a few choice words that'd make the devil blush. Lanie ran off.

Ray touched his cheek, spit on the ground, and turned his attention back toward the lake.

Chapter Three

The bluegrass band started to play just as I got the last mini cupcake placed on the cupcake stand. They were perfect, bite-sized treats filled with chocolate and vanilla cream that were perfectly paired with the different wines offered to the guest. I'd even made cute little signs that showed which pastry paired well with which wine.

It was nice to see the residents of Rumford come out and enjoy the last bit of the afternoon sun, listen to some good music, and hang out with one another while raising money for a good cause. For a Sunday, the winery grounds were busy and full.

Even Cat Fraxman was socializing more than I'd ever seen her do, and she was smiling the entire time. It was strange not seeing her head stuck between the covers of an open book.

Perry and Tammy Dugan strolled over with wine glasses in their hands. Perry reached for one of the cupcakes before Tammy smacked his hand away.

"Please, help yourself." I laughed at the brother and sister duo. I was always envious of siblings since I didn't have any, though you might consider Bitsy more of an annoying older sister than a mother. "I've got plenty more."

"If you insist." Perry flashed that bright white smile. He was very different from his father, and he didn't work for the family business like his sister. He was a lawyer and with all the rumors I'd been hearing today, it looked like he was the only member of the family who wouldn't be affected by the sale of the land.

"What is that?" Tammy pointed to a plate inside the glass display.

"Mud puddles." I opened the door and took one out, placing it on a napkin as I held it over the case for her. After she took it, I pointed to the sheet I'd made up. "Are you drinking Cab?" I asked, guessing that her glass contained Cabernet Sauvignon.

"Beaujolais, Cabernet Sauvignon, Bordeaux, Merlot, and Zinfandel go well with a mud puddle?" Tammy looked at the list and down at the napkin in her hand.

"Smile!" Lizbeth Mockby, the editor of the *Rumford Newspaper*, hid behind her camera and snapped a few photos of the brother and sister with their pastry treats in the air. "For Goodness Cakes Bakery, right?" She looked at me over the top of her glasses for confirmation.

"Yes. Thanks." I was happy to take all the free press I could get.

Lizbeth didn't bother to acknowledge my thanks; she

moved like a little flea, hopping from person to person, snapping photos along the way.

Excitement and pride rose from my stomach to my throat, almost making me tear up as I saw all the happy faces not only glad to interact with one another but also to enjoy my pastries. Everyone told me I'd outdone myself.

Every time Tammy took a bite of the cookie, she followed it up with a sip of her wine. Her face relaxed and a smile crossed her lips. A satisfied gurgle even escaped her throat. This was the exact reaction that made me love baking so much. It was the satisfaction and happiness baked goods brought to people that made me feel like I was making some sort of difference in the world, making it a happier place one pastry at a time.

"Delicious." Perry smiled.

"I think you're right." Tammy nodded and popped the rest of a cookie in her mouth, slowly chewing every savory bite before she took another sip of wine. "Perry," she whispered, "you must try this. Amazing."

Tammy held the napkin out for him. He took the mud puddle off the napkin and took a bite.

"This cookie is amazing." His eyes were gentle. "Tammy is right. You're a pretty amazing baker."

"Tammy, do you know where your father is?" Reba's eyes snapped between Tammy and Perry after she walked over. "Cat Fraxman is desperately looking for him. She's not a happy person right now. I think Ray told her."

Their attention quickly locked on Cat Fraxman and

Ray Peel. Cat and Ray seemed to be having a very heated discussion, her voice rising above the band and laughter of all the guests. Perry and Tammy headed that way, and I watched as Ray's face contorted when they reached him.

While I rearranged and added some pastries to keep the display looking full and pretty, I could see Bitsy scurrying my way.

"You didn't go home and change?" Bitsy's brows knitted together. Her eyes bore into me with each step she took in my direction.

"I think you look just fine." My dad, Robert, stood next to her. "Bitsy, she's working."

He'd obviously just come from work, because he had on the three-piece suit that he used for trials.

Out of the corner of my eye, I saw Ray storm off toward the vineyard, cursing under his breath.

"She needs to work on settling down. Where is Carter anyway?" Bitsy's disapproval of my lack of interest in getting married was written all over her face. But ever since I'd started dating Sheriff Carter Kincaid, Bitsy had been dropping off bridal magazines in my mailbox on a weekly basis. "Robert, none of us are getting any younger, and I'd like to be able to run around with my grandchildren on my own two feet instead of them pushing me in a wheelchair." Bitsy let out a very loud and exhausting sigh.

"You talk about me like I'm not here." I looked between them. "I'm here for a job, not to attend or donate, or to be on a date with Carter."

I wanted to remind Bitsy exactly why I'd moved back to Rumford from New York City, though falling in love with Carter was a bonus. He'd gone to school with Charlotte, Madison, and me, but wasn't a standout like the boys we'd hung around with. He was quiet, reserved, and observant—qualities I like much more now that we are older.

Since he had the title of sheriff and came from what Bitsy would call "good stock," she'd been pleased as punch when we started dating.

"Smile for the camera," Lizbeth chimed in on her way back over to us.

"Where have you been?" Bitsy gave Lizbeth a scowl. "You were supposed to be at the Junior League last night, taking pictures for the society page. We raised over two thousand dollars."

"Yeah. I got a little tied up, but I'll be sure to get a photo of you and the league members today with the check. I'll definitely put you on the society page." Lizbeth knew the right words to say to Bitsy.

Bitsy perked up and nudged my dad. I was standing on the other side of him for the photo, and he jerked away from Bitsy.

"Robert, smile with your mouth slightly open, and show your teeth," she instructed him. "Not the the fake pull-your-lips-apart kind. Actually, think of something that will make you laugh."

"Like the thought of you gardening?" I asked, and Dad busted out laughing.

"Good one." Lizbeth grinned.

"I want to see it. I don't think I was smiling." Bitsy rushed over to Lizbeth's side and tried to get a glimpse at the digital screen that gave a preview of the photo.

"It's fine," Lizbeth assured her but held her camera close her.

While the two of them debated whether or not Lizbeth was going to show Bitsy the photo, I tugged Dad toward the For Goodness Cakes bakery counter.

"Would you like a Nanner mini pie?" I asked, putting on my sweet-as-pie face because Cat had walked up.

Before he answered, I took out a mini graham cracker pie shell, knowing it was hard for Bitsy and Dad to refuse any sort of homemade treat from their daughter. Especially Nanner mini pie.

"You've got to be so proud of Sophia coming back to Rumford after all of these years and reopening the old bakery." Cat clasped her hands in front of her and rocked back on the heels of her black flats.

Bitsy rejoined us after Lizbeth found someone else to capture.

"Mm-hmm," Bitsy's lips snapped together, and she nodded her head.

"We are very, very proud of our daughter, even if she hadn't come back to Rumford. But there's no denying we are pleased she's come home to live." Dad always had the right thing to say. "Have you tried Sophia's Nanner mini pie?" Dad offered his mini pie to Cat, but she politely declined.

"I'm excited you're here and hope you still plan on giving generously to the library addition. Especially since you are in the Friends of the Library Club." Cat wasn't so subtle in asking for money.

"You can rest assured we have our check." My dad patted the front pocket of the suitcoat before he took one of the Heart of Rumford cookies.

"I hope it's big," Cat chirped.

Dad dropped the cookie, and Bitsy quickly picked it up.

"Blow it off. It ain't dirty." She popped the cookie in Dad's mouth. "Sophia needs all the people here she can get. I noticed no one was in her bakery today. This will be good advertisement."

I gave Bitsy the stink eye. It was best to ignore her. She knew I wasn't going to say anything at the fund-raiser.

"Dad, can I talk to you?" I asked him.

He looked at Bitsy like he needed her permission.

"I'm going to go say hi to the girls from the Garden Club." Bitsy excused herself.

"What's going on, kiddo?" My dad treated me like I was still a teenager.

"I wanted to ask you about intellectual property law. I was cleaning out the bakery office, and I found the Fords' old recipe journal. It appears to be really old, and I'd love to recreate some of their recipes. Is that illegal?"

"It's true you did buy the bakery, but morally I think you know what you need to do." His head tilted, and his soft eyes looked down at me.

"I was afraid you'd say that." A sigh escaped me. "I did try to call them, but I guess I could stop by their house."

"They'd love that. I wonder, do they know you were the one who bought the bakery?" He asked a good question. Everything with the sale had been done through their lawyer and Madison, since she was the real estate agent.

"Thanks, Dad." I gave him a quick hug and let him go enjoy his evening.

Cat was still waiting for me.

"Are you okay?" I asked. Tears lined the ridges of her lower lids, and if she blinked, they would flood right on over and mess up the pretty makeup she wore.

"No." Her jaw tensed as she swallowed back that wall of tears. "Ray Peel said he wasn't able to give the donation he'd pledge to give."

"How much is he donating?" I asked.

"Much less. Like nothing. Nada. Zip. Goose egg." She held her fingers tips together in the shape of a zero.

"But—but," I sputtered, "what about the half million?"

"That man." She spat out the words. "I swear . . ." She started to say something but stopped herself. Her eyes became flat and unreadable. "Karma is a bitch."

Of course, after Cat had stormed off, I'd kept my eye on the crowd and how many people seemed to give her checks for donations. I had to give her credit because she'd taken the donations with a smile on her face, though I knew she was dying inside. She seemed to be holding it together when the entire addition to the library was crumbling in front of her eyes.

From what I'd heard, there had to be a certain amount pledged before the bank would even give the city the loan to build the addition. It was rumored that Ray Peel had made the pledge as long as his name was on the new addition. Of course, it was hearsay. Gossip around town spread like butter on a hot, fresh, out-of-the-oven biscuit.

"Did I miss anything?" Charlotte asked as she hurried next to me, shoving her purse under the counter. She pushed her hair back with her hands and grabbed the apron I had brought for her to put on over her clothes.

"Did you ever," I responded, pointing her face toward Cat. "Ray Peel has not only pulled his funding for the project, but he's also planning on selling the land. Oh . . ." I pointed my finger in the air toward her. "Remember the lady who ordered the pastries for the wine convention?"

Charlotte nodded.

"She was here, and she smacked Ray." I watched as Charlotte's eyes grew big. "You missed a lot."

"Okay." Her jaw dropped. "The land is no big deal, but the funding? What's going to happen with the library addition? And why did that lady smack him?"

I shrugged. "I guess they'll have to pay on the loan from the bank." I looked at my watch and noticed it was already eight-thirty. I didn't want the offices to close before I got my money.

"Maybe you can get some inside scoop while you're

here." I untied the apron from around my waist and hung it on the corner of the display case. "I'm going to go get my check from the Dugans before they decide they can't pay me. Do you think you can hold down the fort?"

"Absolutely." There was a gleam of excitement in her eyes. There was nothing Charlotte loved more than good gossip; she'd have all the answers before I got back.

It was that strange time of the day when it isn't quite dark, but it was past dusk. The sun had set on the rolling hills on the horizon and painted the sky with a burnt orange and dark blue. If I didn't hurry, it'd be dark before I got back, and the vineyard would become a maze.

I hurried down the row of the grapevines, and it took a lot of willpower for me not to pluck off a grape. I loved grapes. Especially when I put them in a dessert to sweeten it a little more. Or threw some in a baggie and put in a freezer for a nice garnish to a cocktail at a catered baby or bridal shower. It was the little touches that made the catering business so special and kept customers coming back.

Being around the grapes, the setting sun, and the entangled vines had my head swimming with creative ideas. My foot got hung on an old, tangled, dead grapevine. I tried a couple of times to jerk my foot out. Without success, I felt myself start to tumble. I put my arms out to gain balance, grabbing a ripe grapevine on my way down. Unripened grapes cascaded from the vine one by one as my hand slid down, following suit with the rest of my body.

"Oh, no!" I screamed when I realized I'd not fallen on

top of a soft piece of ground, but on top of and face-to-face with Ray Peel. A wide-eyed and blue-lipped Ray Peel. "Ray?" I frantically called out his name and put my hand on the front of his shirt. "Ray?" I asked again when I didn't feel or see a rise and fall of his chest. "No, no, no," I pleaded and put my ear up to his heart to see if I could even hear a heartbeat.

Nothing. Ray Peel was dead.

Chapter Four

"Sophia," Carter Kincaid said, running his hand down his face. He looked at me and inhaled a deep breath. It wasn't the endearing look I was used to seeing on his face. The kind of look that told me he was so happy I'd moved back to Rumford and that he had fallen in love with me. "Don't move. I need to call dispatch."

Nonetheless, being the girlfriend of the sheriff actually came in handy tonight. Calling Carter on his private number from my cell phone probably wasn't the best idea since this was an official I-need-you-right-now sheriff's call. I should've run back to the winery and called for help, but he was the first person I'd thought of.

"This is Sheriff Kincaid. Can you please send the coroner and a few officers to Grape Valley Winery? We have a homicide. Blow to the head." He used his formal work voice that sent shivers up my spine. He moved in front of me when he saw me staring at Ray.

I tried not to stare at the lifeless body, but I couldn't

45

help noticing the blood dripping down the side of his temple and the look of fright that'd stiffened on his face.

"Tell me exactly what happened." Carter brought me out of my thoughts. His brown eyes grew still and serious.

"I . . . I . . ." My mouth was dry. I gulped, licked my lips, and tried again. "I was walking from the winery to the office so I could get my check from the Dugans before they went out of business."

I looked down at my hands. They were shaking. I clasped them together to try to get them to stop. I couldn't take my eyes off Ray. Carter took his hand and cupped my chin, bringing my gaze back to him. I blinked a couple of times to come back to the present and out of the images in my head.

"Anyway,"—I cleared my throat and continued to look at Carter, which seemed to calm my nerves and ease my stomach—"I was admiring the scenery when I fell and tripped over Ray." My voice cracked, and I could feel the sting of tears as they rolled down my face. "I should've called nine-one-one so it was on record, but you were the first person to pop into my mind." I gave my head a little shake. "I'm sorry. I should've—"

"You did fine," he assured me.

The sirens were getting closer and closer. Soon the guests of the fund-raiser would know what'd happened.

"The fund-raiser wasn't going as well as Cat had wanted it to, and now this." My voice lowered, I started to ramble, as I always did when I was nervous.

46

"It's okay. You didn't know what to do." He tried to break the tension with a thin-lipped smile. "Forensics and the coroner are on the way, so we can start to investigate." He pointed away from the crime scene. "Why don't you wait over there?"

In an instant, he went from boyfriend to sheriff. Fright swept through me as I watched Carter's flashlight going over and around Ray's body. Deep breathing was the only thing keeping me from jumping out of my skin. The question of who could have done such a thing stabbed at my heart.

"Who could do this to you?" I asked when I glanced back over at Ray.

I squinted when Carter flashed his light in my eyes, and I drew my hand up to shield it from blinding me.

"What did you say?" he tried to ask over the loud sirens and squealing tires in the background. I said it again.

"I can't hear you. Hold on," he said. He went back to looking over Ray.

It wasn't long after that that the crime scene was swarming with officers and guests.

"Sophia, what happened?" Bitsy ran up to me. My dad, Charlotte, and Cat weren't too far behind her. "We heard the sirens."

"I was going to see the Dugans, and I tripped over Ray Peel," I spoke in a suffocated whisper and wrung my hands together. Suddenly, I was very cold.

"Is he okay?" Bitsy's head bobbled back and forth as she tried to get a better look.

"No, Mother. He's been murdered," I informed her.

"Don't tell me." Bitsy's eyes met mine. "You found him?"

I nodded my head.

"Oh, Sophia." Bitsy's disapproving tone was apparent. "Not again."

"I'm afraid so." Like I said, this wasn't my first experience with Carter in a similar situation. The head chef at the Rumford Country Club—RCC for short—had been murdered the week of Charlotte's wedding. It wasn't as if I'd been truly trying to solve the crime. I was trying to make sure that the RCC didn't shut down, so Charlotte could still have her dream wedding. What's a best friend to do?

But when I'd gotten in the killer's line of vision and been run off the road, it was Carter who had to come to my rescue.

"What's going on?" Perry Dugan rushed up and peered above the crowd. Tammy and Giles were behind him.

"Ray Peel's been murdered." Charlotte relayed the story to them. In fact, she told everyone who walked up about what happened and my part in it.

Cat didn't seem too impressed. I watched as she walked back to the winery.

"Are you okay?" Perry asked me. "You seem to be shaking."

"I am?" I asked. "I guess it's my nerves."

"Why don't you come back into the office, and we'll get you a blanket," Perry suggested to me. Tammy's head nodded rapidly in approval.

"Yeah," Tammy said, wide-eyed, and motioned for me to follow her. "I can't believe that Ray has died."

"Died? He was murdered." Images of Ray Peel's expression haunted me. "He was surprised too."

I couldn't help but look Tammy over—her hands, her clothes, any sign of a struggle, or anything she might have used to hit him on the head. I glanced around the ground as we walked, but the darkness was setting in fast, and it was hard for me to find any sort of big object she might've used.

"Well, we'll go to the office and get you a blanket." She held the door open for me and led the way.

She sat me down in a chair in the reception area and told Reba about the murder. I couldn't help but take my focus off Tammy and watch Reba's reaction, since she'd already lied to me today about the Flip-Flops.

Reba did that whole nodding and shocked expression thing before she ran off toward the back of the building. Tammy made a phone call and glanced up at me a few times before she turned her back and finished the conversation.

Reba came back up front with a plaid red blanket draped over her arm and a cup of something steamy in her hand.

"Here you go, Sophia." She set the cup on the small table next to me and laid the blanket on my lap. "You can warm up with a cup of tea. Herbal to calm the nerves."

"Thank you." I was grateful for the hospitality.

For the next hour or so, I sat there and watched the door of the offices barely close before they were ripped opened and yet another officer would walk in. One of the offices had become a makeshift sheriff station. Carter was running the operation as if the police were on a secret mission. He'd gotten the layout of the winery from blueprints Tammy had, and he dispatched deputies, along with dogs, to search the property for anything and anyone.

Giles Dugan rushed into the winery offices. He looked around, and when he saw Carter talking to Tammy in the makeshift office, he headed back there. He and Carter shook hands. Giles's expression was serious, and he kept nodding his head in agreement to whatever Carter was saying.

Then it started. The shock of the murder started to wear off and crazy theories about who could dislike Ray Peel so much that they wanted to wipe him off the face of the earth hit me like a brick. Tammy Dugan for sure wanted Ray Peel gone from the winery. Now that he was dead, what would happen to the vineyard?

Chapter Five

The sound of a crash startled me awake. I flung off the covers and reached for the flashlight on the bedside table because it was the only thing I had to protect me from whoever or whatever had made that sound.

The stillness of the pitch-black darkness surrounded me as I lay still and tried to hear anything above the sound of my heart pounding in my chest. All I could think about was whoever killed Ray Peel could now be after me since I was the one who'd found Ray. Did the killer think I'd seen something?

Out of pure fright, and hoping whoever was in my house wouldn't notice that I'd turned on my bedside table lamp, I slid out from the comfort of my bed. I gripped the flashlight in case I needed to whack someone. I peered out the bedroom door and down the hall. The glow from the table lamp I kept on in the living room didn't show any shadows from an intruder or anything out of place. It wasn't like I lived in a palatial estate; it was a four-room house that had once been a small carriage house before a developer bought the land and built a neighborhood on it. So if someone were in the house, it'd be hard to miss.

Meow. Duchess, my cat, ran across the counter.

"Duchess." I let out an audible sigh when I saw one of the cupcake stands from the fund-raiser that I'd brought home, now on the family-room floor. "Did you knock that off the island?" I asked her, as if she were going to talk to me.

She'd already beat me to the splattered cupcakes and tried to lick away the evidence. She looked up with her big blue eyes and charmed me as she batted them.

"You can't have that, sweet girl." I put the flashlight down on the island and picked her up, flipped on the kitchen lights, and walked into the pantry to grab a scoop of her kibble. "This is much better for a middle-of-the-night snack."

I rubbed down her fur a couple of times to get the slight purr I loved to hear, and then put her down. I watched as she ate up her food, and was very grateful there wasn't an intruder in my home.

"I guess I should've checked your bowl when I got home." I grabbed the role of paper towels and walked back around the island to clean up the mess. "You're a good girl."

She pranced around the kitchen for a few more minutes, brushing against my leg until she'd had enough.

It'd taken me a couple of hours to fall asleep after I'd gotten home from the winery. Carter hadn't let anyone leave the crime scene without giving them a time to come down to the station for an interview and to make a statement. I assured him I was going to be okay, and he didn't need to stop by my house after he was finished doing the initial investigating. I didn't really give him a time that I'd stop by the department. I knew I'd see him at some point during the day, and he'd definitely call me if he needed to see me right away.

I noticed the time on the microwave—four AM, which only gave me thirty more minutes to sleep until I had to get up to get ready to go to the bakery. It truly was not worth getting back into bed. It was best to just get ready and head on into the bakery to help get my mind off Ray's murder.

Duchess ran down the hall and jumped into the window seat to clean herself, and I flipped on the coffeepot to brew while I jumped into a hot shower to wake me up.

Spring mornings in Kentucky meant it was still chilly, but the afternoons were warm. After pouring more kibble in Duchess's bowl and filling her water bowl, I grabbed a light jacket.

"You're in charge, Duchess. Run off any would-be killers." I said, only half-joking, and headed out the door.

Charlotte and her husband, Brett Ponder, lived across the street in a cute gray Cape Cod house. Brett was a developer who bought old run-down property and neighborhoods in small towns to revitalize them. He'd been instrumental in working with the land developer in turning the place where I lived into a neighborhood, making it into one of the most desirable areas in the mid-income range—not like my parent's fancy gated community on the outskirts of town.

There was a light on in Charlotte's house, and I couldn't

help but notice her looking out the window. I just so happened to look back over at her house when I got into my car. Charlotte was standing on her small porch with the front door wide open, staring at me.

"Sophia, is that you? Gawd, I hope it's you standing next to your car," she called across the street, trying to squint through the dark. "It is you." She straightened up.

"What are you doing? Go back to bed," I called back in a hushed whisper.

"Oh, good. You're up and at 'em." She darted off the porch and ran across the street in her bare feet. "Early bird catches the killer."

"Catches what?" I'd obviously misheard her, because she fanned her hand in the air. "You're going to catch a cold. What is wrong with you?"

"I've been up all night, thinking about Ray Peel." She gnawed on her bottom lip. "Who do you think killed him?"

"I don't know. But I've been thinking about it too," I told her.

"That's what I was hoping you'd say." She fidgeted uneasily back and forth on her feet. "I think Madison is a suspect."

"Madison?" I laughed at first, then realized she was serious. "Our best friend, Madison? As in Madison Ridge?"

"Do you happen to know any other Madison?" she asked. "Yes, our Madison."

"Why do you think that?" I asked and wondered where on earth she'd gotten this crazy idea. "Or let me guess: the gossip telephone game has begun."

Anytime there was some juicy gossip, the phone lines remained busy. It wasn't enough for people to gossip. No, no. They had to talk and talk about it. Run over it, and then put it all in reverse to run back over it until the gossip was beat into the ground and smashed so it didn't resemble anything like the truth.

"Last night, after you left, I overheard Tammy Dugan talking to Carter. I heard her say something to Carter about Madison having an argument with Ray right before you found him. And no, I haven't talked to him since I left the winery."

There's no way Carter thought that Madison could kill anyone. We were all friends.

"I wonder what Tammy overheard them say." It was impossible that Madison had killed Ray. At least, the Madison that I knew. "Never mind that." I blew her off. "I'll talk to Madison and see what's going on. But for now, you keep this between you and me."

"Got it. And you're going to ask Carter, right? Because if Madison is in trouble, she needs us." Charlotte's shoulders seemed to relax a little as I nodded in agreement. Of course I was going to ask him. As soon as I talked to him, but I would let him call me since I got up before the crows of roosters.

"I've been waiting up all night for you to wake up," Charlotte said.

"Now you can go back inside and snuggle up with Brett for a couple of hours before you have to be at work." I winked and gave her a quick hug.

"See you soon, boss." She hurried back across the street, and the lights in her house were already off by the time I'd started to drive down the street.

Now that I was back in Rumsford and a little older, I wasn't going to take my hometown for granted anymore. Downtown was so charming. It wasn't your typical small town with old brick buildings one after the other. They were all different shapes and sizes.

Rumford, being one of the oldest towns in the state, had the charm of a Southern city while needing little construction to keep it updated. It was one of those old Kentucky mining towns where the miners came and built a city with all the houses in a row. Unlike most Kentucky towns, Rumford had made it through all the transitions and remained a viable town.

The old homes had been transformed into cute shops and city buildings that lined both sides of the street. They'd replaced the large sidewalks a few times and had updated the carriage lights with dowel rods that held beautiful baskets of seasonal flowers along with a seasonal banner.

Each shop had a grassy patch in the front or on the side, since it'd been reconstructed from an old house. Some had small picket fences to add character while others had homey front porches as well as colorful awnings with the shop name printed across the front. A few of my favorite shops I'd frequented since I'd been home were the Family Feud Diner, Small Talk Café, Peacock and Pansies Clothing Boutique, Back-en-Thyme Flowers, and Sassy and Classy

Salon. They were all within walking distance of For Good-ness Cakes, but the coffeehouse was right next door, which made it easy to deliver their daily order of treats and do some events with them.

I'd also done some collaborative work with Back-en-Thyme Flowers for different social occasions. I'd really found my groove after I'd gotten over the hump of the first murder I'd happened upon. And now my groove seemed to have hit a roadblock.

My normal routine was to turn the ovens on as soon as I walked in the door. After that, I'd get the donuts out of the freezer, as well as some of the other desserts that I'd premade, but not baked yet. Today was no different—or so I thought.

"What on earth?" The oven was stone cold when I opened it to slide in a few of the racks of donuts. I looked at the oven knobs and realized I hadn't turned them on; my mind had been on other things. Madison. "Let it go, Sophia," I said to myself out loud.

Before too long, the ovens were baking, the timers were dinging, and the warm smell of cinnamon, sugar, and nut-meg filled the bakery, bringing a cozy comfort to my soul. It made me feel a tad bit better about Charlotte's claim that Tammy had overheard a heated argument.

The knock on the front door made me jump. On a differ-ent day, I'd have just looked up, but the thought that who-ever had killed Ray was out there put my nerves on edge.

Dolores Master and Ella Capshaw had their noses pressed

up against the door. When they noticed they'd gotten my attention, both waved.

I unlocked the door and flipped the "Closed" sign that hung on the door to "Open."

"Good morning." I stood back as they pushed their way inside.

"Sophia, are you open?" Dolores asked. She and Ella walked right on in whether I was open or not.

"I am now," I muttered and then smiled. "Come on in."

There was no need to encourage them. I quickly closed the door because there was still a bite in the air. My skin pricked with goose bumps.

"I was so busy getting all the freshly baked donuts in the display case that I forgot to unlock the door." Technically it wasn't a lie. I could be on autopilot and bake.

Dolores abruptly stopped in the middle of the bakery, stuck her nose up in the air, and took a couple of whiffs. She looked like she'd just stepped out of *Southern Woman's Magazine*, with her brown hair swept up in a bun on top of her head, a black mock turtleneck, skinny jeans, and a pair of black flats. Even though it was a simple outfit, somehow Dolores took sophistication to a whole 'nother level.

"It always smells so good in here." Ella's smile reached her eyes when she glanced over the freshly baked donuts that'd just come from the oven.

She was just a few years older than me, but much more fashion forward, making me feel a little frumpier with my khaki pants and white button-down. Granted, I did try to spruce myself up with a pink scarf tied around my neck to make myself feel a little bit better about being the one to find Ray, but no pop of color was going to brighten that doom-and-gloom feeling deep in my gut.

"I'm working on making some coffee too." Though Small Talk Café was right next door, I still made regular coffee because I loved it. "Y'all take a look around, and I'll be right with you."

While they took a gander at the morning's specials, I filled the stainless-steel coffeepot with water and carefully measured out the freshly ground coffee that I'd bought from Jessie Pearl Longley, the owner of the Small Talk Café.

"Good morning," Bitsy trilled when she walked into the bakery. "I'm not sure if it's the chill this early spring morning or the fact there's a killer on the loose." She rubbed her arms vigorously.

Bitsy's eyes drew up and down Dolores—a clear sign she was assessing her and comparing herself to Dolores. They were around the same age, but Dolores had always outdone Bitsy in the fashion department, which really put a burr under Bitsy's saddle. Many times, Bitsy wanted to take me shopping after church on Sunday because she'd see something Dolores had worn and felt she herself needed something new for the next week. Bitsy was a right-now person: she got something in her head, and she wanted to do it right now. As a teenager, I'd groan and moan that I wanted to spend time in the kitchen baking, but she'd insist that I had to get new clothes and become a debutante.

"I heard," Dolores Masters said, and her face lit up with a curiosity as she nodded toward Ella Devon Capshaw. "Can you believe it?"

"I'd believe it. Ray Peel was probably caught with his pants down," Ella replied. Her blue eyes narrowed speculatively.

Ella was good at throwing stones at a glass house. It wasn't too long ago she'd been a suspect in a murder—well, suspect on my end. It proved to be false, but she was known to have had an affair or two.

"With who?" As much as I tried to stop myself, I just couldn't. The thought of what Charlotte said about Madison being a suspect wasn't just a breeze flying by—it'd taken root in my bones and chilled me to the core.

"I did hear the other day that he and Reba Gunther were seen together, huddled up in the corner table at that new Eye-talian restaurant in town." Ella's accent dripped with Southern charm.

"Café Italia?" I asked. "I've been wanting to go there because I heard the waiters walk around singing in Italian."

"Yep." She snapped her fingers and nodded. "That's the one. I mean huddled up in the corner. As in row-mantic." Her lips pressed into a duckbill.

"By the other day, how long ago?" I asked because in Rumford when someone said *the other day*, that could've meant any time between now and three hundred and sixty-five days ago.

"Lordy be, Sophia," Ella snarled. "Just the other day."

"Mm-hmm," Dolores ho-hummed, and she walked down

the length of the glass display case. "What have you heard, Bitsy?"

I busied myself with to-go boxes so I could listen in without interruption, because I'd already made Ella mad. Then I wondered if Carter and I could make a reservation at Café Italia. While we were there, I could talk to the staff and see if anyone else saw Reba and Ray. Reba sure didn't seem too upset when Tammy took me into the offices last night. If they were an item, I'd think she'd have been pretty upset.

I sure was curious to what Ella had heard. I'd been gone so long from Rumford that I wasn't clued in on all the gossip, and I still couldn't shake the idea Madison could be a suspect, even if Charlotte overheard the ridiculous notion.

"Ask Sophia," Bitsy boasted. "She's the one who found him."

Now, Bitsy would've never been proud to say that in public, but she knew she had something Dolores didn't have. The inside scoop. Not necessarily the gory details of Ray Peel's murder, but the fact that I was the one who found him. In Bitsy's book, this was a one-upper.

"I'll have a cup of that coffee with one of your Cherry Flip-Flops while you tell me about it." Dolores's long nail tapped the glass case.

"And I'll take a little information on who you think did it." Ella stared at me with cow eyes.

"You might as well make that a few coffees." Bitsy sat down on one of the bar stools I had butted up to the long bar top that I'd put in on the right side of the bakery just for customers who came in for a quick dessert, even though we weren't a café.

Bitsy plopped her designer bag on the bar and shimmied her shoulders back so she sat straight up. She carefully crossed her legs at her ankles and folded her hands in her lap. Her face beamed from the knowledge that she knew something Dolores didn't.

"Really, it's nothing." I filled three mugs with coffee and carried them over to the three nosy women, along with three Cherry Flip-Flops. "I was going from the winery to the offices through the vineyard. It was almost dark, and it's so hard to see at that time of the night."

The Cherry Flip-Flops were my version of a turnover, only better. The cherry filling oozed out the sides, and the vanilla icing melted into a perfect stream across the top. The tartness of the cherries and the sweetness of the icing along with the fluffy pastry were perfect to wake up the morning taste buds.

"Go on," Dolores's expression didn't hide her nosy side. "Don't leave out a single detail." She dug her fork into the fruit-filled pastry.

"I was enjoying the beautiful night when I fell over him," my voice trailed off.

"Fell on him." Bitsy nodded with arched brows.

"You didn't." Ella's face curled at the thought.

"I did. Nose to nose." I tapped my finger to my nose.

"Were his eyes open?" Ella asked.

"Yes. Frightened eyes." I gulped and couldn't help but wonder what Ray had seen right before he was murdered.

"How did they kill him?" Dolores brought the steaming cup of coffee up to her mouth. The curl of steam made her question seem more eerie.

"Hit him over the head." I sucked in a deep breath. When Megyn Oslica came in, I waved hello and then returned my attention to my gruesome story.

"We were on my way out to the fund-raiser, since Grant was going to give a big donation. Running late of course." Ella had recently started to date Grant Livingsworth. She winked. "You know he's got all these write-offs since he's such a success in the food industry." Grant owned the Piggly Wiggly, Rumford's only grocery store. "Grant had to swerve to miss a car that'd crossed the line as they were speeding away from the winery, and I spilled wine all over myself."

"You were drinking wine in the car?" Bitsy drew back and looked at Ella.

"What? You act like I'm an alcoholic." Ella had yet to learn to take Bitsy's comments with a grain of salt. "We'd just been to dinner, and I wasn't going to waste a single drop of the fifty-dollar glass. Call me a hillbilly, but I took that glass of wine right on out of that restaurant." Ella lifted her nose and shook her hair in place.

"Do you know what time that was?" I asked, just in case it had something to do with Ray Peel's murder.

"Well . . ." She opened her purse and dug down in it. She pulled out a piece of paper. "Here's the receipt from the restaurant." She handed it to me. "As you can see, we spent over two hundred dollars on food and drink. That Grant," she bragged, "he spoils me."

The only reason she'd offered me the receipt was the pure fact of the total. She loved to boast about Grant Livingsworth's money and how he spared no expense when it came to her. Still, I was only interested in the time. My eyes scanned down and noticed it had been stamped eight forty-five last night. I clearly remembered looking at my watch before I found Ray, and it had been eight thirty.

"What kind of car?" I asked.

"You sure are asking a lot of questions." Her lips pursed. "Silver. I think it was silver. Grant even said how pretty the car shined. Or something like that."

"Good morning," Megyn greeted us after she'd stopped briefly to talk to some customers. She was the mailman—or mail lady, actually—for the downtown area of Rumford. "Just a couple of things today?" she asked when she picked up the few stamped bills I'd stuck in the wire basket that was my mailbox.

"That's all." I walked over, and she put my mail on the counter.

"I see you made the paper again." Her eyes focused on my mail. She pushed the plastic wrapper with the rolled-up newspaper in it toward me. "Not in a good way either."

"I told Sophia she has to stop finding all of these dead bodies," Bitsy whined. "Murder magnet. That's a reputation you don't want."

64

"Two dead bodies. Not *all*," I corrected her. "I can't help it. I didn't plan either of them."

"It doesn't seem like it. At least not in there." Megyn shrugged. "See you tomorrow."

My brows knitted in a frown. Was Bitsy right? Did everyone think I was some sort of murder magnet?

"I've got to get to work." I rolled my eyes and set the mail aside, paper included. I didn't want to even open the paper to see what Megyn was talking about. I'd been there last night and knew all about Ray Peel. I knew the truth and didn't need to read about. Relive it. "Dolores, what did you want to order for the meeting today?"

"I wanted to see if you had some tea cookies with a little flower on top of them. We'll be discussing the flower swap. Jessie said that your spring collection would pair nicely with her black tea."

"I do have a nice sugar cookie I infuse with some black tea that you'll love." It was going to be good to head back into the kitchen and start something from scratch. "I'm actually going to make some for the wine convention, and I can do a double batch so I have some for you."

"Wine convention?" Ella asked.

"I'll be right back." I held up a finger and hurried through the swinging door between the kitchen and the bakery.

Charlotte was busy rolling out the dough for the tea cookies.

"Did anyone call this morning about the wine convention?" I asked, wondering if Lanie had cancelled the convention, not only because of Ray's death but also because of the conversation I'd overheard at the winery before Ray was murdered.

"Not a word. The phone hasn't even rung." She used the flower cookie cutter for the shapes of the tea cookies and quickly placed the cutouts on parchment paper on the baking trays. "Strange, right?"

"Yeah. Maybe everyone is busy talking about Ray. Which reminds me, I've got some new information to tell you that might just help Madison." I grabbed Lanie's business card from the magnet on the chalkboard. "But first, I need to call this lady to make sure she still needs the items for the wine convention."

"I hope she does, because we're going to have cookies and cake out the wazoo if she doesn't." Charlotte put the cookies in the oven. "Would there be a reason she wouldn't?"

"The convention is supposed to be at the winery, and if it's closed due to the investigation, then I kinda need to know that." I left out the conversation I'd overheard between Lanie and a breathing Ray. There was no need to alarm Charlotte and get her juices going any more than they already were with Madison. "Speaking of Ray, have you heard from Madison?"

"No. I thought you were going to call her." She set the timer on the oven.

"I haven't had time, but I will on my way out to the

winery." I slipped the business card in my pocket. "Do you have it all under control?"

"You know I do." Charlotte was priceless. "But I thought we were going to talk about Madison."

"We will. Let me get a few things done, and I've also got to stop by the station to give my statement." I grabbed my purse and my phone.

"Don't worry. I've got it all under control," she assured me.

Not that I didn't trust that she did. I was procrastinating. I might have been having all sorts of images in my head from finding Ray, but reliving the event by giving all the details to Carter was something I wasn't looking forward to. Don't get me wrong: looking at Carter and spending time in his arms was better than getting a set of real pearls as a gift, but reliving the details of finding someone dead wasn't my cup of tea.

The sheriff's department was on the edge of town. It used to be downtown before the department grew and needed more space. Considering the edge of town was about a five-minute drive, which included getting stopped by a couple of stop signs, I was there in no time. I took the opportunity to give the Fords a call about the journal.

The sheriff's department parking lot was filled with white news vans, and camera crews had their lenses set up directly at the entrance. No doubt they were there because of Ray Peel. After I pulled into the parking space, I turned the car off and grabbed my phone. I quickly looked up the Fords' phone number from my contacts and hit the "Call" button.

"Hi, this is Sophia Cummings, the woman who bought the bakery. I was wondering if I could talk to Dixie Ford?" I wasn't sure who answered the Fords' phone. It wasn't the slow Southern accent that I remembered Dixie Ford greeting me with when I was a child and went to the bakery with Bitsy.

"Who did you say this was?" the much younger voice asked.

"Sophia Cummings. I bought the building where the Ford's Bakery was located," I said and watched out the window as some of the TV news crews went live.

"Granny Dixie is busy. You'll have to call back later in the day." The phone went dead. I pulled it from my ear and looked at the screen.

"Well, I'm going to leave my number." I hit the "Call" button again.

"What do you want?" The bite in the girl's voice came through the phone loud and clear.

"I need to talk to Mrs. Ford about the recipe journal I found at the bakery." There was a silence on the other end of the phone. When it seemed like it was too long of a pause, I continued, "Can you please give her my phone number?"

"What is it you got?" she asked.

"I found their journal with their recipes. You know the Maple Long Johns they baked? Even though I know that since it was left with the property, I technically get to keep it, I wanted to make sure it was okay with them if I duplicated the recipes. Because if it's not . . ." I rambled on, but she stopped me.

"What's your number?" she asked in a flat voice.

I rattled off my number, satisfied. She actually said goodbye before hanging up on me again. With two boxes of sweets from the bakery, I headed into the sheriff's department, ready to get this interview process over.

"Mornin', Sophia," Effie Glass, the secretary, greeted me when I walked in. Her eyes fixated on the boxes I'd brought with me.

"Good morning, Mrs. Effie." I'm not sure why, but everyone referred to her by her first name. But that's the way it was, and it was going to stay that way. I took one of the boxes and set it on her desk. "I brought you some donuts this morning."

"Sophia Cummings, how on earth did Rumford ever survive without your delicious treats?" Mrs. Effie was so great at making everyone feel good. She only stood about four feet six inches, and she had to be in her late seventies.

"We survived somehow, Mrs. Effie." Carter had turned the corner. "I might've been single all my life, but we survived."

"Why, Sheriff Kincaid, are you eavesdropping on us girls?" Mrs. Effie teased. He flushed.

"I don't think I've ever seen you blush." Mrs. Effie looked between him and me. "I think you two are the cutest couple who've ever come from Rumford. And that includes my mister."

"We are mighty appreciative of your kind words. And I do think Carter hit the jackpot." I winked and blushed when the handsome sheriff's eyes raked over me. "But I'm here to give my statement."

"Honey." Mrs. Effie opened the box and pushed it toward me. "I heard about you finding another dead body. You might need to get a job here. I'm retiring, so you can just slide on into my spot."

"You're retiring?" I was a little surprised to hear this news. "Who's going to keep these boys in line?"

"I think you'd be perfect to replace me." She winked.

"That's enough, you two. Don't encourage her, Mrs. Effie." Carter stepped in. "I have a difficult enough time trying to convince Sophia not to stick her nose in official business."

Mrs. Effie shook the open box in my direction again. "No, thank you. I had plenty while testing them as I baked them. You enjoy."

"Are you ready?" Carter asked and motioned for me to follow him.

The department was just like any other time I'd been there. The sheriff's deputies were busy on the phone or talking to one another.

"Here you go." I set the rest of the boxes down next to the coffee station they had by the big watercooler. "A few treats for all of your hard work."

The deputies thanked me and rushed over to get one before they were all gone. They knew anytime I came, I came with treats. Not only did it make me feel good to bring them, but I loved how it made the atmosphere less stressful. It amazed me how something I'd made with my own hands brought so much comfort to people.

"Have a seat." Carter shut the door behind me when I

walked into the interrogation room and he sat down in one of the wooden chairs behind the steel desk. The darkened window he had me face didn't go unnoticed.

"So formal?" I asked. "Last time we did this, it was at my house." I referred to the interview he gave me after I'd found Emile.

"Yeah, well, I got in trouble for all the loose ends in that one." He dropped a file down on the table and took a seat across from me.

He opened up the file. His pronounced cheekbones and clearly defined jawline disguised the dimples I knew he had when he gave a big smile. While he shuffled through the papers, I let my mind wander back to high school, when Carter had been so different.

Though we hadn't hung out with the same crowd, I clearly remembered him being a really nice guy. When I came back to Rumford and got into the little pickle of Emile's murder, I realized Carter Kincaid had grown up into an amazing man who just so happened to be single.

"Has the investigation been intense?" I asked.

"Let's just say that I'm looking forward to a night off." His eyes slid over my way.

"Does that mean I'll be seeing you?" He worked really odd hours.

"I'm off tomorrow night." And the dimples showed up, melting my heart. "Would you like to go out to supper?"

"I'd love to." I returned the smile, and my heart fluttered.

"Great." His chest lifted as he sucked in a deep breath.

"Let's get this over with." He pushed the button on the microphone. "We are taping this interview with witness Sophia Cummings. Sophia is owner of the For Goodness Cakes Bakery. You were hired to cater the desserts for the Heart of the Town fund-raiser, correct?"

"Yes," I stated.

I adjusted myself in the seat so I could really focus on what he was going to ask me instead of focusing on him.

"Why were you going back to the offices?" he asked.

"I went back to get payment for the catering I'd done for the event." I wasn't sure how much he wanted me to elaborate, so I stuck with simple statements.

"Tell me exactly how you found Mr. Peel."

"It was a pretty night, and I'd decided to cut through the vineyards to go to the offices. I wasn't paying attention to my feet, and I tripped over Ray Peel's shoes and landed pretty much on top of him." The image of his face shattered my concentration.

"Go on." Carter's soft voice comforted me. "It's okay."

I swallowed, my lips forming a thin smile.

"His face . . ." I paused and licked my lips. "His face had a very scared look on it."

"Can you tell me what you did after you tripped on him?" Carter didn't care about the look on Ray's face. He just wanted the facts.

"I called your cell phone. It was the only thing I knew to do." I found myself apologizing again for not calling the dispatch. He smiled. I added, "I knew you'd know what to do."

"You did fine," he said. A vague light passed between us.

"Within minutes, you showed up. You checked Ray out, and then you told me to stay put while you called for backup." It was exactly how I remembered things.

"While you were waiting for me to get there, did you hear or see anything or anyone?" he asked.

"No." I shook my head.

"Nothing like footsteps?" I shook my head. "Shuffling of feet?" he continued to ask.

"Nothing that I recall." I tried to remember anything, but my mind couldn't dredge up any sights or sounds—just the look on Ray's face, tattooed on my memory.

"The Grape Valley Winery was paying you? Or was it Ray Peel?" he said, changing his line of questioning.

"The Grape Valley Winery." I watched as he wrote down what I was saying. "I'd never talked to Ray Peel about the event. I didn't even know he had anything to do with the winery other than owning and leasing the land to the Dugans. When I saw he had an office at the winery, I did think it was strange." I stopped myself because I felt a yammering coming on.

"Was there any reason you felt like you weren't going to get paid for the event?" he asked and looked up at me.

"I was a little concerned since I'd overheard Ray was selling the land, and this was my first big event. So I'd put a lot of my own money into it, and I'd like to be paid."

"You've not been paid as of today?" he asked.

"No. But I'm heading out there after this so I can be." All of a sudden, I felt like I'd done something wrong.

"Sophia Cummings, did you kill Ray Peel because you'd heard about the winery being sold and were afraid you weren't getting paid? Did you confront Ray Peel about it in the vineyard and when he said he wasn't going to pay you, did you kill him?"

My jaw dropped.

"You just wait a cotton-pickin' minute," I warned, letting out my you're-not-gonna-mess-with-me Southern roots. A sickness came over me. I felt the rush of tears sting my eyelids. "Of course I didn't kill him."

"There's no need to get upset. It's just a standard line of questioning. I have to ask everyone." He closed the file and pushed the "Pause" button on the microphone. "I know you didn't do it, and I'm sorry I had to ask that. But last time I got reprimanded for not getting a formal statement from you on tape."

"Last time," I muttered. "I can't believe we are even saying that. Do you have any suspects?" I asked in hopes he'd say something about what the law enforcement stance was on Madison being a suspect.

"You know I can't tell you, Sophia." His head tilted, and his voice faded, losing his steely edge.

"I thought I'd ask. You know, give the customers something to gossip about," I joked and got up when he did. I headed toward the door. "I did hear a rumbling that you might have a few suspects."

I was hoping he'd tell me about Madison. That way I'd have something to ask her about instead of assuming she was a suspect. This wouldn't be the first time Charlotte got her gossip signals crossed.

"Sophia." He stopped me and shook his head.

"Did you check Ray's house for any clues?" I asked.

"Yes, and nothing turned up. I'll pick you up tomorrow night around six." His tone was firm.

"Only if you take me to Café Italia." I'd decided right then that I just might look into some of the things I'd heard.

"A few of the guys said it was good," he agreed.

"I'll be ready." I sucked in a deep breath and turned around, so he didn't see me squeeze my eyes shut and smile so big I couldn't get my lips to close. He made me feel like a teenager all over again. It was such a new feeling for me.

The hall was crowded with familiar faces from the fundraiser. When I walked past the other interrogation room, I noticed Madison was sitting in a chair like the one I'd been sitting in. She was crying, and a deputy was standing over her. I figured he was accusing her of killing Ray Peel.

"Madison is a suspect?" I gasped when the reality of what Charlotte had told me earlier was confirmed.

I turned on the balls of my feet. Carter almost ran into me. He grabbed my elbow and dragged me next to the watercooler. I blinked in anticipation of his answer, even though I could read what was going on here.

"Madison? Are you joking me?" I threw my arms in the air. "There's no way." I shook my head in refusal to even think it.

"It doesn't look good for her." He let go of my arm. "She

was seen with Ray by a few people. They were having a heated argument."

"You know she didn't do this." I kept my voice low when some deputies walked past the watercooler to get a cup of coffee and a sweet treat. "There were so many other people who—"

"I don't know. But I'm going to figure it out. We didn't find any murder weapon." His cool and aloof manner irked me. How could he even think Madison could do this? "It doesn't mean you need to figure it out," he warned. "Madison is simply here to be questioned."

My brows knitted. "But the look—" I started to talk really fast because the look he was giving me meant I was trying his patience. "Ray's face looked so surprised. He wouldn't've been surprised at Madison. He'd just been with her."

"Don't get involved. We are talking about a killer here." This was the second warning Carter had given me.

"She's my best friend. I know her. She's got two small children. She'd never do anything to harm a soul." As I stood there listening to him babble on about how in desperate times people do things we'd never imagine them to do, I got dizzy when I remembered the conversation Madison and I had had at the fund-raiser.

"That Ray Peel, he's a jerk. If I weren't a good Southern girl, I'd strangle him with one of the grapevines out there."

Carter grabbed my arm. "Are you okay?" he asked.

"I'm fine." I brushed it off. There was no way I was going

to tell him what I'd remembered until I talked to Madison. Plus, there was the whole Reba romance thing. I had to figure some of this out before I opened my big mouth. "I haven't eaten much since last night. Low blood sugar or something."

"Have one of your cookies." He grabbed me a cookie.

"Thanks." I stuffed it in my mouth. As much as I wanted the cookie to comfort me, it didn't. I had to figure out who'd killed Ray Peel, because I knew Madison couldn't've done it, no matter how mad he'd made her. "I'll see you tomorrow night."

I couldn't get out of the sheriff's department fast enough. I filled my lungs with the clean spring air. Taking several deep breaths before I got into my car did clear out a bit of the fog.

"Think, Sophia," I said out loud, hoping to bring back some sort of clarity to anything about that night. "The winery."

It was clear I still needed to go and get my check. This was the third time I'd tried. Reba Gunther was just the person I needed to see.

Chapter Six

The flurry of activity that'd taken place at the winery less than twenty-four hours ago had died down to a couple of cars in the gravel lot.

There was never a better time to have a box of Flip-Flops like the present. I was going to have to use them on Reba if I was to get any information about Ray Peel's decision to sell or any truth about her and Ray dating. As hard as I tried, I couldn't stop from looking over at the vineyard. Particularly the spot where I'd tripped on Ray.

When I stepped into the winery, I noticed Tammy and Giles in Ray's office. They looked up and saw me, and Giles walked over and shut the door.

"Hi." I held out the box of sweets to Reba, who was sitting in the chair behind the desk. "These are for you. I figured you could use a little distraction."

Nervously she picked at the edges of her pixie cut. Her jaw clamped down with each chew on the piece of gum in her mouth.

"You know," she said, leaning in on her elbows and whispering, "I don't think my fantasy vacation to go would give me a distraction. It's just awful what happened to Ray." She reached over the desk and patted my hand before she took the box. "You must be horrified. Two bodies." She tsked.

"Two?" My eyes popped open.

"Chef Emile and now Ray." The corners of her mouth dipped. "You must be some sort of death magnet."

"Death magnet?" I gulped. "I sure hope not."

This wasn't the first time I'd heard someone say this to me, and it sure wasn't the legacy I wanted to leave in this world. I'd much rather have "baker extraordinaire" behind my name.

"And to think—Madison Ridge." Reba stopped and dabbed the edge of her eye. "Her mama must be so upset. Speaking of mamas, how's Bitsy and them?"

Them. She meant my daddy.

"They are fine." I had to get back to the subject at hand. "Back to Madison. What were you saying about her?"

"It's no secret she wished some sort of harm on Ray after he said she was nothing more than a trailer-park trash real estate agent." Reba tucked her lips together and frowned. "I know she didn't sell a lot of upscale real estate and really worked in the poorer side in Rumford, but he didn't need to call her names."

"It doesn't make her a killer." This was a bleed and I had to put a stop to it. "It appears everyone has already tried and hung Madison before there's even an investigation."

"You think it's a coincidence she said she'd love to kill him to more than one person right before he just so happened to be killed?" Reba's face contorted.

Tammy Dugan's heels clicked along the floor and headed toward us.

"I'm going out for a few," she said to Reba. She nodded politely at me. "I hope you're doing okay, Sophia."

"I'm fine. Thanks." I couldn't help but think of why she'd tell Carter that she really believed Madison had done it. I couldn't let Tammy get away. "I'd really like to talk to you if you have a minute."

"Not now. I'll be back soon," Tammy called over her shoulder and rushed out the door.

"What about Giles? Do you think he could've been so mad at Ray?" I blurted it out and brought Reba back into the conversation we were having before Tammy ran past us. "He'd have the most to lose if Ray sold the property. Shouldn't he be a suspect?"

It made perfect sense to me. Giles Dugan had more motive than anyone. If Ray had sold the property, he wasn't going to renew Giles's lease, hurting Giles's income in the process.

"Mr. Dugan is a man of integrity. A man of honor. He'd never lay a hand on anyone," Reba looked over her shoulder. "Look at him now. He's back there trying to hold it together while his son's best friend is down at the morgue with a blow to the head." She dabbed both eyes this time.

"I didn't know that Ray and Perry were friends." It was news to me, but news nonetheless.

"How else do you think Giles got the land? One night the boys were drinking at the bar. Perry was telling how his dad had this crazy idea to make wine." She scoffed. "Who in Kentucky makes wine? Bourbon, yes. Tobacco, absolutely. But wine?" She shrugged. "It was Ray who came to Giles the next day and said he'd heard all about his crazy notions. Right then and there, Giles quit his job at the factory, and Ray leased him the land. That, my dear Sophia, as they say, is all she wrote."

"How did Perry feel about Ray selling the land?" I asked.

"I don't know nothin' about it. I just know Giles said that Perry was devastated by Ray's death." She frowned. "We all are. Ray might've been a complete jerk to some, but here he was like one of the family. Like one of the employees." She waved her hand at me. "I'm sorry—what was it you came here for?"

"My check." There was so much information swirling in my head. "I've not been paid for the fund-raiser."

"Oh." She pulled back and glanced behind her shoulder. "Tammy has the checkbook with her. Do you think you could come back in a couple of days when the shock dies down?"

"Yeah. Absolutely," I agreed.

"Hello." Megyn, the mail carrier, walked into the building, gripping the mail in her hand. "There you go."

"Megyn, I didn't know you came out here," I said and watched as Reba gave her some mail.

"I do all of the downtown stores and a few of the out-of-the-way places like here. I don't mind driving around, especially as the seasons are changing. The Dugans don't really care if I get here early in the morning or late in the night." She leaned in. "How's it going around here?"

"Very sad." Reba's lips quivered when she offered a weak smile. "Would you like one of Sophia's fabulous Cherry Flip-Flops for the ride back into town?"

"I'd love one." Megyn looked into the box. "I'll take the one with all the filling oozing out."

"Good choice," I said and waved her off. Then I turned back to Reba. "Can I ask you another question?"

"You certainly have a lot of them." She looked up from under her brows.

"Why did you give Ray Peel the Cherry Flip-Flops when you told me you'd gotten them to give to Giles when you came into work? I mean, you said you had something to do before you went to work that day." I watched her body language.

She was definitely a little fidgety, and her eyes darted back and forth to different items on her desk, which told me I'd struck a nerve somewhere.

"I see your mother is starting to rub off on you," she

said and laughed as if she were joking. "When I got to the office, Ray was here, and he noticed the box. I offered him one because I was nice. That's all." She pushed her chair back from the desk and stood up. "If you don't mind, I've still got a job to do while the winery is still open."

"About that: I overheard Ray telling someone that the winery was going to be shut down after the fund-raiser last night. It looks far from shut down," I said.

"I don't know anything about that. All I know is the sheriff's department has been in and out all day. Taking computers and papers." She tapped her fingertips on the top of her desk. "If you'll excuse me, I need to check on Mr. Dugan."

"It looks like he's busy shredding papers." My eyes grazed her shoulder and looked back into the office through the partially open door. "I'm guessing those are papers the sheriff's department didn't want."

"It was good to see you. I'll let Tammy know you'd like your check." She turned and walked off.

"Do you happen to know if the wine convention is still going to be here tonight?" I called after her.

"No." She stopped and shook her head. "Now, I did hear it got cancelled."

"Lanie Truvinski was the woman in charge of the convention. Do you happen to have her paperwork or signed copies of the venue?" I asked.

"I don't because I didn't handle that one." Her eyes narrowed. She glared at me, or at least from the distance she was from me it seemed like her stare was intent.

"I thought you handled all the venues that rented the winery?" I asked.

"I do, but this was a special occasion. Ray Peel asked Mr. Dugan if he could do it himself." She lifted her chin in the air. Her gaze drew down her nose.

When I started to walk away, I mustered up enough courage to ask, "How well did you know Ray?" This time my tone was a little louder than normal.

She stopped.

"That's an odd question." She raked the edges of her hair and walked back toward me. "I mean, of course I knew him because he was in here, but not well enough to know much about him."

"I was asking around town about the new Italian restaurant." I looked up at the ceiling like I'd forgotten the name, but I was trying to get her to respond. She was as cold as ice. "Café Italia. Yeah. That's it. Anyway,"—I shook my head and smiled—"someone told me to ask you about it because they'd seen you and Ray there."

I left out the cozied-up part and the corner table, because, by the look on her face and how the blood had drained, she knew what I was talking about.

"Who said?" she asked.

The phone in my back pocket buzzed. I pulled it out and saw it was Charlotte. I gave Reba the finger wave and scurried out the door.

"I can't remember," I called over my shoulder and made a mental note about her behavior. "I'm glad he enjoyed the

Flip-Flops, though. At least that's what he told me." I knew I'd left her there with a question in her mind about what I knew. Or at least I'd gotten her attention. Her odd behavior didn't go unnoticed. I wasn't sure what all of this meant, and she wasn't going to tell me . . . yet.

I stepped out into the sun. As it warmed my face, and before I answered the phone, I sucked in a deep breath of fresh air that you could only get in the country.

"Hi, Charlotte. Is something wrong?" I had to ask right off the bat because Charlotte rarely called me during the working day.

"Sophia, get back to the bakery. We have a problem." The tone in her voice alarmed me. She hung up the phone before I could ask what was wrong.

I threw the car in gear and drove as fast as I could.

Chapter Seven

Excitement and anxiety mixed in the core of my body. When I drove past the bakery and turned down the alley to park in the back, I noticed there was a line of customers out the door.

The back door of the bakery was propped open, the oven timers were going off, and loud chatter filtered through the swinging door. On my way into the bakery, I turned off the timers and looked in the ovens to get out whatever was in there so it wouldn't burn. Beads of sweat gathered on my forehead from the heat in the kitchen.

"What are those?" I asked myself and bent down close to one of the pans. I looked at the lump of dough Charlotte had concocted into something unrecognizable. "Charlotte?" I called.

"In the shop!" she hollered back.

I grabbed an apron and tied it around me on my way out the swinging door. My awaiting public needed me.

Charlotte's eyes glittered with panic after I pushed through the door. "You could've told me about the coupon," she whispered.

"What coupon?" I asked and watched as she iced some of those lumpy things I'd taken out of the oven.

"The Ford's Bakery Maple Long Johns coupon." She sat the bag of icing on the counter and dragged out a copy of the *Rumford Journal*. The one I'd not paid attention to this morning when Megyn dropped it off with the rest of the bills.

"What the heck?" I grabbed the paper and took a good long look at a coupon that read "Free donut with the purchase of a Ford's Bakery Maple Long John."

"I didn't do this," I exclaimed.

"Tell them that." She was busy icing the rest of her lumpy dough. "I had to come out here to finish the decorating because we're so busy."

The line had grown longer since I'd arrived. People were starting to get a little antsy and peering over one another to look at me.

"Is that . . . ?" I pointed and questioned.

"My version of the Long John? Yes," she replied with heavy irony. "And my version of the maple icing."

Panic struck me deep when I turned around and saw all the people were holding a coupon, staring at me, and gossiping among themselves. The looks on their faces weren't happy, and I'd noticed a few of them were checking their watches or phones.

For some odd reason, I felt a bit of relief when Carter pushed his way through the door. He too had a paper stuck up under his arm. His eyes met mine. Without saying it, I was screaming for help inside, and he must've seen it.

"I'm assuming you didn't think people would see your coupon?" he asked.

"I didn't put that in the paper. I have no idea how it got in there." I sucked in a deep breath.

"Someone did." He turned back to look at the line. "And these folks are here to collect."

"I'm trying." Charlotte was on the verge of tears.

I took a bite of her version of the famous Long John that the citizens of Rumford were dying to have, and the dough was still sticky inside.

"I can't help it. I'm doing my best." Her voice was fragile and shaky.

"Don't worry." I wanted to reassure her so she wouldn't be upset. That wouldn't help anything. "I've been trying to duplicate Dixie Ford's Maple Long John all my life in the kitchen, and I've never gotten it right." I tried to chew the rest of Charlotte's version, but I just couldn't do that kind of injustice to my taste buds.

She'd tried so hard. Maybe making the Long Johns just wasn't her thing.

"We can't do this." I spit the remaining donut in a napkin and threw it in the trash. "Can I please have everyone's attention?" I walked around the counter and waited for everyone to gather inside. "I'm sorry for the confusion. We didn't put a coupon in the paper. I'm not sure if the editors at the *Rumford Journal* found an old ad from years ago, but

I do feel terrible about this. I'm more than happy to honor the coupon with the delicious and fast-selling peanut butter and jam sandwich cookies."

There was a murmur that blanketed the bakery, and soon heads were nodding in agreement.

"Thank you so much. I promise I'll try and get this worked out." I looked at Carter and let out a sigh of relief, and then I looked at Charlotte. A cry of relief broke from her lips.

"These are awful." She laughed and dumped the pan in the trash.

For the next hour, Charlotte and I filled the customer's coupons and even took a few orders for some birthday cakes and special-order cookies. Carter told me he'd be back because he needed to talk to me. Charlotte flipped the sign on the door to "Closed." I hated to do it, but somehow this coupon was put in the paper and the only way to stop, gather my wits, and figure things out was to close for the day.

"What are we going to do about the peanut butter and jam sandwiches you just gave away?" Charlotte asked after the last of the customers had left the bakery. "Didn't that woman already pay for those?"

"We aren't going to do anything." I knew she was referring to the special-order made by Lanie Truvinski and the wine convention. "I was at the winery trying to collect payment for the fund-raiser and found out the wine convention had been cancelled."

"That woman didn't call you to cancel?" Charlotte's eye widened.

"Not a word. But I plan on calling her." It might've worked out for the good that she didn't get the order because I wasn't sure how I would've gotten all the coupon customers happy, but I still didn't like her skipping out and not calling me. "I guess I need to give her money back."

"No, you won't. That money is fair and square yours. You held up to your end of the deal. Don't let her get away with it." Charlotte leaned against the counter. "I'm going to go clean the mess in the kitchen."

"Thanks so much, Charlotte. I have no idea what I'd do without you." I squeezed her arm. "I'm sorry this happened."

"Do you really think it was a mistake on the part of the *Rumford Journal*?" She asked a very good question.

"I might have an idea." I stewed on it for a second. "Bitsy," I gasped when I recalled her saying I could use some more customers.

"Bitsy is a hoot and a holler and a lot of things, but would she put a coupon in the paper for something you don't make?" Charlotte asked and walked through the swinging door.

I followed her. Both of us started to clean up the doughy mess she'd made from trying to come up with a recipe for the Long Johns.

"I didn't want to say anything because it would make you really excited, but I found the Fords' journal with all of their recipes in one of the desk drawers in the office." I would've shown her, but I'd left it in my car, along with my purse, after I'd gotten panicked from seeing the line of customers and ran into the bakery. "When she came in yesterday morning, she mentioned we could use some more customers."

"We're always closed on Sundays." Charlotte washed the baking trays and put them away.

"I reminded her. But then I made the mistake of showing her the Fords' journal." I took another tray from her and dried it before putting it back where it belonged. "The Maple Long John recipe is in there."

"And why aren't we making them?" Charlotte wanted to know.

"Because I'm not sure if it's my property to replicate, and that's what I wanted to ask Bitsy. I wanted to see what her thoughts were on it. I'm going over to their house for supper tonight, and I'll find out if she put the ad in or not. In the meantime, I'm going to call the paper." If she did do it, she'd not be able to deny it to my face. If I called her, she'd lie and I wouldn't know it. It was the face-to-face she wasn't good at.

"If the Fords wanted it, they'd have taken it." Charlotte said exactly what I'd thought.

"I did call them, and some young girl answered the phone." I grabbed the peanut butter, eggs, and butter out of the refrigerator. As long as the coupon was still circulating, I had to make enough peanut butter and jam cookie sandwiches to last. Since they were pretty easy and a lot could be made at one time, it was a perfect substitute. "She said Dixie wasn't available to talk."

"I bet it was Patsy's daughter." Charlotte worked alongside me with the dry ingredients: the flour, baking soda, and sugar. Just like the ingredients for this cookie, Charlotte and I worked perfectly together. This made the process go much faster.

"I didn't know Patsy had a daughter." Patsy was the Fords' only daughter and had been in school a few years ahead of me. They were just another family I'd not kept up with while I was away. The only people I had kept up with were Bitsy and Dad. I rarely made it home because in the food industry you rarely get a day off.

"Yeah." Charlotte's brows rose. "She got pregnant right out of high school. You don't remember that? Everyone was talking about it. Even the chickens under the porch knew that."

"No. I guess my head was stuck in a flour and sugar sack all through high school," I joked. "But I do remember she was a wild one." I remembered how many times Bitsy would tell my dad how she felt sorry for the Fords because Patsy was always in trouble.

"Apparently, the apple doesn't fall too far from the tree. I heard down at the salon that Patsy leaves her daughter with the Fords all the time. That's why I bet it was her."

"She didn't have very good manners." I got all the ingredients ready to make the icing while I gave Charlotte all of my wet ingredients to be mixed in with her dry ingredients.

Both of us looked over our shoulders when the back door of the bakery opened.

"You're not going to believe this." Madison stepped in and slammed the door. "I'm the only suspect in the murder of Ray Peel. Sophia, I need your help."

Chapter Eight

"Now, calm down," I encouraged her. She looked like she was about to raise all sorts of hell, with her face a dark flush and her eyes narrowed.

"That—that—that—" She spit out the words but couldn't wrap them around her tongue.

"That what?" Charlotte asked.

Madison pointed her finger at me and shook it.

"That boyfriend of yours!" she blurted out. "He accused me of killing Ray Peel. The nerve." She crossed her arms in front of her body and jerked them tight to her. "And you're going to help him realize it wasn't me."

"Did you have the murder weapon?" I asked.

"Heck no." She looked at me like I didn't believe her, and then turned to Charlotte. "Charlotte, you believe me, right?"

"Of course I believe you, and so does Sophia." She nodded.

"Yes, of course I believe you. I don't think you could do

it, but Carter must have a really good reason to believe that you could've been involved." I was about to say something I was sure I was going to regret. "It's up to us to find the real reason someone did it."

"You mean the killer? Yeah. You did it once. You can do it again." She wasn't going to take no for an answer.

Not that I should've been surprised that Madison was a suspect since I saw with my own eyes what went on when I was at the sheriff's department giving my statement earlier in the day. I was a baker, not a sleuth like the ones on the television shows that I loved to binge-watch on a lazy weekend afternoon.

"We'll all meet at your house since it's your boyfriend who got me into this mess. Plus, you don't have a husband or children to worry about like Charlotte and me." Madison made it real clear that I was alone in that department just like Bitsy loved to do.

"Fine. I've got to call Bitsy and let her know that I'm not coming for supper. She's going to be all sorts of mad." I dragged my phone out of my back pocket.

"We're out of here, then." Charlotte tidied up the kitchen and put the baked goods for tomorrow in the refrigerator or freezer before she left.

"I'll just follow you to your house." Madison wasn't about to let me out of her sight.

"You're going to love what's for supper," Bitsy said over the phone. She wasn't going to be happy when I had to tell her that my plans had changed.

"I love you—remember that." It was my way of buttering her up before I gave her the news. "But I'm not going to be able to make it over tonight."

"Oh, goody." There was an uncanny delightful tone in her voice. "I can only assume that you aren't coming because you and Carter are going to be spending some time together. Oh, Sophia"—her smile was so bright, I swore I could see it through the phone—"I can't wait until I see you come down the aisle."

"Okay. You can stop right there." There was no sense in letting her think Carter was the reason I was cancelling. "No, I'm not going on a date with Carter. I'm going to spend some time with my friends."

"I was looking forward to a good home-cooked meal." I left out that Charlotte was going to grab takeout Chinese and meet us at the house. There, we would put our heads together and try to come up with anything we'd seen at the Grape Valley Winery. "We need to come up with some other people for Carter to check out who'd have reason to kill Ray Peel."

I had a few in mind but decided to wait to say anything until we all got together.

"You mean to tell me that you're going to spend time with criminals? Killers?" She sounded so appalled on the other end of the phone that I could almost see her holding her hand to her chest in disbelief.

Without even having to ask who or what situation she was talking about, I already knew.

"You and I both know Madison didn't kill Ray Peel, so get that out of your head." I had to defend my friend.

"That's not what I heard at the Garden Club meeting that you didn't attend today like you said you were going to. Thank goodness, Charlotte arrived with Dolores's order made for the meeting. We have another one in a couple of days, and I told them you'd be there." It was amazing how Bitsy went from one subject to another, and each time made me feel guilty.

"I hope the ladies enjoyed the treats." I'd completely forgotten about it after the afternoon I'd had. "I'll call you soon." I needed to get off the phone with her because I felt like I was a dog chasing my own tail. Our conversation always went around and around.

"Sophia," Bitsy whined. "I see you less now that you live here than when you lived in Manhattan."

"That's not true," I retorted. "I just saw you this morning. Which reminds me, why on earth did you put a coupon in the paper for a Ford's Bakery Maple Long John?"

"What?" she snapped.

"The coupon," I said again, but a little bit louder.

"What coupon?" she asked in a tone such that I almost believed her.

"The coupon in the *Rumford Journal* you put in to bring in more customers to the bakery." I reminded her of how she'd made that comment.

"I wouldn't use a coupon, much less come up with one

to give something away for free. How do you run a success-ful business giving away free food?" She made a good point.

It was true. Bitsy didn't ever use or cut coupons.

"You didn't put a coupon in the journal?" I asked and heard a shuffling of papers on her end of the phone. "Page three." I could tell she'd gone to retrieve the *Rumford Journal* and was thumbing through it.

"I ought to slap you silly when I see you." Bitsy would never lay a hand on me, but her words were more effective. "You know better than that. Now, the real question is who is trying to put you out of business? Robert!" Bitsy screamed so loud in the phone, I had to pull it from my ear. "Robert! Someone is trying to make Sophia go bankrupt."

"Bitsy. Mama. Mama," I continued to call after her when she didn't pay any attention to me. "No one is after me. Bankrupt? I took care of it."

There was no sense in me trying to even talk to her. She wasn't having it. If someone wronged me, she was always the first one by my side.

"Heavens to Betsy, Sophia." She came back to the phone. "What on earth are you saying?"

"I'm saying if you didn't do it, maybe the paper acciden-tally pulled an old ad." It was probably just as simple as that.

"Here, talk to your daddy." She didn't give me a second to protest.

While jumping into my car and waiting for her to give

the phone to Dad, I noticed how the carriage lights downtown had turned on and gave a warm glow to the sidewalks and fronts of all the shops. There was a light breeze tonight that made the banners hanging down from the dowel rods sway. I hoped it wasn't a sign that a spring storm was coming.

On my way out of downtown, toward my neighborhood, it had gotten darker from the lack of streetlamps. A feeling of home swept over me as I turned onto my street.

"Honey, what's this business about someone wanting you to go bankrupt?" My dad was now on the phone.

"Nothing, Daddy." I turned off the car and leaned back in the driver's seat. "Bitsy is getting all worked up over a mistake at the newspaper. That's all. I'll go see Lizbeth Mockby in the morning."

Lizbeth was the head honcho at the *Journal* and it didn't surprise me one bit. She loved all things news.

In my gut, I knew there was no mistake. Not in today's world. It was just another thing on my list to get to the bottom of.

"If that's all it is." He didn't sound so convinced.

"Yes. That's all it is," I confirmed and watched as Madison pulled up behind me in the old station wagon. "Give Mama a kiss, and save me some leftovers. I'm sorry I can't make it tonight."

"It's alright, honey. I know you've got your own life, and we are very proud of you." Daddy was always so complimentary to me. "And thank you for the treats you sent home today."

"You're welcome." I grabbed my bag and opened to car door to get out. "Bye, Daddy."

We hung up, and I slipped the phone into my back pocket. I'd get in touch with the *Journal* in the morning.

"Are you okay?" I asked Madison. I wanted to get the real low-down before Charlotte got there and ask Madison about the conversation she and I had before I'd found Ray.

"I can't believe they think I killed Ray Peel." She shivered. The situation had gone from making her mad to her coming to the realization that she could be charged. We walked to the front door of my little house. "I have two children and a husband to think about. I can't even clean the kid's boo-boos when they get hurt. Blood makes me ill."

"Carter told me that they still haven't found the murder weapon." I gave her a squeeze on her arm to show her I supported her.

I handed her the keys to my door while I plucked a couple of the dead flowers from the window boxes. I loved the small flower bed and the flower boxes under the front windows of my house. Those were just a couple of the things that gave my home so much character and made it so cozy. I'd worked really hard to keep the pink and white wild cosmos, teal forget-me-nots, purple coneflowers, a few red poppies, and black-eyed Susans alive because I enjoyed watching the butterflies flutter around. I was lucky that the landscape was perfect, and I loved it exactly the way it was when I bought the house.

I walked to the small water fountain feature on the right side of the door. One of the river rocks was making the flow of the water go all wonky, so I moved it to the side to unplug the clog, letting the water go back to flowing down the fountain and into the pool of water at the base.

"He didn't tell me that," she grumbled on our way into the house, still worrying over my comment about the murder weapon.

Duchess ran up to us, rubbed on our ankles, and ran to the kitchen. It was her way of saying, *Hello, now feed me.*

The kitchen had sold me on the house before I even knew I was in the market for one. When I'd come back to Rumford for a visit that turned permanent, this house had been for sale, and I'd agreed to bake some chocolate chip cookies in the kitchen for Madison, so her clients would smell them when they came to tour the house. I instantly fell in love with the shiplap walls, but the repurposed screen door with the chalkboard that led into the biggest pantry I'd ever seen in a house made my buying the house a foregone conclusion.

Since I needed a place to stay while I was in town, and Madison didn't have a buyer, she and I had agreed to do a contract like the Airbnb ones that were so popular. A week later, I'd decided not to go back to New York City and to stay in Rumford instead, making it a no-brainer for me to buy the small house that was the perfect size.

"And that's why I need you." She put her hands on my kitchen counter island and leaned forward. "Carter is in love with you, and I need you to convince him that I didn't do it."

"I know you didn't do it." At least the Madison I knew couldn't. "But he has to have some sort of reason to believe it."

"That alone should be enough proof." Madison's jaw tensed.

"Carter said he was going to subpoena the phone company and see if he can get anything that might've been erased. There was nothing at Ray's house." I offered a sympathetic smile. "It's going to be a few days until the phone records come back. Until then, we need to figure out other people with motives. Maybe check out a few. Why does Carter think you did it?"

"He thinks I did it because Ray Peel turned me down to be the real estate agent for the land. Ray said I was a hillbilly real estate agent with hillbilly clients," she snarled. "I'm not saying I'm glad he's dead, but Ray Peel was crooked as a dog's hind legs."

"Madison," I gasped. "He said that you were a hillbilly? I knew you were upset, but you never told me what about. Only that you would strangle him with the grapevines if you could."

"Right!" She threw her hands up in the air. "Strangle him, not hit him over the head," she said, as if those words were proof of her innocence.

"Please tell me that you didn't say that to anyone else

but me." I closed my eyes and waited for her to answer. I had a nigglin' suspicion that she'd let her loose lips spread bad words about Ray and how he thought mean things about her business.

"Tell anyone but you what?" Charlotte had let herself in the front door. She had a brown bag in each hand. The smell of Chinese food wafted across the room and made my stomach gurgle in delight.

"That she wanted to strangle Ray Peel, right before he died," I said and opened one of the bags, taking out the little containers filled with the yummy food.

"You said that?" There was disbelief on Charlotte's face. When Madison nodded, Charlotte said, "Well, no wonder you're a suspect."

"Just because I *said* it doesn't mean I *did* it. I didn't do it." She dragged over one of the containers. She snapped the wooden chopsticks apart and stuck them in the food.

The three of us stood there with our heinies leaning against my kitchen counter and dug into the food. All of us were deep in thought.

"I've got some people we can look at." I put the container on the counter. "Lanie Truvinski."

"Thank god for her order, or we'd have been in trouble today." Charlotte continued to stuff her mouth.

"No." I shook my head and walked over to grab the chalk on the ledge of the chalkboard on the pantry door. "Suspect and motive," I said and wrote the two words at the top. "Lanie Truvinski." I wrote her name under suspect.

I stood back and looked at what I'd written.

"Okay." Madison pushed up, to stand. "Who is Lanie Truvinski, and how did she save you from being in trouble?"

"Bitsy put a coupon in the paper for a free Long John. And when Lanie didn't follow through with her order—" Charlotte started to tell Madison about the whole mess.

"No. That's not it," I interrupted. "Lanie Truvinski and Ray Peel knew each other." Under motive I wrote that she was friends with Ray and this wasn't the first time he'd betrayed the friendship. "You saw her. Remember the lady you thought was a high-end real estate agent at the winery?"

"Yeah." Madison nodded her head, her eyes lowered. She walked over with a sudden interest.

"Ray had promised to let her use the winery for the annual wine tasters' convention. I overheard him tell her he was closing the winery that night, and she said he'd promised her she could have the convention there. She smacked him across the face, and I've not seen her since." It was all starting to come back to me. "Now I can't find her. I've called her several times. Reba told me the convention had been cancelled."

"Write that down." Madison pointed her finger at the board. "Do you think anyone else heard or saw this happen? She could have motive."

"Well, Catherine Fraxman might have, but . . ." My heart dropped. "She was standing there when you told me you wanted to strangle Ray. Remember, she said thank goodness you were a good Southern girl?"

"Then it was Cat who told Carter I said that. Hussy," Madison muttered. "Carter wouldn't tell me who told him, but I knew it wasn't you."

"Think," I encouraged them. "Did you hear or see anything? The smallest of things."

"What about Cat?" Charlotte asked. "Did she get the money from Ray that he'd pledged?"

"Oh, right!" I clapped my hands together. Duchess took off like a jet. "She did say Ray wasn't able to give the money, and she was mad. She said she believed in karma."

"So that's two people we can look into besides me." Madison took the chalk from me and wrote down Cat's name.

"But what about Tammy and Giles Dugan? They'd have the most to lose if their business was taken away." I shrugged. "Why not put them on there?"

"I'd overheard something about Tammy's son going to a fancy college while I was at the fund-raiser. She was bragging on it." Charlotte jarred my memory again.

"Bragging on it?" I asked. "She was mad before the event When I tried to get my check the first time. She said that she hadn't been saving tuition for him. We need to get the lease agreement."

"Why?" Madison's brows furrowed.

"Because we need to know what, if anything, is in it for the Dugans if something happened to Ray." I wrote down on the chalkboard to get the agreement. The motive could be in it.

"I thought Giles was set for life." Charlotte threw it out there.

"Giles might be, but what about the kids?" Madison asked.

"Kids? I hardly think Tammy or Perry are kids. Besides, Perry is a big-time attorney. He doesn't need his dad's money." Charlotte took the chalk from Madison. "But Tammy sure would be affected by it. She'd not only lose her job but her income. She worked at the Piggly Wiggly for years as a cashier before the winery took off. I'm sure she wouldn't want to go back to that. I think you have someone there to look into."

All three of us stood back and looked at the chalkboard, with silence hanging over us.

"And"—I gnawed on my bottom lip "Ella Capshaw told me today that she'd heard Ray and Reba were cozy in the corner table at Café Italia. That new place."

"Really?" Madison drew back and looked at me funny.

"I asked her about it, and she got all weird and nervous like I'd hit a nerve." I looked between them. "Like she was hiding something."

Madison went ahead and wrote Reba's name on the board too.

"My pantry door should have my grocery list on it, not a list of murder suspects," I half-joked to lighten the mood.

"There's no way I can go see any of these people." Madison looked at me.

"*You've* got the in." Charlotte looked at me too. I was in a friendship sandwich.

"How do I have an in?" I wondered.

"You can deliver cookies and treats." Charlotte made it seem so simple. "You've got that knack."

"Right. You helped figure out Emile's death." Madison threw that horrid memory at me. "And people feel comfortable with you. They tell you things."

"If that's the case, you two need to leave so I can do some baking." I nodded at their idea. It wasn't so bad.

"You're the best." There was a twinge of hope in Madison's eyes.

"Don't get too excited," I warned.

"I know you're going to help me. If not for me, for my children." She threw the biggest guilt trip on me.

Now there was no way I could refuse.

Chapter Nine

When you're not a police officer or any kind of investigator, there is something so strange about waking up to a chalkboard covered with the names of people you know who might be a killer. The next day, after I'd gotten ready for work and filled Duchess's bowl with kitty kibble, I couldn't stop looking over the names.

"Cat Fraxman," I said—the first name on the list. "What did you say to Ray Peel when he told you he wasn't going to donate the half-million dollars you needed to pay off the construction loan?"

I leaned back on the farm sink and faced the pantry chalkboard, talking to it like it was some sort of crystal ball that could show me the answer to my question.

Meow.

Duchess trotted up to me and sat down by my feet. She lifted her paw and began to lick it. I bent down and picked her up.

"What do you think?" I asked her and rubbed my hands

down the exotic, long-haired white Persian feline that had been Bitsy's baby for a few years after I left home. Duchess decided that I was her human after I moved back to Rumford. I was shocked when Bitsy actually brought Duchess to me when she figured out why Duchess had stopped eating and wouldn't come out of my childhood room.

"Which one of those did this nefarious crime?" I gave her a quick kiss on the head and put her back on the floor. She scampered off to smack the gray toy mouse with the bell on the end of its pink tail.

Since Duchess wasn't going to give me any insight, and Charlotte had agreed to go into the bakery for the early shift so I could do a little snooping, it seemed appropriate to start with the first name on the list. But not without pulling a few baked treats from the freezer that I'd made ahead of time. A couple of seconds in the microwave, and no one would ever know I'd made them a week ago.

"Good morning," I trilled when I opened the sliding glass door to my parents' back deck. Bitsy was sitting in one of the chairs overlooking the gorgeous view of the ten acres of untouched land behind their home.

"Sophia." Bitsy turned in her chair and smiled. The pink puff ball on her small-heeled, slip-on pink house slippers peeked out from the hem of the quilt laid over her lap. "What a nice surprise. Let me get you a cup of coffee."

"That sounds great," I said.

Bitsy got up and neatly folded the quilt, placing it on the seat of the chair.

"I'm so glad to see you this morning," she said, and we hugged each other.

When I'd left Rumford ten years ago, I was quite young, and our relationship was a bit volatile. She didn't want me to move, but I wanted to see the world. When I'd moved back a few months ago, it was like our relationship hadn't grown, and we picked right up where we'd left off. It was a little touch-and-go because she was still trying to protect me from the big bad world, but she quickly realized that I wasn't a little girl anymore. No matter how much I'd grown, I was still her daughter—but an adult—and she'd finally started to treat me like one.

I followed her into the house and noticed the piles of plastic planters stacked at the bottom of the steps. I slid my gaze to the other side of the deck and looked down at the landscaping. Pops of purples, white, pinks, and yellows dotted the black mulch.

"What's going on with the planters?" I asked Bitsy when I walked into the house.

"What on earth do you mean?" She avoided looking at me by busying herself and getting me a cup of coffee.

"There's a stack of used brown plastic planters at the bottom of your deck steps," I said. "Like someone bought them from a store and replanted."

The island was in the shape of a half-moon and took up half of the kitchen. It had been a perfect gathering place when I was growing up. We'd had a lot of conversations at that island, and I'd done a lot of homework there, but my best memories in this kitchen were about the baking. I'd been making creations since I could remember. When Bitsy and Dad built the house, Bitsy had to have the latest and greatest. No expense was spared on the kitchen. The interior decorator insisted they'd love the tall white cabinets and the white tile floor as well as the big island. Bitsy did love all of that, my favorite things were the industrial kitchen appliances that Bitsy saw as decorations and I saw as the perfect tools to create the best possible pastries.

I dragged the steaming cup of coffee across the island and pulled it up to my lips as I leaned my hip on the granite.

"Who knows." She shrugged and topped off her mug. "Your father is always finding things around here to throw away."

"They don't belong to the pretty gerbera daisies, at least I think they're Gerber Daisies," I eyed her through the steam of the coffee and took another sip. "Because I'd hate to think that you'd try to pass off daisies you didn't actually grow from seedlings at the Garden Club annual flower swap."

Slowly, she turned her shoulder toward me, her head following. Her eyes snapped and not in a good way.

"Sophia Cummings," she gasped. "I can't believe . . ." Her jaw dropped, she closed it, it opened again, she shut it. "I don't have time for this nonsense. Is that what you came over here for?"

"Fine." My brows rose. "I just noticed and asked. I wasn't accusing you of anything."

Though, from the way she responded, I could tell I was

onto something. Now it was just one more thing on my plate, to figure out how to get her not to pass daisies off as her own.

"Actually, I came over to ask you about Ray Peel and the Dugans." With my foot, I scooted one of the stools away from the kitchen island and sat down.

"Don't tell me that you're sticking your nose into something." She lowered her chin and looked down her nose at me. "I told Robert that I was worried you were going to do it again." She referred to my dad.

"I'm not doing anything again." I gnawed on my bottom lip. "Sort of."

"What does that mean?" she asked.

"Madison is a suspect. And I know she didn't do it." I ran the pad of my finger around the rim of the mug.

"Oh, dear." Bitsy's brows furrowed.

"That's why I asked you about Ray Peel and the Dugans. Did you talk to them at the fund-raiser?" I asked.

"I talked to Tammy Dugan, but not the rest of them. Ray was a bundle of nerves that night. He wasn't really engaging in conversation at all. I figured he was nervous about giving so much money away. I know I'd be as nervous as a cat in a roomful of rocking chairs." She sighed. "I can't believe Madison is a suspect."

"Did Tammy say anything?" I asked.

"About what?" Bitsy's head tilted to the side.

"Anything about the winery?" I tried to be nonchalant in my questioning, but I could tell Bitsy's radar was on full alert.

"No. I asked about her son and that fancy college I'd heard he was going to, and she said he was excited."

"She didn't say he wasn't going?" I clearly remembered her telling her father that without the income of the winery, she couldn't pay what her son needed to go to the Ivy League college.

"What are you getting at?" Bitsy knew me well enough to know I was digging around.

"I need you to keep your nose in the gossip circles of your clubs." I leaned over the island. "Madison had a meeting with Ray Peel. He was selling the land the winery sits on. The winery lease is up, and he wasn't going to renew it with the Dugans. When I went to get my check for catering the fund-raiser, I overheard Tammy telling her father that her son couldn't go to the school if she didn't have the job."

"How does this make Madison a suspect?" she asked.

"He'd made fun of her because her clientele isn't as wealthy as he is, and he didn't believe she'd have the contacts to sell such an expensive property." I shook my head. "But that's not the problem. I think the Dugans have more motive to have killed Ray than Madison."

"What do you want me to do?" she asked.

"I want you to listen to the gossip and ask around if anyone has heard anything about the sale of the property. You run around with all those rich people. You know what they're going to be talking about," I suggested.

"Are you saying that we need to investigate?" There was an upbeat tone in her voice as she straightened up her shoulders.

"I'm . . . um . . ."

"This is great! You're finally including me." She rubbed her hands together. Her eyes grew big. "We can call it . . ."—she hesitated before a grin as big as the day is long crossed her lips—"Operation Merlot."

"Wait." I pushed myself off the stool and stood, trying to figure out exactly how she'd just turned this into an investigation with her involved. "Not an investigation."

"Sophia, who do you think you're talking to?" She sent me a sly eye. "I'm your mother. I know you better than anyone, and I can see that little noggin of yours is filled with crazy ideas about how you're going to get Madison off the list of suspects. You need me."

"But this is not . . ." I stopped when I could see she wasn't buying it. "Operation Merlot does have a good ring."

"I'm pretty witty when I need to be." She lifted the mug to her mouth and with a wry smile took a drink. "I'll meet you at your house tonight to discuss what I find out."

"You can't do that. Carter and I are going out to supper at the new Café Italia." I looked at my watch. It was almost that time of the morning when he usually called. If he called while I was at my parents', he'd know something was up because I never went to my parents' house this early in the day. "I've got to get to the bakery," I told Bitsy and left out the minor detail that I was going to stop by the library to ask Catherine Fraxman, the Rumford librarian, a few questions.

"Then when are we going to get together and compare notes?" she asked.

"I'll call you." I gave her a kiss. "I set some treats over there on the table."

"You love to fatten us up." She winked before we gave each other a hug goodbye.

The Rumford Library had always been the town's heartbeat, and that's how the committee had come up with the name of the fund-raiser. Clubs, groups, and government committees used the library's conference room to hold their monthly—sometimes weekly—meetings. This was one of the reasons for the expansion. There'd been talk of a new government building, but it would change the charm of Rumford, and that wasn't a compromise the citizens wanted to make. In a unanimous vote, the townsfolk had decided to invest in the library so that the entire town population would benefit. That included the expanded children's section. Anytime children were included, the entire town was on board.

Rumford, being the small town it was, meant that it only took me a few minutes to get across to the south side of town, where the library was located.

The one-story library was actually pretty big and long, but the addition of a second floor was going to be so nice. The double sliding doors that led into the library opened automatically, and the smell of print books circled around me, bringing wonderful memories of my childhood and causing me to glance to the right, into the children's library, where the short shelves, bean bags, and computers waited for the children.

The reference desk was directly across from the children's section.

"Sophia, what are you doing here?" Catherine was behind the desk. She lifted the ruffle on the edge of her blouse sleeve and looked at her watch. "You're a little early for Friends of the Library. Like two days early."

Friends of the Library was the club that Bitsy had started after she and a group of her friends started meeting there for book club. She'd drag me to book club on a regular basis, and when other people in the community came into the library and noticed our group, Bitsy realized there was a need to spread the word about books and what the library had to offer. This was one of her many proud accomplishments she liked to boast about.

"You know what they say about the early bird." I pulled a bag of the Flips-Flops out of my purse. "You get the first fresh batch of the day."

Technically it was freshly out of my freezer.

"Uh-oh." Her eyes lowered. "You're buttering me up for something. I've seen you use this trick on other people."

"Cat. We've been friends for a long time. I'm here to make sure I've got all the notes correct on my list of items you want me to make for the ribbon-cutting ceremony." I pulled out the list. "I mean, it's been a while since we made the list."

"I thought I signed off on the list a few weeks ago." She opened up the bags and took one out. She pointed to the list in my hand. "On that paper too."

"Yeah, but I just wanted to make sure. I mean, I've lost

a lot of money in the past couple of days, and it's not a habit I need or want to get into, so I'm double checking with everyone." Wow, I surprised myself, pulling that lie out of nowhere. Not that I was totally lying. I was out of a lot of money since I'd yet to be paid by the Dugans. Then there was the whole Lanie Truvinski thing. Though she'd given me a partial payment.

"Tell me about it." She looked over to the construction workers coming through the door with their gear, getting ready to start their day. "I've got to meet with the Friends of the Library to let them know Ray Peel didn't . . ." She shook her head. "That doesn't matter now. The poor man is dead."

"Yeah. I can't believe it. I'm so sorry he didn't give you the donation. Do you know why he decided not to donate?" I asked with a sudden urge to know the answer.

"He said he'd talked it over with his financial someone or other and that it wasn't going to be a good donation for this year. Or something like that. He said all sorts of other stuff too, but all I heard was he wasn't giving the full five hundred thousand." Her voice cracked. "If that was the case, we'd have been doing way more fundraising drives. Now we're going to have to pay some sort of fee for turning the construction loan into a building loan since we didn't have all the funds to build upfront."

"Did he mention the name of his financial advisor? I need some advice about the bakery." I really hoped she'd heard him say something.

"No. I mean, he could have, but I was so mad at that point I couldn't even think straight." Her jaw tensed.

"What did you say to him?" I asked.

"What could I say? I walked up to him at the fundraiser and told him how I'd gotten one of those big checks made with the five hundred thousand dollars printed on it. After I announced his big donation, I was going to have him sign the fake check and hold it up for the newspaper to take a photo. I was even going to name the new children's wing after him. I was going to announce that too. It was all planned out, and he ruined it," she spat.

"I'm sorry." I gave her as much sympathy as I could without making her realizing I was being nosy.

"I don't mean to speak ill of the dead, but between you and me, he'd wronged too many people. I was warned. I knew better." She sighed.

"Warned? By who?" I asked.

"Reba Gunther," she snarled.

"Reba?" I asked, once again connecting Reba to Ray. Only this time Cat was connecting Reba to Ray in an unfriendly sort of way, while Ella Capshaw had put Reba and Ray together romantically.

"She said something really strange about the winery," Cat said. "The other day when I was there to see Ray about doing the speech for the ribbon cutting, since I was going to be naming it after him due to the big donation." She rolled her eyes. "Anyway, I can't dwell on that. A dead man ain't gonna give me any money now." She let out a deep sigh.

"What about Reba?" I hurried her along.

"When I was there, Ray was in a pretty heated meeting with Giles. I asked Reba about it because Reba knows everything going on in that place. She said the lease was coming up, and Ray had put in the new lease that he got fifty percent of the wine sales." Her words nearly stopped my heart. "Apparently, Ray knew Giles wouldn't go for it, and it's why he put the clause in the agreement."

"Do you know anything about contracts? Lease contracts?" I wondered if I could get my hands on the contract between Ray and the winery.

"Like what?" she asked.

"Is the actual contract public?" I knew that Cat would know since she'd been involved since the beginning.

"No." She shook her head. "If there was a sale of the property, you'd be able to get the deed and bill of sale from the courthouse, but not a contract. That's probably with the lawyers, though."

"I wonder who their lawyers are?" I'd assume that since he was a lawyer, Perry would be his father's.

"I have no idea." She looked at me with a suspicious eye. "Why are you asking about all of this?"

Madison was the police's number-one suspect, and I just knew she didn't do it.

"You know what?" I looked at my watch. "I've got to go, but I'll be back, and we can go over that list for the ribbon-cutting ceremony then."

"But I won't have time later," Cat called after me before

I headed out of the door. "You're the one who needs to go over it. Not me."

"I'll call you." I waved over my shoulder.

As I hurried to my car, I dragged my phone out of my bag and scrolled through my favorites to find Carter's name.

"Good morning," he answered in his slow Southern drawl. "How did you sleep?"

"Fine." I got into the car and started it up. "Did you talk to Reba Gunther about Ray Peel?" I asked.

"Seriously?" He didn't sound happy with me.

"Good morning. I didn't sleep much because I'm so upset about Madison being your number-one suspect." I knew he wasn't going to like that I'd been investigating.

"You aren't snooping around, are you?" he asked me. My silence was his cue to continue speaking, "Please, Sophia. Let me do my job," he pleaded on the other side of the phone.

As he talked about how dangerous it was for me to get involved, I watched all the construction workers file through the sliding doors of the library. With each one, I saw dollar signs that Ray Peel's money could've been paying for. Now it was all debt the Rumford citizens were going to pay for.

"I've got to go, but I'll be over to pick you up at six. Got it?" he asked, seeming fairly confident that I'd listened to him.

"Got it." I dragged the phone from my ear and hit the red button. I hadn't gotten a thing he said, and I wasn't going to just sit back and let Madison go to jail.

Chapter Ten

"You agreed not to look into things?" Charlotte looked up from the sink, where she was cleaning the batch of peaches I was going to be chopping up to put in the Peachy Surprise Bites—my take on peach pie.

Instead of going to see Perry Dugan after I left the library, I went back to the bakery. I knew he'd be in today to order the birthday cake for the winery for Reba Carol's fortieth birthday. Charlotte was holding the fort down, but I needed to think, and baking was the best way to get my mind flowing with ideas.

"I didn't agree not to look into anything." I sliced the peaches in half, then quartered them before I began to dice them. "He didn't wait for me to say anything. He just said he'd pick me up at six."

"And now Bitsy is involved?" She grabbed a white towel out of the drawer and hand-dried each peach before she put it in front of me.

"Operation Merlot." I stopped chopping and looked at

Charlotte, laughing. "At first, I thought she was kidding, but she wasn't. When I asked her to snoop a little bit, she was all for it."

"Knowing Bitsy, she'll find out everything you want to know." Charlotte walked over to the industrial refrigerator and took out the chilled butter that the recipe called for.

When you used chilled butter, it created pockets of air in the dough and when you put it in the oven, those little pockets steamed and helped the dough rise, giving the perfect airy fluffiness my Peachy Surprise Bites were known for. Otherwise, they'd be flat and boring.

"It gives her something to do besides being in here all day asking questions." I combined the sugar and water in the pot while she sliced the butter and started to combine it with the flour and dry ingredients. "I found some freshly planted flowers in the back of her house and a few used pots stacked up next to the back porch steps."

"I don't think I've ever seen her participate in the exchange," Charlotte said, looking over the top of the electric mixer. "Like *ever*."

"I wonder what made her want to do it this year?" I knew I couldn't let her look like a fool. "Do you know when they're having another meeting?"

"I'll check on my phone once I get the dough rolled into balls." She flipped off the mixer and put her hands in, grabbing enough dough to make into small balls. I flattened the dough balls and put the chopped peaches in the middle.

"Speaking of the phone, I need to call the newspaper

and check on how that ad got in there." I pulled out my phone and scrolled down to find the paper's phone number. I hit the green "Dial" button. "Lizbeth Mockby, please."

Lizbeth and I had gone to school together. She'd gone to college and gotten her marketing degree. From what I'd heard, she'd come back right after she graduated, taken over the marketing department at the newspaper, and then moved her way up to being the number-one reporter.

When her voicemail picked up, I said, "Hi, Lizbeth. It's Sophia Cummings at For Goodness Cakes Bakery. Can you please give me a call?" I rattled off my number.

The bell over the front door dinged. I put my phone back in my pocket and rubbed my hands down the front of the apron, untying it when I pushed through the swinging door.

"Perry." I was a little shocked to see him standing in the bakery, because I'd lost track of time and had yet to come up with a plan for questioning him. "How are you guys doing?" I asked.

"Fine. Why?" he asked.

"With the murder at your winery, I just figured . . ." I stopped and smiled. He didn't seem to be paying much attention to me, between looking over his shoulder and checking his watch. "Anyway, I can't wait to show you some cakes."

"Great. I'm excited to see what you came up with because I really enjoyed tasting your pastries at the fund-raiser the other day." His eyes lit up as a smile curled across his face. He pulled up his sleeve and looked at the time yet again.

"I'm glad you enjoyed it. Let me grab a notepad." I walked over to the glass counter and pointed to one of the displays. "While you wait, I want you to try one of these macarons. Reba loves them, and I think we can incorporate those in some way."

I grabbed a paper napkin and took off the dome of the cake platter Charlotte had arranged, with all the bright, spring-colored macarons on display. It was that time of year when people came in for a light and fluffy dessert. The colorful, airy macaron was the right choice with a fresh cup of coffee.

I walked back into the kitchen to grab an order pad.

"I totally lost track of time." It was something I shouldn't be surprised about since baking allowed my mind to wander. "Perry Dugan is here for his appointment for that cake order for Reba," I said with an exhausted sigh, and I picked up the dry erase marker, marking through his appointment time. I grabbed the order pad. "Do you think it'd be tacky if I asked if Reba and Ray were dating?"

"Yes. But who cares." Charlotte smiled. "You're never going to know unless you ask. And we are in the throes of Operation Merlot," she reminded me.

On my way back out to take his order, I decided I could just make it seem like I was being nosy.

"These are real good, Sophia." He wadded up the napkin and threw it in the trash can at the end of the counter.

"Thanks. Macarons are fun, and we can color them in her favorite color." I gestured for him to sit down at one of the small café tables like I did with all my clients who made special orders. There were a couple of photo albums of cakes I'd done for clients and for the restaurants I'd worked in.

He sat down, and I grabbed one of the albums, flipping through it until I found the cakes I'd had in mind.

"We can make her a chocolate macaron cake that can be three tiers high or even in a pointy shape." I indicated a couple of cakes. "If we do the tiers, I can outline each one with different colored macarons. If we do a cone shape, I can cover it with macarons like this one."

He leaned in and looked at the photos.

"What's her favorite color?" I asked.

"I think she'd like this color." He pointed to the light blue color that was the same color as Tiffany's blue box that was so famous. She likes sprinkles too."

"Why don't we do a three-layer chocolate macaron cake with this light blue icing. I can melt chocolate on top and let it drip down the sides. Once it's nice and hardened, I'll make some light and hot pink macarons to decorate the top. Around the bottom of the cake, I'll add some sprinkles and a few more macarons for decoration." As I spoke, I watched his eyes start to brighten in agreement with me.

"How is Reba doing now that Ray is gone?" I asked and started to write up the ticket for the order.

"What do you mean?" His mouth took on an unpleasant twist. "Why would Ray Peel's death affect her?"

"Well, I'd heard they were pretty close. Going on dates and things." I shrugged and stood up.

"No. They weren't dating. My father has a strict policy against employees dating. He said it makes for a bad workplace. I don't know where you heard that, but I don't think it's true." He stood up and adjusted the buttons on his suit jacket.

"Hmm. Maybe I misheard. Still, how is she doing now the lease is up on the winery?" I continued to probe.

"The lease isn't up at this minute. I'd been working with Dad and Ray on a new lease." His expression stilled and grew serious.

"Ray had talked to Madison about being the agent. I have to say," I said, busying myself behind the counter to look like I wasn't being so nosy and focused on his answers, "I was shocked that Ray took back his donation. Said he was having money issues and wanted to sell. I thought the winery was doing great."

"It is. That's the problem when you don't own the land. The landlord sees how well the business is doing and up goes the rent." He pulled his wallet out of the back of his dress pants.

"Do you regret making the deal over a beer?" I asked.

"How did you know that?" His head tilted.

"Reba told me. She said that you and Ray were best friends." I could see his nostrils flare slightly as he tried to keep his composure. What nerve had I struck? The one where Reba said they were best friends? Or how Reba told me about the lease?

Without even looking at him, I could feel the tension in

his muscles flex. I used the pen to circle the price of the cake and handed him the receipt. I bent down to get the calendar from underneath the counter. "You can pay for it when you pick it up. When do you need it?" I asked, standing up.

The bell over the door dinged. Perry was rushing down the sidewalk in front of the bakery.

"What was that about?" Charlotte asked over my shoulder.

"I think I hit a nerve, but I'm not sure where." My eyes lowered as I watched Perry jump in his fancy sports car and zoom down the road. "But I do know that Reba Gunther might know more than we think."

"Like what?" She took one of the macarons from the pile on the cake plate before she put the domed lid back on.

"Well, he did say that Giles didn't allow employees to date, but Ray wasn't an employee—or was he?" I turned to face her. "When Perry was picking out her cake, he didn't just pick out a cake like any guy would. He actually hand-picked her color and told me she liked sprinkles."

"What does that mean?" Charlotte asked.

"Sprinkles are an intimate detail when it comes to putting them on cakes. Special cakes. Only someone who knows you really well would say that you love sprinkles." I smiled real big. "I think Perry is in love with Reba."

"Oh, shut up. She's like twice his age." She started to count out loud using her fingers.

"He's thirty. She's turning forty. Not that ten years is a big deal, but something was strange when I asked him about Reba and Ray. Like it was news to him, what I'd heard about Ray and Reba going on a date." There was something there; I just couldn't put my finger on it.

The phone rang. She grabbed it. "For Goodness Cakes, Charlotte speaking."

She handed me the phone.

"Lizbeth from the paper," she whispered.

"Hi, Lizbeth. Thanks for calling me back." I had to put the whole Reba thing in the back of my head for a minute.

I quickly explained to her about the coupon.

"No, it was the right one," she said, as if she hadn't made a mistake. "I printed it exactly how you told me to."

"I never called and put in an ad." Had she lost her mind?

"It was on the note you left on my desk with the payment," she said. "I've got it right here."

"What are you talking about?" I asked her and heard paper shuffling through the receiver.

"When I got to work the day before the ad ran, there was an envelope with a note from you and cash to pay for it." She sighed. It read, "*Please put this ad in the paper exactly as I've written it.*'" She began to read off the ad that offered the coupon and a free Long John.

"I didn't place the ad," I said. "Can I come down and look at it?"

"Yeah. It's your ad," she said.

"I told you that I didn't place the ad. I didn't write out an ad, and I didn't come to the newspaper office to deliver the ad." It was plain and simple.

"If you didn't do it, who did?" she asked.

"I don't know, but I intend to find out. I'll be down there to get it." I hung up the phone.

"Well?" Charlotte asked.

"Someone is trying to send me a message." I swallowed hard and squared my shoulders. "Only, I don't know who, and I don't know what message they are trying to send. But I'm about to find out."

I grabbed my bag and made sure Charlotte could finish up the Peachy Surprise Bites. Trying to figure out who killed Ray Peel was going to have to wait. It was now a priority to find out who was messing with my business and my life, and why.

Chapter Eleven

The *Rumford Journal* wasn't too far down the street from the bakery—just a couple blocks north. They'd taken an old gray clapboard house like those owned by most of the merchants on Main Street, gutted the inside, and made it into offices for writers and editors. The actual printing was sent out by courier to a larger Kentucky city. The *Rumford Journal* was a biweekly paper, and I knew if I got in front of Lizbeth quickly enough, I could get a retraction for the next issue.

"Hi, Sophia!" Lizbeth yelled over the ringing phones and chatter. "Come on in." She waved me over.

When I walked in, I couldn't help but notice she was looking for something. Picking up different files, looking under stacks of papers, and crawling around on the floor.

"I've lost another earring." Her voice echoed from underneath her desk. "I give up." She got up and dusted her pants off. "I don't know why I wear earrings to work." She lifted her right hand to her right ear and felt the earring she did have. "I get on the phone and rest the receiver between my shoulder and ear. The back of the earring pokes me, so I take it out, and then I lose it."

"Occupational hazard," I joked.

Lizbeth hadn't changed much in the last ten years. She'd been the student who loved to run for all the offices and have a hand in all the groups, and who took pride in doing the announcements. When she graduated, I'd heard she still went back to the high school to help them with the paper.

"Here's your envelope." She sat down at her desk and dropped the envelope on top. She shoved a pencil in her black hair, which was pulled up in a tight bun.

"That's not mine." I picked it up and opened it. "I didn't write an ad or send you money for one."

"Someone did you a favor. That's a few-hundred-dollar spot." Her dark eyes stared at me.

"No one did me a favor. Someone wanted me to fail, but the joke was on them." I read the ad that had been typed and then printed out. "Someone who didn't want anyone to know their identity."

"Really?" She leaned in and took an interest. "This could be a story on its own." She sat back in the chair and drummed her fingertips together. "Tell me what happened when this came out."

"What do you think happened?" My face contorted. "Charlotte called me and told me there was a big line at the bakery. I hurried back, and they all had this coupon. They wanted their Fords' Long John. I don't bake or sell Fords' Long Johns."

"It was explicitly stated in the instructions it was for that specific donut." She licked her lips. "I sure do miss those Long Johns."

"We all do," I muttered, not feeling any better. "Originally, I thought Bitsy had done it because she came in and said I needed customers."

"Do you?" Lizbeth asked.

"Do I what?" I questioned, a bit confused.

"Need customers?" she asked.

"No." I shook my head. "Bitsy came in on a Sunday, when I'm not open."

"Continue." She appeared to be taking notes.

"I told the customers that you must've put in an ad from years ago because I didn't place an ad." That got her attention.

"You put this on my shoulders?" Her brows lifted. "I don't make mistakes with my paper."

"Someone did. It wasn't me. I was out a lot of money because I had to make good and give them something free." I lied a little. A little white lie never hurt anyone. At least telling that to myself made me feel somewhat better. "That's not what's important. I need to know who dropped this off."

"Is someone mad at you?" she asked.

"What? No. Ridiculous." All the one-word sentences came out of my mouth like darts.

"Really?" She dragged her glasses off the desk and slid

them up on the bridge of her nose. "I heard you found another body. A dead one, to be specific."

"Are you saying that someone is trying to send me a message?" It wouldn't've been the first time.

"I heard the last time you snooped around, after you found that dead body, someone tried to run you off the road." There was a snarkiness to her voice.

I gulped and reached down to rub my shin. I'd been out for a run when Emile's killer veered their car toward me, sending me a very clear message to stop looking around. *Veered* is being polite. I was almost the next victim in that case. But all of that was in the past.

"Listen, why don't we put a retraction in the next issue. In order to do that, I want you to give me an interview and place a new ad because I don't want the subscribers to think we made a huge mistake. That's not good for business." She was playing hardball.

"Right now?" I looked at my watch and wondered how Charlotte was doing alone at For Goodness Cakes. It was already getting to be late in the afternoon, and it was almost time for me to go home and get ready for my date with Carter.

"Yes. The next issue will be out in the morning, and I need to fill some space." She grabbed a pad of paper, pulled the pencil from her bun, and started the tape recorder. Whether or not I wanted to do an interview, she was going to get it.

"When did you know you wanted to be a pastry chef?"

She asked that and a few other basic questions I'd been asked before in interviews. Then the questioning turned to what I'd say was the real meat of the interview and why she'd wanted me to do it. "For Goodness Cakes—love the name, by the way—was contracted to do the Heart of the Home fund-raiser given by Grape Valley Winery."

I swallowed because I knew what was coming next.

"Can you give me a detailed account of exactly how you found Ray Peel?" She pushed the tape recorder a little closer toward me, to the edge of the desk.

I hesitated. She must've sensed I was a little uncomfortable because she pulled a file out of the wire basket on the credenza behind her desk.

"According to the police report"—she pushed her glasses even further up on her nose—"you were going back to the winery to get your payment when you tripped over Ray."

She pulled her glasses off and put one end in her mouth, easing back in the chair; she was going to wait me out.

"Since you have the police report, I guess I can tell you. Ahem." I cleared my throat and told her exactly what had happened.

"Do you have any idea who would want Ray Peel dead?" she asked.

"Why would I know that?" I questioned.

"I don't know. Maybe because your boyfriend is Carter Kincaid." Her voice escalated. "And I'm sure he gives you some tidbits."

"No. Nope. I don't teach him how to bake, and he

doesn't share with me how to solve murders." I pinched my lips together.

"What about your best friend Madison?" she asked. I could tell she was trying to read my body language. I made sure I sat perfectly still and showed no facial expressions. "I heard she was the number-one suspect."

"That's ridiculous." I threw my hands in the air and all the body language I'd tried to stuff inside came flooding out. "She's a mother of two and a very important, up-and-coming real estate agent who'd never hurt a fly, much less kill someone."

"You and Sheriff Kincaid are not agreeing on this matter?" She was poking the bear with her direct questions, and it worked.

"Of course we aren't," I blurted out. "Madison only wanted a chance to be Ray's real estate agent."

"Why did Ray Peel need a real estate agent?" she asked.

When I'd walked into the newspaper office, I'd had no intention of permitting myself to fall for Lizbeth's tricky way of getting people to talk. She'd done it over and over when we were younger, and now she'd done it again.

"Do you think Catherine Fraxman did it? Because I heard her parents took out a second mortgage on their house for the initial loan of the half million, and Ray Peel was going to pay them back. Any truth to that?" She tapped the eraser of her pencil on the desk. "I'm sure they can't really afford to pay a double mortgage."

"Where did you hear that?" I asked, enlightened by this bit of news.

"I've got my sources." An evil grinned flashed across her face.

"I've said too much." I grabbed a piece of paper and a stray pencil on her desk. I scribbled the new words for the ad and left it on the desk. I knew my flapping lips were going to get me in trouble. "Here is the new ad. Please run it in tomorrow's paper."

"It'll be in print before you even wake up." She seemed very pleased with herself, which stuck with me until I got home.

That wasn't the only thing that stuck with me. If the bank was open, I'd stop there and see Bill Bellman, the loan officer, to find out exactly what he knew. He'd know for sure if what Lizbeth said about the Fraxman's taking out a second mortgage was true. But why would they do that? Unless Ray Peel had promised he'd pay them back. No wonder Cat was so upset. It had to do with her family's livelihood, and that would make a Southern girl mad. But mad enough to kill?

I was so deep in thought, I found myself parked in my driveway without even realizing I was already home.

"Good evening." I bent down and picked up Duchess.

She'd greeted me at the door with a happy purr. With her snuggled to my chest, I headed into the kitchen, turning lights on along the way. The days were getting longer, and I knew the spring weather would be turning into the warm sunny summer.

"How was your day?" I asked Duchess. I looked out the window over the farm sink and watched the ducks swimming in the lake behind my house. "Mine was interesting. I still don't know who put the ad in the paper. But someone did."

I sat her down and watched as she pranced around my legs. She was as silent and graceful as a trained ballerina. She was truly a duchess.

"I had a meeting with Perry Dugan." I walked to the pantry and retrieved a scoop of her kibble to put in her bowl. She sniffed and batted a couple of pieces before she started to eat. "He ordered the birthday cake for Reba, and it wasn't just any birthday cake."

I closed the pantry door and looked at the chalkboard list of possible suspects.

"He knew her favorite color, and he knew her favorite cake. I did too, so it wasn't that surprising, but for a man that isn't involved in the company . . ." I thought about how strangely he'd reacted when I'd asked him about Reba and Ray. "He also said Giles didn't allow employee romances, but why would he say that about Ray?"

I picked up the chalk and added Reba's name to the list of people I needed to check out. The employee-relationship situation seemed pretty strange, so that was the first thing I needed to find out about. I also added the little bit about going to the bank to see Bill to check out what Lizbeth had told me. I wrote "Operation Merlot" at the top of the suspect list.

The clock on the stove read 6:00 PM when the knock at the door brought me back to reality. It had to be Carter.

Duchess ran in front of me, and when I opened it, there stood Carter with a bouquet of roses and a big smile.

"I'm looking forward to just a relaxing night and catching up." He held the flowers out in front of him. "Are you ready?"

"I've got to get changed." I looked down at the dirty clothes that were dusted with flour and other baking ingredients. I pulled the door wide open. "Come on in."

Duchess meowed and batted her big brown eyes at him.

"You're the cutest little girl." He handed me the flowers before he picked up Duchess. "Do you think I forgot something for you?" He put his hand in his pocket and pulled out a little bag of catnip.

She jumped out of his arms and circled around his feet.

"I'll let you give her the treat while I go get changed." I smiled and headed down the hall to my bedroom.

Luckily, I had a lot of cute dresses that I'd gotten in boutiques while I lived in Manhattan. Things you couldn't buy in Rumford. When we went to the new Italian restaurant, I was going to wear an electric blue shift dress that went perfectly with my strappy black sandals. On the way out of my bedroom, I grabbed the black shawl to slip around my shoulders in case there was a nip in the air after we'd eaten. You never knew about the seasonal weather in Kentucky. One minute it was warm, and the next was chilly.

"She's going to love you forever," I called down the hall toward the kitchen as I walked into the bathroom to run the brush through my hair.

I hurried up when I didn't hear anything, and found Carter standing in front of the chalkboard.

"Operation Merlot," Carter murmured satirically. "Are you kidding me?"

I exhaled loudly in exasperation.

"I know you told me to stay out of it, but I think you're looking at the wrong person." It was going to be hard to keep my mouth shut.

He shuffled his feet, licked his lips, and ran his hand through his hair—all signs that he wasn't happy with me at all.

"I like you—I really do." He turned to me. His dark eyes narrowed as he frowned. "But I can't have my girlfriend going around and trying to undo everything that her sheriff boyfriend has done in a homicide case."

"I know." I did know, but I couldn't stop myself. "It's just that there's so much more that keeps coming up about this winery and the relationships."

"The evidence is the evidence, and right now it all points to Madison. More people have come forward saying she was seen at the scene, arguing with Ray. She also told several people she wished him dead." His jaw tensed. "I'm not saying there's not more out there, but you've got to let the department do the job we were trained to do."

"I know. I should stick to baking." My face softened and I grinned. "Then look into these other things." I stepped forward and pointed to the names. "Tammy has the most to lose. Her son was accepted into an Ivy League college, and I heard her say that she had to have the winery job in order to send him there. If Ray was going to kick them out, then she'd have no job but her old grocery job from before Giles opened the winery."

"What about Cat?" he asked. "What on earth did she do?"

"She was counting on the money to pay off the loan. Though I don't know what type of loan it was. It just seemed she was pretty upset. Money is big motive to kill someone, right?" I asked.

He peered at me intently.

"What?" I asked, my eyes darting back and forth from his.

"You," he whispered.

A tingling feeling hit the pit of my stomach as I watched his obvious examination and approval of my dress.

He walked over and pulled me into his arms.

"You're really cute when you do all this amateur sleuthing." My heart pounded with each word he spoke. "What if I look into some of these things for you tomorrow, but tonight we get to enjoy us?"

He didn't give me time to answer before his lips touched mine, leaving me with a kiss that was sweeter than any dessert I could make.

Chapter Twelve

Café Italia was definitely not what I'd expected. The outside of the old Victorian home I'd driven by and seen all my life was no longer the house I remembered. Long gone was the clapboard siding, replaced with cement painted an orange-yellow. The windows were outlined in red, with black shutters on each side.

The two-story home once had a double front porch with rocking chairs. The Southern charm had been replaced with red fencing and small café tables topped with checkered red table clothes. They'd used streetlamps with circular frosted glass to create what, in my mind, Italy would look like. Flowers and greenery hung from large flower boxes on the side of the house.

"This is beautiful." My mouth gaped open as I stared out the window. "Very romantic."

"Do you think this is what Italy really looks like?" Carter asked and put his car in park.

"In my head, yes," I sighed. I couldn't wait to get inside.

Like a true Southern gentleman, Carter got out of the car and ran around the front to open my door.

"After you." He took my hand and helped me out of the car.

Both of us continued to look around the outside on our way up to the side door, which had been turned into the front door of the restaurant. The café tables were occupied, and the food on the plates made my mouth water.

When we walked inside, a heavy curtain the same gray color as the building was neatly pinned to one side. The entire inside was open. The red brick walls and wood flooring were exactly what I'd always pictured an authentic Italian restaurant would have. The high bench seating, upholstered in red, wrapped around the entire restaurant, with dark wooden tables set for four people.

The chandelier lights set in large beams were dimmed to help set the ambience, along with the lit candles in the center of the table. The place settings included striped red cloth napkins, huge wine glasses, and water glasses.

"Table for Kincaid." Carter held two fingers up when the hostess asked for our reservation. I continued to look around.

"Right this way," the hostess said. I recognized her voice.

"Jane, how are you?" I knew her from the Rumford Country Club.

"I'm good. You're going to love the food here." She grabbed two menus and turned on the balls of her feet.

"Are you still waitressing at the RCC?" I asked and followed her to the table.

"Yes. I'm doing both. It's a little difficult on nights like tonight." She put a menu in front of each us as we sat down. "I wasn't supposed to work at the RCC tomorrow, but they had someone book a quick wine convention or something and needed the help."

"Wine convention?" I asked.

"Yeah. Some sort of national tasters or something." She shrugged. "I don't know." She looked between Carter and me. "So, you guys are still an item?" She dragged her finger from him to me.

"We are." Carter picked up the menu and looked it over. "I'm glad you're doing well."

"Yeah, I heard you weren't so good." She looked at me and shifted her weight to her right hip.

"Me?" I asked. "The bakery is doing great."

"No. I mean another body." There was a glint of wonder in her eye. "Remember when we found Emile dead?"

"How can I forget?" I sighed. "I'm fine. I'm sure Carter will figure out all the particulars with Ray's death."

"Mm-hmm." Carter didn't take his eyes off the menu. "Can you bring us a bottle of the house red wine?"

"Sure." Her mouth held a tight grin. It was apparent Carter didn't want to talk about Ray Peel, but I did.

I watched Jane disappear around the corner and couldn't help but notice the bathroom sign also pointed that way.

"If you'll excuse me, I need to go to the ladies' room," I said.

Carter looked up from his menu and nodded. I couldn't tell if it was a suspicious eye he was giving me or if it was the dark shadow due to the low lighting. Without looking back at him, I darted down the hall to find Jane.

I peeked my head into the bathroom just to see what it looked like. It was unisex, and looked just like my bathroom at home. Nothing special. No big deal.

There was a swinging door between the shop and the kitchen like the one at the bakery. I rose up on my tiptoes and looked through the galley window in the middle of the door. Jane was standing next to the workstation and looking down the line of dishes. It appeared she was trying to find the ones for her customers.

"You'll never know unless you ask," I said, giving myself my own little pep talk. I looked over my shoulder before I pushed through the door, and all the kitchen staff turned.

"Sophia." Jane's brows arched up high on her forehead, her eyes darting between me and some of the other employees of Café Italia. "Is something wrong?"

"No. Can I talk to you?" I jerked my head to the right in a gesture indicating a need for some privacy.

"Um . . ." She pulled her hand from one of the plates. "Sure." She turned to the guy next to her, who was dressed in the same uniform of black pants, black shirt, and white apron. "Brad, do you mind taking table four their appetizers?" She pointed to another door off the kitchen. "Let's go in there, Sophia."

Once we were in the dry ingredients pantry and she shut the door behind us, I knew I had limited time before Carter became suspicious.

"Just like before, one of my friends is a suspect, and I know she didn't do it." I bit my lip. "I heard Ray came in here the other night with someone. Have you seen him in here?"

"Yeah. He was actually part owner." Her words stopped me in my tracks. Part owner? "The house wine is from the Grape Valley Winery. He was a silent partner." She leaned in and whispered, "He was here all the time with different women, and he drank a lot."

This put a whole new spin on what I was going to ask her.

"Did you know any of the women?" I asked.

"It's so dark in here." She shook her head and rolled her eyes up as though she were thinking.

"What about short red hair? Fortyish?" I'd hoped to place Reba here with him.

"No. But I do remember nails." She wiggled her fingers in front of her.

"Nails?" I asked.

"Yes. This really high-fashion woman who put the ladies of the RCC to shame was with him a few days ago, and I clearly remember her nails because she was raking them down the back of his neck," she said.

"Blonde?" I asked. She nodded. "Lanie Truvinski."

Jane snapped her fingers. "That's her name. I knew it was something different from names around these parts. She was something. She was trying to get him to do something with the winery. I tried to linger, but I think Ray knew I was being a tad bit nosy, so he kept sending me for silly things like extra napkins. It wasn't until she threw a glass of wine on him and stormed off that he said to me, *'People only want me because of my money.'*" She used a deep voice to imitate Ray Peel's.

"He said that to you?" I asked, hoping this would be a good lead.

"Yep," she said. The door flew open, a waitress came out, and both of us jumped. Jane continued, "Lizbeth from the newspaper was here that night, doing some shots for the restaurant. I wonder if she got any. I saw her talking to Lanie after she stormed off."

"Sorry." The waitress looked more shocked than us. "I need some sugar."

"I need to get back to work." Jane grabbed a bag of sugar and handed it to her. "Sorry I can't be more helpful."

"You were more help than you know." I gave her a quick thank-you and asked her to keep what we'd talked about between her and me. I also made a mental note to check the paper and see if there was something about the Café Italia's grand opening. "You know how weird Carter was about me snooping with Emile's death. I just want to check things out for myself."

We walked back out into the working kitchen. The chef was calling out food and putting the dishes on the pickup island. There were people rushing around with trays and yelling out orders.

"If you can get your friend cleared, like you did Evelyn Moss, it'll be worth it." Jane grabbed a big, round black tray and put a couple plates of spaghetti and a loaf of bread on it. "If your friend is innocent." She hoisted the tray onto her right shoulder.

"She's innocent." I pushed the door open to the restaurant dining room and held it for her. "When did you say the wine convention started tomorrow?"

"Ten in the morning. Barely enough time for me to get my eyes peeled open." She laughed and hurried down the hall toward the dining room.

I waited a few seconds before I walked back out, because I didn't want Carter seeing me walking out with her.

"Are you okay?" he asked and stood when I walked up. He was such a Southern gentleman. He put his hand on the back of my chair and scooted it in when I sat down.

"I'm good." I offered Jane a fake smile when she walked over with the bottle of wine Carter had ordered.

Jane opened the wine and let Carter take a sample sip from his glass after she poured it. He gave his nod of approval.

"Do you know what you'd like to eat?" Jane asked and carefully poured the two glasses of wine.

"What do you suggest?" I asked.

"The fried ravioli is amazing and pairs well with the house red," she noted and pointed to the daily special. "I also suggest the simple spaghetti and meatball. It's one big meatball, but I can give you two if you want to share your dishes."

"That sounds good." Carter nodded in agreement.

"We'll do that. Thanks, Jane." I handed her my menu. As she walked away, I said, "She's such a nice person."

"And did she have any insight for you?" Carter asked. My jaw dropped. "Do you really think you were fooling me with the whole 'I've got to go to the bathroom' bit, then minutes later you walk out a few seconds after her?"

I opened my mouth to explain, to try to get myself out of deep water, but was saved by singing waiters approaching our table. The three male voices, all deep baritones, harmonized. Their operatic style nearly brought tears to my eyes, even though I had no clue what they were singing about.

The way they moved their bodies to the rhythm of their voices, with outstretched arms and wide palms up to the ceiling, was a performance in itself. It truly was worth coming here just to hear them.

"Amazing." Carter clapped along with the rest of the restaurant.

"Very romantic," I said with a wink and smile, which was good because it prompted Carter to lean over and kiss me.

"I never saw this as my future." He gestured between us. "In high school, I would lose my mind and fumble for the right words to say when we passed."

"You were very shy in high school." I had few notable memories of Carter from high school. "I just remember how nice you were to everyone."

"And I remember how beautiful you were and that you never conformed to anyone's beliefs but your own." He reached over and took my hand in his. "That's one of the qualities I love most about you." He looked me in the eyes. His face stilled. "You aren't going to leave this investigation alone, are you?"

"You're right. I have never conformed to what people want me to be. Bitsy wanted me to be a debutante. I followed my passion to be a pastry chef. You wanted me to stop snooping about Emile, and I helped figure out the killer." I slipped my hand out from under his and picked up my wine glass. "I've always been very loyal to my friends, and I can't just sit back and not try to figure something out."

"How do you know that I'm not following up on different leads?" he asked and played with the stem of his wine glass.

"I don't know. You don't share that with me." I took another drink of wine.

"Right now, the guys are at the winery with a search warrant."

"They are?" This was the best news I'd heard all day. "That's great."

"The Dugans are fine financially. There's no reason for any of them to have killed Ray. Reba Gunther did tell us in her interview that Ray and Giles had an argument a few hours before Ray was killed." He picked up his glass and took a sip.

"Just because they are financially set doesn't mean they didn't kill him in a crime of passion." I used words that he'd said to me against him.

A shrill voice jolted me, and I looked across the room toward the sound. A waiter had tipped his tray a little too much, causing food to land in the lap of a woman who was seated. The surprised look on her face jarred to mind the memory of Ray Peel's expression the night I'd found him.

"Are you okay?" Carter's warm hand covered mine.

A shiver traveled up from my toes, along my spine, and down my arms.

"Your hand is cold." He picked my hand up and vigorously rubbed his hands over mine. "What's wrong?"

"When I found Ray Peel, there was a look on his face that was so surprised and frightened that it has stuck with me," I said. I tugged my hand out of Carter's and picked up my glass. "It was as though he was so shocked to see the person." I shook my head and took an even bigger gulp of wine, draining the glass. "His face. I can't stop seeing his face."

"As a lifelong citizen, I've known Ray Peel a long time. There's one thing I know about him. He kept his gun strapped on his ankle, and I'm not sure why he didn't have it on him that day. I couldn't even find it in his house when I searched it." Carter picked up the bottle and emptied the last of it into our glasses. "He was very particular. He took my conceal-and-carry class. I wonder where that gun is?"

149

"Did he sell it?" I suggested.

"It would definitely be out of character for him, but if he did, I could find his gun through the gun register database and see if we can trace the serial number." He leaned back in his chair. "And I'm really hoping those phone records will show something."

We stopped talking once Jane walked up with our food.

"This looks so good." I let the aroma of the tomato, basil, and cheesy goodness waft up to my nose. The cheese oozed out when I cut one of the fried raviolis in half with my fork. "You get the first bite for being such a wonderful boyfriend."

I put the fork up to Carter's mouth. His face melted into a warm, satisfied smile. All thoughts and talk of Ray Peel's murder vanished while we enjoyed more wine, more food, and a few more romantic songs.

That was, until we made it back to my house, and it looked like a tornado had gone through it.

Chapter Thirteen

"Stay right here," he said and drew his finger up to his mouth, gesturing for me to be quiet.

He pulled up his shirt and took out the gun from his concealed holster. He was always packing heat. I gulped and tried to stop the escalating heartbeat I could feel taking over my entire body.

Carter tiptoed into the house with the gun drawn in front of him. Outside, I nervously tried to look around in the darkness. An eerie feeling swept over me. Then it turned to fear with the thought that Duchess might've gotten out.

"Duchess!" I couldn't stand it any longer. I stepped into the house and called for my trusty feline again. "Carter, can I come in?"

"It's all clear." His words were accompanied by a burst of light as he began to switch on the lights in my house, exposing my ransacked belongings. The couch cushions had been taken off the couch and thrown on the floor. It looked like someone had dragged their arm down the coffee table and pushed all my knickknacks off.

The contents in the kitchen drawers had been dumped. All of my ingredient containers full of flour, sugar, and oats had been unscrewed and dumped all over my counters. When I didn't notice Duchess in the kitchen near her bowl, I began to panic.

"Duchess!" I screamed and ran toward the bedroom. "When it would lightning and thunder, she always runs under the bed."

My only thoughts were for her safety.

"Sophia, don't touch anything." Carter hurried after me.

But it was too late. I'd flipped on my bedroom light and crawled to my bed, where I pulled up the bed skirt and looked under. Duchess's big blue eyes batted as if she were saying, *What about me? Where have you been? I'm scared.*

"It's okay, Duchess." The reality of what had happened to my cute and cozy house, and what could've happened to Duchess, set in and jolted my heart with pain. "Come here, sweetie."

She wasn't moving.

"Please come here." My voice cracked and tears stung my eyes. "Please," I begged.

"Sophia." Carter's warm hand touched my back. "Let's give her some space. She knows you're home, and she'll come out when she feels safer."

"Okay." I sat back on my heels and wiped away the

tears. "Okay." I shook my head and took his strong hand as he helped me up.

The shock of it all left me a little wobbly. Carter swept me into his arms.

"I'm so sorry," he continued to repeat over and over, snuggling me tighter as he walked down the hall. I wrapped my arms around his neck and let myself be sad for a few more seconds until he set me down on the couch in the family room.

"If someone thinks they can scare me away from helping Madison, they've got another thing coming." The anger erupted inside of me, replacing the scared and helpless feeling as the words seethed out of my mouth.

"Wait just a second." Carter bent down and looked me straight in the eyes. "This is not good."

I swallowed hard, lifted my chin, and met his gaze.

"If you think that I'm going to sit around here and be scared because I've gotten a little too close to the truth about Ray Peel's death, forget it. They've only fueled my fire more." I looked around my family room.

"I'm calling this in." He stood up and pulled out his cell phone. He walked around the room and looked at items as he talked on the phone. I got up as well. "Don't touch anything," he reminded me.

I wasn't going to disturb anything, just in case they could pull prints.

"They were looking for something. Nothing is missing.

Not even the chalkboard is touched." There was something strange about all of this.

"What on earth could you be hiding that someone wants?" he asked and carefully stepped over items on the kitchen floor.

"I don't know, but I can tell you it was a deliberate break-in to find something. If this person knew anything about kitchen gadgets, all of these are very expensive, and you can't get them at stores around here. If they were trying to rob me, they would've taken these things. They were looking for something."

"I think it was the killer, and they came in here to see if you had any information on them or ties to them. Who have you told about looking into things?" he asked.

"Besides Bitsy, Charlotte, and Madison, I told Cat Fraxman, Lizbeth Mockby, Jane, and Reba." I gasped and looked at the chalkboard. Reba's name was blurred where something had rubbed across it. "Do you think that Reba came in here?"

"Why would Reba Gunther want to break into your house?" Carter asked and looked toward the front door when we heard it open, followed by heavy footsteps.

"Because she knows there's something going on out at the winery. She's the eyes and ears of that place. She knows more than what she's telling. Her loyalty to the Dugans is strong." The more I talked, the more I believed my words. "Not to mention there's a big rumor circulating that she and Ray had a thing. Which is fine since they were both single, but it was kept a secret."

"Her alibi checked out. She was in the offices of the winery the entire fund-raiser. Cat Fraxman took every donation as she got it, and Reba kept a running tally. Reba also continued to work and send emails. She has a solid alibi for the time of Ray's death." He put his hand up to stop me from protesting. "The guys are here to do their work. You can go in there and make some coffee and sit at the table while we do our job. Let me try to figure out who came in here."

"It was someone who wanted me to know they are watching me." I clenched my jaw to kill the sob in my throat as I watched the deputies walking around in my private space and taking notice of what had been touched by the intruder.

The team of deputies walked around and continually asked me to take a look and make sure nothing had been taken. Carter spent a lot of time looking at me and asking if I was okay, which of course I wasn't. Someone wanted something they thought I had, but what?

"Sophia!" Bitsy's voice echoed through the entryway and spilled into the family room. "Aren't you that Spivey boy?" I heard her ask. "You better let me in, or I'll call your mama," she threatened. She scurried into the family room, swatting at the deputy that was trying to stop her.

"She's fine." I motioned the officer back, but he kept pursuing her. Carter waved him off, and he finally desisted.

"What on earth did I hear about someone ambushing you when you came home?" she asked.

"Ambush?" If I weren't still a little shaken up, I'd have laughed. "Who said that?"

"Ella Capshaw called and said that she'd heard over Grant's police scanner that someone had broken into your house while you and Carter were here." The lines between her eyes deepened with worry.

"First off, Carter and I weren't here and secondly, we came home to find the house torn up. No one ambushed us." I could see her face relax slightly. "But someone did come in. To find what, I don't know, but something."

"Carter, what are you going to do about this?" Bitsy asked. "This is a little too close for comfort."

"Seeing as how I can't seem to get the two of you to stop snooping with your little Operation Merlot, it seems that someone knows Sophia is looking into matters and sending her a clear message to stop." His brows arched, and he looked at Bitsy. "I suggest you give your daughter some advice and tell her to stop, because she won't listen to me."

"Don't even try." I put my hand up and warned Bitsy when I saw her mouth fly open.

"I'm going to stay here tonight and sleep on the couch to make sure she's okay." Carter slid his gaze to the sofa.

"You'll do no such thing." Bitsy wasn't about to let any sordid tales of Carter and me sleeping under the same roof before marriage take over the gossip circles. It nearly killed her when I'd moved in with my ex-boyfriend in Manhattan, even while living away from the wandering eyes and gossip of Rumford. "I'm going to spend the night with my daughter, and we'll call if we need anything."

Carter knew better than to argue with Bitsy. No one ever won when they went up against her, not even the sheriff.

She plunked down in a chair at the table and hugged her purse in front of her. While she looked around at all the deputies, I got up and opened my freezer to get something for the guys to munch on. The chocolate chip cookies would be fine.

Instead of microwaving them to thaw, I turned the oven to a low temperature and put them on a baking tray. I took out the fresh coffee beans I'd gotten from Coffee Talk and used the grinder to make a nice blend of coffee with a little dash of cinnamon. Not only did the brewing coffee make the house smell good, it sent a lot of happy feelings to my gut and reminded me that everything wasn't so bad. Nothing had been taken, Duchess was okay, and all the people I loved were still alive.

"Help yourselves, please," I told a couple of the deputies who were taking photos of the mess in the kitchen. Careful not to disturb anything, I took a few of the coffee mugs out of the cabinet and set them next to the coffeemaker and the warm cookies. The chocolate chips had melted and dripped with goodness, making my mouth water.

The officers started to gather in the kitchen. I couldn't help it—I did eavesdrop a little as they talked amongst themselves. They found nothing threatening and all came to the same conclusion that I had: someone was looking for something they thought I had. But what?

"We are wrapping everything up." Carter walked into the kitchen and sat down at the table next to Bitsy and me. "Can you think of anything you might have, or might have taken, that could make someone come in here and do this?"

"I don't know." I shook my head. "If it had to do with Ray, I don't have anything but—" My eyes bolted open. I jumped up and grabbed my bag.

"But what?" Carter asked.

"Nothing." I took my hand out of my bag. "It's nothing. I was trying to think if I remembered anything strange at the bakery, since everyone has been talking about it."

There was look in his eye that said he didn't believe me.

"Can I get a statement?" Lizbeth stood in my family room, her hair still in a high bun. A pair of large black glasses magnified her eyes. She held out a tape recorder in her right hand.

"What are you doing here?" Carter asked.

"Police scanner." She took a step forward. When I saw her eyes focus on the chalkboard, I scooted in front of it. There was no part of this I wanted her to print in the paper. "Do you think this has to do with Ray Peel's murder? It's no secret Sophia Cummings found him and that she's trying to investigate the murder on her own, since her friend, Madison, is your number-one suspect."

"That's a lot of speculation." Carter lips curled up, a slight laugh escaping.

"Not according to Sophia herself." She looked at the tape recorder and hit a couple of buttons, playing back my voice from when I was in her office, asking about the ad.

I watched as Carter closed his eyes and took a few deep breaths.

"That's enough." He held his hand out to Lizbeth to stop the tape. "There's nothing here to see. There's no evidence this is tied to the Ray Peel case. There was nothing taken according to Miss Cummings."

"Do you think this is a clear message to scare Miss Cummings, so she'll stop putting her nose into something that doesn't concern her?" Lizbeth might be good at her job, but she had some gumption to come to my house after hearing that scanner.

I'd finally had the last straw. "I'm fine. My home is fine. There's nothing here to see."

"It looks to me like there's a lot to be seen. Not to mention Reba Carol's name has all but been completely erased from that board." She pointed.

"Sheriff, we're all done here." The deputy came up and interrupted us.

Lizbeth wrote down a couple of things after she looked at the chalkboard again. Carter was too busy with the paperwork from the deputy to even pay attention to her anymore. But I followed her out the door.

"Lizbeth." I stopped her.

"You want to go on record now?" She stared at me from the small front porch in the front of my house.

"I wanted to ask you about Lanie Truvinski." I let my words settle. In the TV shows, they always give sources some space to answer questions.

"Who?"

"Carter and I went to Café Italia for supper tonight. I ran into Jane, the waitress from the RCC who also works at Café Italia. She mentioned you'd been there for the grand opening and you saw the blonde woman and Ray fighting." I asked, "Do you recall that?"

"No. I was there, but I didn't see a fight." She flipped through the notepad she had in her hands. "What was her name?"

"Lanie Truvinski," I said and tried to get a look at the words on the page she was reading, but it was too dark outside.

"No." She shook her head. "I got a couple of reviews from customers, and I didn't even bother putting it in the paper. It wasn't as big as I thought it was going to be. I told them they should get a food critic in there to drum up some business."

"They were packed when we went," I told her. "Are you sure you don't remember talking to a blonde lady about this high?" I used my hand to show how tall Lanie was. "She's super elegant." Lizbeth shook her head. "That's so odd. Jane said she saw you talking to her."

"Well, if I did, she didn't give me her real name, and she certainly wasn't memorable." Lizbeth shrugged.

"Did you happen to take any photos of that night?" I wondered if Lizbeth had snapped some action photos and in the background I might find a couple shots of Ray and Lanie together. Lanie and Ray had had a fight. I'd seen it with my own two eyes, and now she hadn't returned my calls or even asked for a refund. Where was Lanie?

"Why do you keep asking these questions?"

"I guess I just want to know what Ray Peel was doing the night before. I can't seem to figure it out." I sucked in a deep breath.

"That seems like the least of your worries, by the looks of your house." Lizbeth cocked her head to the side, and she looked inside the wide-open door. "Come on. I know you and Carter talk. Can't you tell me if he's got any other suspects?"

"He doesn't discuss this with me. If anything, he wants me to stay out of it because of this right here." I nodded toward my house.

"By the looks of the chalkboard in there, you've been digging around." She put her pen to her paper. "Do you want to tell me what your thoughts are? Who do you think could've done it? Because it appears you're working hard to get Madison off the hook."

"No one." I shook my head and thought about Lanie. "But if you look through your photos from that night, I might have something for you." I tried to entice her.

I wanted to find out what Lanie knew on my own, by taking her pastry order for the wine convention to the RCC in the morning. The idea that she'd killed Ray had started to infiltrate my mind, leaving me with no choice but to confront her myself.

"Can I talk to you for a minute?" Carter asked after he stuck his head outside.

"I'm out of here, but I'll look in my photos for you and get back with you," Lizbeth said.

"Yeah. Come by the bakery, and I'll give you something good for your belly." I turned to Carter.

"Are you sure you don't have any idea who would do this or why?"

"No, but I'll think on it." I rose up on my toes and gave him a kiss. "Thank you for a really nice date. I really liked that place."

"The company was better." He let me off the hook. "You and Bitsy get some rest. If you remember anything—I mean *anything* . . ." He couldn't've stressed it enough. "You better tell me."

"I will." I crossed my heart with my right hand and crossed the fingers of my left hand behind my back. The lights of a car driving down the street forced us both to look. He didn't question me any further.

Charlotte came running across the street in her pink jogging suit.

"Bitsy called and told me everything that happened," Charlotte gasped, catching her breath.

"She's inside." I pointed behind my shoulder.

"Hi, Carter," she trilled before she rushed inside.

The car had come to a screeching halt. Madison jumped out.

"Just like high school: one of you needed help, y'all came running." Carter watched Madison bolt through the front yard and up to the porch.

"Bitsy called." Her eyes slid between Carter and me. "What?" she asked him. "You think I did this too?" She shoved past him and headed inside the house.

I didn't stand outside long enough to watch his car pull down the street like I normally did, for fear that the person who ransacked my house was still out there and watching me.

* * *

"Finally," Bitsy said.

She'd already replaced the cups of coffee with big glasses of wine for everyone. Duchess too seemed to be relieved that the officers had left. She finally had come out from the bedroom and sat in Bitsy's lap.

"Go on." She gestured with her pointer finger. "Grab the chalk. It's time for Operation Merlot to go into full investigation mode."

I quickly told them about how Jane from the RCC was working at Café Italia. I wrote down all the particular details about Lanie and Ray, including all the tension between them.

"What on earth do we have on Cat Fraxman? She's always got her nose stuck in a book." Bitsy rolled her eyes.

"I think that when you're as passionate about your job and the welfare of the library as Cat is, it's a little personal when someone gives that organization half a million dollars and then snatches it away," I said.

"Not to mention the fact that she didn't do anything different than Madison or Tammy Dugan did." Charlotte was right.

"For the umpteenth time, I didn't do it," Madison responded defiantly.

"Honey,"—Bitsy took another swig of the wine—"I might've hurt the man if he'd called me real estate scum."

"He didn't say I was scum. He said I didn't have the right clientele to purchase the land." She glared at Bitsy. I was envious that she could get away with giving Bitsy attitude. If I gave Bitsy the same look, she'd have had a hissy fit and would've given me a good tongue-lashing.

"I know—*we* know—you didn't do it. Have a cookie. I did find out that the Fraxmans took out a second mortgage on their home, under the assumption the money Ray Peel donated would pay off their mortgage and the library would be free and clear."

"I think you need to check that out because to me that's a pretty clear motive to kill someone." Charlotte nibbled on the cookie.

"I heard they were going to have to file for bankruptcy." I couldn't imagine how Cat felt about it. Her parents were so kind. To even think they'd mortgage their lifelong savings to help out their daughter made me want to go to the bank first thing in the morning to see if Bill Bellman knew anything."

Everyone continued to eat and drink as I walked around and talked.

"Cat and Tammy were both at the fund-raiser. Both of them were wronged by Ray Peel, dealing with money." I drew a dollar sign on the board and circled it. "Money is a big motivator for killing someone. Then there's Lanie, whose reputation is on the line. She's gone missing."

"If there's one thing I know for sure,"—Bitsy's words began to slur—"there's nothing like a woman scorned. Your own reputation is all us girls have got in this world. I mean . . ." She pointed to me with same hand she held her glass. The glass tipped to the side, slightly spilling the wine. I rushed over to wipe it up just in time, before Duchess could step in it. "I mean, look at my daughter. I tried so hard to get her to be a debutante, and look at her now."

"I think she looks nice in her dress." Charlotte's eye drew up and down.

"Not the outfit—I mean look at where her life has led her. Right back to the kitchen, cooking for everyone but a man of her own." She hiccupped.

"I bake and I'm happy." This was the same old song and dance between Bitsy and me, and she wasn't going to be happy until I walked down the aisle with a veil over my face. I wasn't sure she'd even be all that happy then. "But that's not why we are here," I said, circling the conversation back around. "We are going to ignore Bitsy."

Charlotte and Madison agreed. Madison poured Bitsy some more wine.

"Just in case," Madison said, winking, "what were you saying about Lanie?"

"Ella Capshaw said something about a car speeding off and almost running her and Grant off the road. What kind of car did she say it was?" I asked.

"Silver?" Charlotte questioned.

"She said she and Grant were late because they'd gone to Café Italia beforehand. She had the glass of wine in the car and spilled it when a car speeding away from the winery nearly ran them off the road." My jaw dropped. I snapped my fingers at Charlotte. "Silver. She did say it was silver. Not only did you and I watch Lanie drive off in a silver car, she and Ray were seen at the Café Italia, where she threw wine at Ray's head and I saw them at the winery in a heated discussion about how he'd promised her the winery and then broke his promise. That's when she slapped him, saying this wasn't the first time he'd broken a promise."

"That gives us something to chew on." Madison's face softened, almost like she was relieved.

"Now that I know Lanie is at the bed and breakfast, I can go see her tomorrow." I put my name next to Lanie's name. "Bitsy?"

"What?" She drew another long sip from the glass.

"Who do you want to go and question tomorrow?" I asked.

"Me?" she asked in a Southern drawl. "I can't possibly go. I've got the Garden Club meeting tomorrow, and I thought you were coming to that."

I ignored her and moved on to Madison.

"Madison? Which one do you want?" I asked.

"I can't go around asking anyone anything. I'm already a suspect, and my job is taking a beating because of it. I've got to get as many clients in houses as I can." She turned her head away from me.

"You know if you're going to be gallivanting all over Rumford, I've got to keep the bakery open," Charlotte was quick to answer.

"This leaves just me to investigate all of them?" I looked at them.

"Operation Merlot," Madison said and held her glass up in the air. Everyone followed. "Operation Merlot," all said in unison.

While they enjoyed the rest of their wine, I'd already figured out who I needed to see first. Reba Gunther. If I didn't get to her before Lizbeth, it wouldn't be good.

After a few more glasses of wine, I'd finally talked Bitsy into letting Madison drop her off at home. I wasn't sure what good she'd do me if the intruder came back in the middle of the night, and I assured her I'd be fine.

"Reba Gunther is first, then Bill Bellman, and Lanie will be my last stop," I said to Duchess as she jumped up on my bed while I peeled back the covers.

Chapter Fourteen

There's no denying that I didn't sleep a wink. I used Bitsy's tried-and-true Preparation H ointment secret while I put my makeup on. *"If it's good for shrinking up things in the nether region, it's good for shrinking bags and wrinkles on the face,"* she'd say.

"Good morning," I answered the phone when I saw Carter's name scroll across.

"Did you put an ad in the paper?" He didn't bother saying hello.

"I did. Why?" I asked and rushed to the front door to grab my paper.

"I just wanted to make sure because there's a big ad in there along with an interview that you gave Lizbeth that clearly says you're looking into the investigation." He didn't sound too happy.

"I didn't tell her I was looking into it. I was saying that I'd . . ." I opened the paper, shutting the door with the toe of my foot. With the phone tucked between my ear and my shoulder, I didn't have to look too far for the interview. It was right on the front page. "Friend Taking Matters into Her Own Hands," read the headline.

"This is why she came around snooping for a scoop last night. You're going to get yourself killed. As much as I've tried to tell you to stop snooping, you just aren't listening," he huffed. "Don't you understand that I'd like to keep you around for a while?"

"I'm fine." I didn't know who I was trying to convince, because this time I was actually a little frightened. Someone had invaded my home, and now this.

"I've had enough. I'm going to send over a couple of officers to just watch your house at night. Understand?" The tone in his voice told me he wasn't going to take no for an answer.

"I understand." I had to give in, but this still didn't mean I was going to stop snooping. I was just going to be a little safer in my home.

"Now that we have that cleared up, I guess you're going to be at the bakery all day filling orders for these coupons?" he asked.

"I guess so." I pulled the phone away from my ear when a call clicked in. "Listen, that's Bitsy. She had a little too much to drink last night. I'm going to take this call."

"Remember, no snooping," he reminded me before I clicked over.

"Take two ibuprofens," I joked in greeting Bitsy.

"You're an evil daughter for letting me drink that much,"

she groaned from the other end of the line. "It's way too early for me to be up, but I've got to take my plants to the Garden Club meeting so we can start to set up for next week's sale. Are you going to come? Because we could really use some Cherry Flip-Flops."

"You mean you told them I'd bring Cherry Flip-Flops?" Though I didn't mind at all making them and donating them to the club, my time just so happened to be limited.

I held the phone with one hand while I scooped out some food for Duchess with the other. Bitsy continued to talk as I walked around and checked all the doors to make sure they were locked before I headed out to the car. It was still dark out at this hour of the morning, but such were the hours of a baker.

Even though I was a little tired, I was on a mission to get some baking done, so when Charlotte came in, she could wait on customers and start working on Reba's birthday cake. The entire drive to the bakery, my thoughts had drifted to the cake. Perry hadn't given me a due date, which was a good reason to go to his office and see what I could find out there. I really wanted to know how the winery could stay open when Ray had planned to put it on the market and was now deceased. And I remembered his comment on the night of the fund-raiser, that the lease was up.

Even if the Dugans wouldn't need the cake for a few days, it took that long to actually make and bake a custom cake. Most people had no idea that the layers had to be fully cooled, and it was even better if the cake was put in the refrigerator for a few days so the icing would go on smoothly.

I turned off Main Street and pulled into the alley behind the bakery. The early morning brought a little frost and extra chill to the air. I hurried out of the car and stuck the key in the lock. The lights flickered a little when I flipped them on after opening the door. The gas ticked when I turned the oven knobs on for preheating. I loved the Fords' old gas ovens and how evenly they baked. In most industrial kitchens, the ovens had a weak or low spot, and I had to learn where they were in each kitchen in order to rotate the items correctly.

I'll flip on the light in the bakery, turn on the coffeepots, and get busy, I said to myself as I mentally went through my morning checklist.

As I pushed through the swinging door, I unhooked the apron off the rack and slipped it over my head, tying it snug around my waist. Brisk air greeted me. My eyes fell on the shattered front window. There was a brick lying on the floor with *Stop what you're doing* spray-painted across it in red.

I know I should've been upset and scared, but I was mostly angry. And I could only think it was because I was getting a little too close to a real breakthrough with the Ray Peel murder.

There was a second when I didn't want to call Carter, but I knew I had to. I didn't want to bring any more attention to whomever was trying to send me a very clear message. I picked up the phone and dialed.

"Carter," I said, my voice crackling, catching me off guard. Maybe I was more upset than I'd realized. "Someone threw a brick through the bakery window."

"Are you okay?" he asked, and I heard his siren start to roar through the phone.

"I'm fine." I backed away from the brick and sat down on one of the stools at the wall bar. "I'm going to wait right here for you."

"I'm almost there. You're going to stay on the phone with me." He wasn't playing the sheriff at this moment. The concerned tone in his voice held some personal element of fear. Carter was being the boyfriend who wanted to protect me. "I'm turning down Main Street near Back-en-Thyme Flowers."

He would be here in no time. The florist was a couple of shops down.

"I see you. Do you want me to open the front door?" I asked.

"Grab a napkin and do it. I don't want to disturb any evidence, though it doesn't look like they came in the front door," he said.

I hung up the phone and got off the stool, plucking a napkin from one of the holders. He was already standing at the door when I got there, and I was careful not to step on too much of the glass.

"Are you okay?" Carter swept me into his arms. There was a deep sadness on his face that I'd not seen before.

"I'm fine. I told you that." I ran my palm along his jawline and gave him a reassuring kiss. "My knight in shining armor," I joked.

"This really isn't funny anymore." He'd turned into the sheriff. "Your house and now your business?"

"It's the window. If they really wanted to do some damage, they would've torn up the bakery. Everything else looks fine." I looked back at the counter. "See? Nothing has been disturbed. I think they just threw the brick, and that's it."

"You still don't have an alarm in here?" he asked.

"It's on my To Do list." I knew he was going to get on me for that one.

"Consider it done." Carter called dispatch.

"Can I turn on the coffee?" I whispered, knowing we both needed some. He nodded.

I looked down at the industrial pots and flipped on the switches. I overheard Carter tell dispatch to get the security company down to the bakery to install an alarm system. It wasn't that I didn't want to do it; I was simply hoping to pay off some things and get some money saved before I did it. There was rarely crime in Rumford, so it wasn't a priority. Now I regretted putting off ordering an alarm, since the crime rate seemed to be picking up.

Within minutes there was a team of deputies in and out of the bakery, taking photos and eating some of the donuts that I'd quickly put in the oven for them. There wasn't much for me to do, so I hid out in the kitchen, trying to get lost in Reba's cake.

While in the dry pantry, I gathered the flour, sugar, cocoa, baking soda, and salt. I sat them on the center preparation island. Since it was going to be a three-layer cake, I wanted to have all the ingredients ready so I could bake all three layers at once. I measured and dumped all the dry ingredients into a large bowl and set it aside. I needed to get all the wet ingredients together.

"What on earth is going on?" Charlotte's voice echoed into the walk-in refrigerator, where I was busy grabbing the vanilla, buttermilk, eggs, and shortening. "Don't tell me someone broke in here too."

She took the carton of buttermilk, dangling from my finger, and the eggs off the top of the pile I was carrying from the refrigerator.

"They didn't break in. They threw a brick and broke the display window." Carefully, I set the items down on the island. "I think it was the same person who was in my house because the brick had a clear message for me to stop snooping, spray-painted in red."

"That's it. Operation Merlot has to stop right now." She smacked her hand on the island.

"That's what I told her last night. I'm hoping she got the message drilled into her head with this situation." Carter had come into the kitchen. Charlotte and I just looked at each other.

"Basic Southern chocolate cake?" Charlotte was able to look at the ingredients and know exactly the recipe.

"You got it." I smiled with some relief, and she took over while I chatted with Carter.

"The guys gathered some things, but nothing showed up when they dusted for fingerprints, so I do believe it was the act of breaking the window with the brick that was meant to scare you." His brows lifted.

"Brick?" I was confused.

"It's a piece of a brick. And it's an odd color." He got me thinking.

"Can I see it?" I asked.

"I'll let you look at it before we leave. I've got the glass guy here already to replace the window. And we've cleaned up the broken glass. I wanted to get it all done before you opened so whoever did this wouldn't get any more attention than they already got from ransacking your house."

"Whoever did this?" I drew back. "Clearly it's the killer. I've stumbled upon something big, for them to ransack my house and break the window."

"And this is where you stop." He put his hand up. "This is where it ends. You're done looking around. I'm not joking this time."

"We're all done out here, Sheriff." One of the deputies stuck his head in the kitchen door.

"Are you going to be okay?" he asked. I nodded.

"I've got Charlotte to keep me okay," I assured him.

"I'll let you know if there's anything pulled off the brick."

He bent down and kissed my cheek. "Let me know if the slightest strange thing happens."

"Like some of the yeast not rising for my donuts? That'd be strange since my donuts always turn out great," I teased.

"You know what I mean," he said, not finding humor in my jokes.

I followed him out into the bakery. He walked over to one of the deputies and took the evidence bag.

"See? It's one of those whitewashed bricks." He stretched the bag across the brick to give me a better look.

"Can I snap a photo?" I asked. When he looked at me questioningly, I said, "I go to a lot of places and deliver baked goods. If I come across a house with similar bricks, I want to have this handy."

"You're not going to go to people's houses on your fancy suspect list to try to match it?" he asked.

"Don't be ridiculous." I rolled my eyes and thought, *Of course I am.*

I took him by the arm and walked him to the door.

"I'll send you a photo," he offered.

"My hero." I batted my eyes. I flipped the sign on the door to "Open" and gave him a quick kiss before he left.

"What on earth did you uncover to hit such a nerve?" Charlotte asked. She stood behind me with the small mixing bowl tightly held to her waist with one hand while she rapidly stirred with the other.

"I don't know, but I don't plan to stop." I glanced up at the clock on the wall. "Is it too early for some wine?"

"Honey, it's five o'clock somewhere," she said.

"Let's go." I grabbed my bag. "Call Madison and Bitsy. Tell them to meet tonight at my house for Operation Merlot," I said to Charlotte over my shoulder on our way out the door.

I didn't know what I was onto, but I knew it was something big for someone to ransack the house and now send me a message at the bakery. With the help of my girlfriends, I knew if we put our heads together, we'd figure this out.

Chapter Fifteen

The Rumford Country Club was my second home growing up. Not because my parents were on the country club board, but because it was the first real job that I'd ever had. I'd worked in the kitchen as a dishwasher, but luckily they let me do some baking as well. Thanks to the bake-off I'd won at thirteen, beating all of Bitsy's friends, Evelyn Moss took notice that I was hanging around her kitchen, always there for the food, and not lying out by the pool with my bikini on or chasing the pimply-faced boys my age. She asked if I wanted to use the kitchen to bake.

It was no accident that I slipped some of those pastries I'd made onto the dessert trays. Then she hired me. Bitsy was beside herself. She had to be put on some sort of medication to calm her nerves because her daughter didn't want to wear pearls and gowns. Instead, I wanted to bake for the girls who did want to wear pearls and gowns.

Still, I owe all my first experiences as a pastry chef to Evelyn Moss. And she owed me a favor too. I had known that she wasn't capable of murdering Emile, the head chef at the RCC, when all the evidence had pointed to her, and I took it upon myself to help her figure out who did murder him with his own cast iron skillet.

The RCC was a private club where members held bonds. Most of the time, the bonds were passed down from generation to generation. The family gatherings and annual events were a timeless tradition. Many times, I'd spent my Easter Sunday here looking for the hidden eggs along the golf course or sitting on Santa's lap in the ballroom. But today I was going to see Lanie Truvinski, and I was going to need Evelyn Moss's help.

The curved sidewalk leading up to the front entrance of the clubhouse was lined with the most colorful display of flowers I'd ever seen at the RCC. The club had strayed from their usual yellow daffodils and added some flowers in reds, whites, and purples. The white brick mansion was on the historic registry and had just undergone a huge renovation, though the large brick stairways on both sides of the massive front porch remained.

It was on the front porch that I'd told Bitsy I'd decided not to go to college and would instead take off on an adventure to find the best pastry school in the world. Call me a coward or a baby, but I knew if I told her in front of all the people she loved to impress, she'd not have her hissy fit until we got home that night.

"Hello," the guard at the gate entrance of the club said after he'd stopped me from driving in. "Member number?"

"One hundred and fifteen," I said, rattling off my parents' bond number.

"Have a good day, Ms. Cummings." He tipped his hat and gestured me on through.

I drove the car around back to the employee parking lot. I'd parked there many times before. Not only did it lead straight to Evelyn Moss's office, it also was a back entrance to the kitchen.

The smell of homemade Southern cooking swooshed through the door when I opened it. The RCC was always busy and served lunch and supper. The new chef was working out well, from what Bitsy had told me. It was a perfect excuse to lead into talking to Evelyn Moss about Lanie Truvinski.

The long hallway had offices on both sides. I knocked on the one with Evelyn's name on it.

"Sophia," she said, looking up from her desk when I pushed open the door. "What a wonderful surprise. Come on in."

"Hi, Evelyn." I entered the office and noticed it was still a big mess. Evelyn wasn't the neatest of people, and I'd never understood her filing system. "Something smells so good." I rubbed my belly.

"I'm not going to complain. The RCC was very lucky with the applicants, and the committee unanimously voted for the new hire." The chair squeaked as she eased back into it, placing her elbows on the arms. She folded her hands together. "Now, I know you well enough to suspect that you didn't come by here to make idle chitchat. What was so important to drag you out of the bakery?" she asked, narrowing her eyes.

"You do know me." I smiled. "I'd heard the wine convention had been moved here."

"Mm-hmm," Evelyn ho-hummed and used the tips of her fingers to push back the loose strands of her brown hair into the half-falling-out bun on top of her head.

"Lanie Truvinski hired and paid me to do the pastries for the event when it was going to be at the Grape Valley Winery." I pulled out the paperwork from my bag and handed it to Evelyn overtop of her desk.

"She is having the convention here. That's the food you're smelling. She came to me in desperation, and I shuffled a few things around to make it happen." She gave me back the paper. "She paid for your services, and I wish I could use you, but you know the rules with the RCC. We have to make all of our stuff in-house."

"That's not what I was trying to do. I understand that. In fact the items she purchased came in handy after someone put a coupon in the newspaper on behalf of For Goodness Cakes for a free Fords' Long John." I sucked in a deep breath.

"You are making their Long Johns?" Evelyn asked, practically salivating.

"No." I pointed at her. "But that reaction is what I want when one of my customers even thinks about one of my pastries."

Telling Evelyn about the coupon only reminded me that

the Fords hadn't returned my phone call. I needed to call them again.

"Then what's the problem?" she asked.

"I'm sure you heard about Ray Peel." I bit my bottom lip. She nodded. "I'm sorta the one who found him." My brows furrowed.

"Sophia," Evelyn gasped, "wasn't my ordeal enough for you? Not that I'm not grateful, and I owe you a lot, but you have no business investigating this."

"Who said I was investigating?" I asked. "I'm just looking into a few things. Madison is the primary suspect, and as you well know, I just can't sit back when I've come across some unanswered questions."

"This is where Ms. Truvinski comes in?" She leaned on the desk and rested her forearms on the edge of it.

"When I was setting up for the fund-raiser at the winery, I overheard Lanie and Ray talking. More of a heated discussion." I rolled my eyes. "It was her slapping him and saying how she should've known he wouldn't keep a promise that caught my attention."

"That must've been right before she nearly hit me in the parking lot with that fancy silver car of hers." Evelyn shuffled through some papers.

"Silver car?" I asked and remembered how Ella said they'd almost been run off the road. "Do you know what time that was?"

"That's why I'm trying to find the paperwork for the event." She moved more things around on her desk, picking up a few folders and stacking them in another spot. "You know I put all the details on there. Including the date and time."

"That's what I need. The time." My eyes swept over her desk to see if I could see anything with Lanie's name on it. "How did she act when you talked to her?"

"First, I was shaken up because she came barreling into the parking lot. She didn't stop at the station, so they were chasing her on the golf cart." Evelyn pulled open her desk drawers and fumbled through them. She continued to talk and look at the same time. "After that, she told me that she had this big fancy wine convention coming to town and the winery was no longer able to do her event. She needed something fast." She looked up at me. "She said money was no object and muttered about how it was going to look for her and that no one was going to make her look like a fool. I just assumed it was Tammy Dugan and Giles Dugan she was talking about."

"Why would you assume that?" I asked.

"No particular reason." She was lying.

"Oh, there's a reason." I put my hand on the desk to get her attention. "I know that people around here gossip. They see the staff here all the time, and the service people start to blend in with the wallpaper. You've overheard something."

The women at the RCC loved to gossip. Especially after a mean game of tennis. They came in for lunch, had a few cocktails, and started chattering. I knew everything about every single person in Rumford when I worked here.

"You know how these women can be." Her brows lifted.

"I'd heard that there was some turmoil over at the winery because Ray Peel had invested in that new restaurant."

"Café Italia. I've been there. What kind of turmoil?" I asked.

"Apparently, Ray hasn't been the best landlord. According to some of the women, I heard he wasn't going to upgrade the filtration system that helped process the limestone underground, which was in the lease agreement. Now the lease is up, and he wanted to franchise the restaurant." This was all very interesting. It made Tammy even more of a suspect. "Ray and Giles had a meeting at the bank. Giles couldn't pull enough money to put down even fifteen percent to purchase the land."

"Really? I'd have thought Giles was doing well since the winery was doing well," I said.

"Honey," she said, holding up a file in the air, "operating a winery is very expensive. It takes years to even see a salary. It's not like us. You can bake and get ingredients practically anywhere. The weather, the soil, and a bit of luck are all part of the grape growing process. Especially around here, where it's all new." She handed me the file. "I just gave Tammy Dugan's son a job as a busboy in the restaurant and on the catering staff because he doesn't even know if he can afford to go to college, much less that fancy one he was accepted into."

I looked down at the contract between Lanie Truvinski and the RCC. It was a standard contract. Lanie had put down a deposit.

"The day you saw her, when she zoomed into the parking

lot, did she seem on edge or nervous? Like she'd just killed someone?"

"No. She was mad, but composed. She said that she didn't have time to find a new place for the event, and she was scrambling to let the attendees know about the change of venue. In fact, Clarice Covington at the Rumford Bed and Breakfast is letting her use the office there to get everything situated," she said.

My head jerked up. "She's staying at the bed and breakfast?"

"Mm-hmm." She nodded. "But I don't think she killed anyone. She doesn't look like she'd get her hands dirty."

"Can you give me a copy of this?" I asked. "I just want to note the time stamp, that's all," I followed up when I saw Evelyn was hesitating.

"Is this something I need to see the sheriff about?" she asked. She reluctantly took the paper and made a copy of it on the printer that sat on the credenza behind her desk.

"No. I don't think she did it, but I do know that between the time Lanie was at the winery and when she got here, a car was speeding away from the winery. It almost hit Ella Capshaw." Not that this proves Lanie did anything to Ray, but it does prove she didn't skip town, which a killer might do.

"You mentioned something about Giles trying to get money to purchase the property." I couldn't help but wonder why Giles would kill Ray. Wouldn't he want Ray alive to keep funding the winery? I understood that Ray was selling, but something wasn't right. "Do you know where Giles tried to get the money? Which bank?"

"Bank? Who said anything about a bank?" She laughed. "Perry Dugan. I heard that Giles went to his son, and Perry said no."

My jaw dropped.

"My exact reaction too." She nodded her head. "Them Dugans are as thick as thieves. But it appears there's a rift in the family."

I stood up and folded the copy of the contract, slipping it into my bag.

"I'm sorry about the RCC's policy about not being able to bring desserts in from outside of our kitchen, but I'm sure you understand."

"I completely get it." I thanked her for her time. "Let me know if you hear anything else from these gossiping women." I winked. "You know how they helped me solve your case. I sure need some information for Madison."

"I'll keep an ear out." She tapped her ear and waved me off.

There wasn't enough time before the Garden Club meeting for me to go see Lanie and Perry.

It wasn't until I'd gotten back into my car and headed toward the county line that I realized I was going to see Lanie first. She'd have the freedom to skip town and leave no tracks. Perry was a different story. He had family and roots here. He wasn't going anywhere anytime soon.

Chapter Sixteen

The Rumford Bed and Breakfast was in a rural area of the town. Clarice Covington had gone to great lengths to make it cozy. Besides the main house with three bedrooms, the dining room, and a common room, there were three cabins on the property, each accommodating a different number of guests.

The cabins weren't close together and had different views of the landscape that Rumford had to offer. I'd heard the couple's cabin had an amazing view of the sunset, and the family cabin had an awesome view of the sunrise. Either way, I'd been wanting to stop by and talk to Clarice about doing some pastries for her guests since I'd seen her buying prepackaged ones from the grocery store. It was a perfect reason to stop by and nose around.

It turned out to be a beautiful spring day. The temperature was at a perfect sixty-four degrees, the sun was shining, and the cardinals were chirping right along with the robins. The landscape around the large main house had been freshly mulched, and the bushes that lined the house had lime green buds on them.

The wraparound front porch of the bed and breakfast had petunias hanging down and was lined with six rocking chairs, all pointed to the west. Between each chair was a small wooden box that contained a quilt for when the air got a bit nippy.

"Sophia Cummings, what on earth are you doing way out here?" Clarice surprised me when she stood up from one of the gardening beds. A shadow drew down her face from the large brimmed, straw hat perched on top of her head. Her eyes slid over to the guest parking. I followed her gaze.

"Is that Bitsy's car?" I asked.

"I doubt it," she said in her sweet Southern voice and fidgeted with the spade in her hand.

"Are you digging up or planting?" I asked.

"Tidying up." She adjusted her body a little more to block my view of the guest parking lot. "What was it that you needed?"

"A couple of things." I'd gotten a bag of Flip-Flops out of my car and handed them to her. "These are for you. If I remember correctly, you love them."

"You have a fantastic memory." She wasted no time in opening the bag and taking one out.

"Can I make some fresh and offer them to your guests?" I asked.

"You know,"—she dragged the hat off her head—"that's

a fantastic idea. But I don't see why you came all the way out here when a phone call would do." She took a quick look over her shoulder.

"I came here for a different reason. I didn't know my mama was here." I knew what was going on without even her telling me. I glanced over to mama's car.

"You know about that?" she asked uneasily.

"Clarice." Bitsy turned the corner with a full-sized fern in her hands and the dirt covered roots dangling down. "Do you mind if I take the—" she stuttered, then stopped in mid-sentence, mid-stride, and practically had to pick her own jaw up off the ground. "Sophia." Bitsy looked between Clarice and me. Her eyes grew big, shock lingering on her face. "What on earth are you doing here?"

"Oh, she knows, Bitsy." Clarice shook her head and squinched up her nose. "You can stop pretending."

Bitsy's shoulders slumped. The fern drooped at her side. She sighed and frowned.

"I was right about the flowers at your house, wasn't I?" I asked.

"I was trying to plant things and grow them myself. Most of the other women do that." She dragged her toe in the grass and didn't make eye contact with me.

"How did she drag you into this?" I asked Clarice.

The door of the bed and breakfast popped open, and a young couple came out. They were holding hands.

"How is your honeymoon going?" Clarice asked them when they trotted down the steps. As they exchanged a few words, I continued to stare at Bitsy, deciding to use this situation to my advantage.

I hadn't come here because I knew she was here; that was just a stroke of luck. I came here to see Lanie or get some information on her. Regardless, I could use this whole situation to my advantage.

"Why don't we go inside and discuss this," Clarice suggested. "My guests are starting to mingle and get going. I don't want them to hear a family tiff taking place between you two."

"It's no tiff. It's a matter of right and wrong. In this case, Bitsy is wrong." I gestured for Bitsy to walk ahead of me. I took the fern and placed it in the grass. "It'll be fine right there."

The inside of the bed and breakfast was a typical old house. To the right of the foyer was a big family room, to the left a big dining room, and straight ahead a staircase to the upstairs. Bitsy and I followed Clarice through the dining room and into kitchen.

Clarice put the box from the bakery on the table before she walked over the stove and took the lid off the big pot.

"Chicken and dumplings for supper. The guests love it. I only wish I had space for more guests. I hate to turn people away when we are the only place in town to stay." She slowly stirred the pot.

While the neighboring towns had small motels, the only major hotels were about forty-five minutes away in the bigger cities.

"There's fresh coffee in the pot. The two of you, sit down."

It was like being in the principal's office. We did exactly what she said.

"I saw you buttering her up." Bitsy's brows rose. "How did you know I was here? Did you have Carter follow me?"

"I can't believe you'd pull Clarice into this. Why did you decide to enter this year when you've never entered before?" I asked and made us each a cup of coffee.

"Those girls at the Garden Club are leaving me out." She huffed and dragged the mug of coffee closer to her once I sat it on the table.

"What on earth are you talking about?" I asked.

"Those young whippersnappers are stay-at-home moms and have nothing better to do than worry about the environment." She turned her face from me, chin turned and lifted into the air.

"And that's how a grown woman acts?" I sighed. "No wonder those women don't include you if you act all high and mighty like this. Besides, you do all the other things like the Christmas extravaganza, the Easter egg hunt in the park, and all sorts of things. They can't afford to hire a landscaper like you do, so they have to participate in these exchanges."

Bitsy sniffed a little and her chin fell back into a normal position. She gulped and sniffed some more.

"Clarice, do you do all your planting?" I asked when she came to join us.

"I do, but it's therapy for me. I don't have children or a husband. I really have no social life, unlike Bitsy and

Robert. Sure," she said, gesturing toward Bitsy, "I go to the Friends of the Library, but I don't fit in with the Junior League. I take care of my plants like I would my children. I nurture them. I feed them. I dig them up in the winter and replant them. It's a process, Bitsy."

"I've already signed up," she whispered. "I can't back out now."

"I have an idea." I looked between the two women. "I'll supply the bed and breakfast with pastries for a couple of months in exchange for the flowers you two have already dug up."

"This is wonderful." Bitsy was all smiles and joy now.

"But," I said.

"I knew that was coming," Bitsy snarled.

"You have to attach one of the bed and breakfast's business cards to each one of the plants and give Clarice credit." Bitsy opened her mouth to protest. I put my hand up and continued, "It's only fair to everyone. You'll say that you joined the exchange because your friend Clarice has the most beautiful flowers and you wanted to share them."

"That's a great idea." Clarice patted my hand.

It was too bad she didn't have any children. She'd have made a great mother. Not that anyone could replace Bitsy, but she could be a pill sometimes, and this was one of those times.

We turned when there was a knock on the kitchen door.

"Come in," Clarice called out.

"Hi, bakery girl." Lanie Truvinski popped her head

around the door. She smiled when she noticed me, then faltered when I didn't return the nice gesture. "I'm assuming you're wondering where I've been."

"You could start there." I got up. "I'll wait for you outside while you talk to Clarice about whatever it was you needed to talk to her about."

Bitsy and Clarice exchanged guilt-ridden looks. Bitsy smacked the table with her hand and muttered something under her breath.

When I got outside, I took the opportunity to sit on the bottom step and let the sun beat down on my face. I watched the happy honeymooners disappear into the woods, holding hands, the bride smiling at her groom. Carter was a great man, but I was nowhere near close to even thinking about marriage, and neither was he—at least it appeared that way. Although our mothers were certainly trying to plan a union between the families.

"I'm so sorry about the whole order thing. I know I should've called, but I figured since I paid in full that you were good and could sell them anyway." Lanie Truvinski started talking as soon as she walked out the front door. "I'm a little short on time. I have to get to the country club because the convention starts this afternoon and runs through tomorrow." She held her keys in her hand and passed me on the way to the guest parking lot. She pushed down on the fob and the silver sports car chirped.

"I have a few questions to ask you about Ray Peel," I blurted out. She stopped.

"What about him?" She turned on her fancy high heels, planted her feet, and put her free hand on her hip.

"How did you know him?" I asked.

"He and I had been friends a long time. Back in our business school days." She sucked in a deep breath and drew back her shoulders.

"I guess his murder came as a shock to you?" I asked and pushed off the step to stand up.

"I'm sorry Ray has died, but he wasn't the nicest person when it came to business dealings. I told him that he was going to regret his selfishness one day." She shrugged. "It appears that day has come."

"How so?" I asked. "Aren't most people who are in business trying to beat out the competition?"

"He would make promises and break them," she said.

"Like he did with the lease contract with the winery?" I questioned.

"To my understanding, the lease was going to be up at midnight the night he died." She looked away. "Murdered." Her voice cracked when she whispered that awful word. "Ray and I were once an item. He made so many promises to me. I even moved to different places around the country with him so he could fulfill his dream of owning a franchise restaurant. Now his dream was coming true, and this happens." She dabbed the corner of her eye.

"Franchise?" This was news to me.

"Yes. He wanted to sell the land so he could open up a

few more Café Italias in different cities." She laughed. "He had a solid business plan."

"If you were so happy for him, why did you slap him?" I wanted to know every detail I could.

"Because it was just another broken promise. He knew I put all my heart and soul into this convention. It's been planned for a year now. When he heard I was in charge of the planning, he wanted the business to come to The Grape Valley Winery because he had a vested interest in the land. Then he went off and opened Café Italia. Just like that." She snapped her fingers. "He changed his mind. Just like he did about us." There was a deep sadness in her expression that spread from her eyes to her lips. She frowned. "I slapped him out of anger, and I had to get out of there to find a new place to host the event. So I jumped in my car and drove as fast as I could. I ended up downtown at the little coffee shop by your bakery. I was coming to see you to tell you that I needed a new venue, but you were closed."

"I was setting up at the winery for the fund-raiser that was supposed to be held that night. The same fund-raiser Ray Peel had pledged to donate half-a-million dollars to, and he decided not to do that, either."

"And you wonder why someone killed him." It was like a lightbulb went off in her head. Her lids lowered. "You think I killed him. That's why you're here."

"I should've been honest with you, but my friend Madison is the police's number-one suspect because he put her down, and she said bad things about getting back at him. But I can't ignore the fact that you slapped him. He did you wrong." I didn't want her to run off just yet. "I heard the two of you fighting. Then a friend of mine said a car just like yours practically ran them off the road as it zoomed away from the winery."

"I know it looks bad that we had a fight, but I can tell you that Ray Peel was breathing and not a bit sad that he did me wrong. As for my driving, I had to find a new venue and fast. I did *almost* hit a car because I wasn't familiar with the curvy country road, but I didn't," she said. "After I went to the coffee shop next to your bakery, there was a woman in there, Evelyn Moss, picking up a coffee. She said that she could move a few things around and host the event. She even bought me a coffee. So I followed her to the country club. I had no other choice. It's not like there are a lot of venues in Rumford, Kentucky."

"I went to see Evelyn. She didn't say anything about see-ing you at the coffee shop." But it wasn't like Evelyn had to tell me her whereabouts either, nor did I ask. "She'll be able to verify your story, even if I tell the sheriff?"

"Yes. I'd never hurt Ray or wish him dead. He has—had—many great ideas, but he wasn't a good businessman. I'm telling you that someone who was in business with him did it." She inched closer to me. "Maybe you need to look into the people who own the winery, because Ray insisted he needed to get out of that lease. He wouldn't tell me why, but he said some really shady stuff went down during all of that."

My phone vibrated in my pocket, and I tugged it out.

"You take your call, because I've got to go." She turned back toward her car. "I just settled up with Clarice because I'm leaving after today's events. But you have my card if you need anything else."

"Hello?" It was Carter.

"Where are you?" he asked. "I just went by the bakery, and everyone is loving the coupon you put in the paper."

"I'm at the bed and breakfast. I won't waste my breath on what Bitsy has been up to, but I do have some information about one of the suspects." It was time to start marking these people off.

"I thought we agreed you wouldn't look into things." There was no negotiation in his voice.

"Sometimes I just happen upon things. Like here at the bed and breakfast. Lanie Truvinski was staying here." I was getting used to stretching the truth.

"Evelyn Moss told me. I have a deputy on the way out there right now. Let me guess," he continued, "you already asked her some questions."

"Yes. She isn't the killer," I said matter-of-factly, "She was the one who nearly ran Grant and Ella off the road because she was mad and coming to the bakery to see me. Only I was at the fund-raiser. She went over to the coffee shop and saw Evelyn Moss there. That's when Evelyn took her to the country club and offered the club for the convention."

"I'm about a step behind you. How can that be?" he asked, and I wondered if he was listening to me.

"Ray Peel was going to franchise Café Italia, and that's why he wanted to sell the land. He needed the money in order to keep his dream alive. I'm figuring you need to look into who was going into business with him. Did you look at his cell phone or computer records?" I asked.

"Of course we did. The cell phone was erased, and we have subpoenaed records from his cell carrier. It takes a few days to get those back. We did get all the papers and contacts for Café Italia, so we have been interviewing some of those people." He suddenly got quiet. "Why am I telling you this?"

"Because you know and I know that Madison didn't do this, and you're doing all you can to figure it out." I looked at the bed and breakfast, where I could hear Bitsy and Clarice chatting.

"Anything else you can tell me?" he asked in a resigned voice.

"Are you beginning to come around to the idea of me looking into things?" I asked.

"I'm beginning to think that no matter how hard I push for you to stop snooping, the more information you get about the investigation. I just need you not to go looking for it." He seemed to be bargaining with me. "This doesn't make whoever broke into your house and threw a brink into the bakery any less of a threat to you. Does that make sense?"

"I'm hearing you say as long as I don't go looking for answers, and people just tell me some information, you're good with that. Right?" I wanted to make sure because I was going looking for things in a sort of different way.

Like with Clarice. I went there to offer her my baked goods and slip in some questions about Lanie and I just happened upon Bitsy's wrongdoings with the Garden Club. And that led me to see Lanie. I could use those situations to my advantage and not feel like I was hiding anything from Carter, though I did know he had my best interest at heart.

"Don't go looking for things," he reiterated. "Want to meet up for lunch?"

"I wish I could, but I've got to get to the bakery and pick up the Garden Club goodies. They're having their meeting before the big plant swap. Of course, Bitsy offered my services. For free." I added.

"Good ol' Bitsy," he laughed. "Gotta love her."

"Someone has to," I joked.

"What about tonight?" he asked. "Dinner?"

"You are making this so hard for me." I knew I couldn't tell him that I was meeting with the girls for Operation Merlot. "I've got plans with Charlotte and Madison."

"Alright. But I'm coming by the bakery in the morning for coffee," he said.

"Great. I'll see you in the morning." I hung up the phone and turned to Bitsy and Clarice, who were wrapping up the roots of each plant in damp seed cloths. "I'll see you at the meeting," I said to Bitsy. "Clarice, I'll be sure to get those pastries to you in the morning."

In the morning, just maybe, if I went to Perry's office early enough, and not too many people were there, I might get a glimpse of that lease agreement.

Chapter Seventeen

The afternoon flew by. I'd gone back to the bakery to get the items for the Garden Club meeting. I was happy to see that Bitsy had taken my advice about the plants and given them to the young moms in the group. She looked a lot happier with herself too. In the end, I wasn't sure if she really would've gone through with her plan to deceive the members of the club because, at the end of the day, we all knew Bitsy wasn't going to get her hands dirty.

"Good evening, Duchess." The house was quiet, and there didn't seem to be any more intruders. Duchess greeted me at the door with her normal prancing around my feet. It was her way of telling me that she needed to eat.

A few rubs down her soft white fur was plenty for her before she led the way into the family room and straight into the kitchen, where she meowed a few times next to her empty bowl.

"You're going to have to watch your weight," I warned. "Soon you're due for your annual veterinarian appointment."

She meowed even louder, as though in protest.

"Okay." I opened the screen pantry door and got a scoop of her food out of the container where I kept her kibble.

"Hello!" Madison's voice echoed through the house. "Where are you? Not tied up I hope."

"I'm in here." I poured the food into Duchess's bowl. "I just got home."

"I was wondering why it was all dark in here." Madison flipped on a few lights on her way into the house. She melted into the couch and let out a loud sigh. "It's been a long day."

"What happened? Not that being a murder suspect isn't enough." I turned the oven on and opened the freezer to get some Flip-Flops out.

"About four of my clients broke their housing contracts with me." Her voice remained steady, and her eyes were closed.

I opened a bottle of pinot noir to go with the sweet treat because it was the perfect combination of sweet and tart.

"Why?" I walked over and handed her a glass of wine.

"Really?" She inspected my face. "Are you serious?"

"I was just hoping for a different reason. That's all." I clinked glasses with her. "Operation Merlot."

The doorbell dinged right before the front door opened.

"Are y'all starting without me?" Charlotte stood in the foyer looking at us. "Or did you have a bad day?"

"Both." I laughed and walked back into the kitchen to get her glass.

"Make it a big pour." She tipped the end of the wine bottle that was in my hand to pour more.

"Here, you do it." I gave her the bottle and finished putting the Flip-Flops into the oven.

Madison joined us. She picked up Duchess and snuggled her tight.

"What would we have done if you'd not come back to Rumford?" Madison moped.

"Lucky for you," I teased, "we don't have to answer that question. And now we have some sleuthing to do."

"Not without me." Bitsy sashayed into the house with another bottle of wine in her hand. "What was the deal with you and the woman who was staying at the bed and breakfast?" She cut to the chase.

"That was Lanie Truvinski, who is probably long gone by now." I set the timer on the oven because once we got to gabbing, I didn't want to forget about the Flip-Flops. I grabbed a piece of chalk off the windowsill and walked over the chalkboard on the pantry door. "Lanie Truvinski and Ray Peel were once an item. They met in business school." I started to make notes under her name. Then I crossed out her name.

"Why did you do that?" The little bit of hope in Madison's eyes went dark.

"She slapped Ray because it was just another veiled promise to her that he couldn't keep. He needed to sell the vineyard for as much as he could get because he was going to franchise Café Italia. That was his lifelong dream, according to her."

"He still wronged her." Charlotte zeroed in on the obvious.

"He did, but with the timing of her activities, and Evelyn Moss' confirmation that they were together, she has a firm alibi." I wrote "Perry Dugan" on the board.

"What's up with that pipsqueak?" Bitsy chimed in. "He thinks he's the best lawyer in town. Robert has had to knock him down a time or two."

"I need to go see him tomorrow." I circled his name.

"The cake just needs finishing touches." Charlotte held her glass in the air. "I made all the macarons while you were playing detective."

"Great. That means I can go in early to the bakery and get it finished. Lanie mentioned that Ray had to get out of the lease. There was something strange with it."

"Like what?" Madison asked. "I do lease agreements all the time."

"I don't know, but I do know the Dugans keep a lot of their stuff within the family. If I can get my hands on that agreement, we might be on to something." I looked at the chalkboard.

"And you're going to do this in the morning when you take Perry the cake?" Bitsy asked.

"My plan is to get there before Perry, get the cake in his office, and then snoop for a minute." I dragged the wine glass up to my lips. "Or until I find something that points to the lease agreement."

All four of us jumped when the timer went off.

203

Chapter Eighteen

The alarm rang too early at four AM. But I knew I had to get Reba's cake finished and the bakery ready so I could head on over to Perry Dugan's law firm and get my sleuthing on. That thought propelled me right on out from beneath the warm covers and convinced me not to hit the "Snooze" button.

Thank goodness for an attached garage. I was grateful to not have to scrape my windows when I noticed the frost all over the grass. The cool temps would soon give way to a sunshine-filled day and the warmth of the bakery oven.

My creative juices were flowing as the landscape rushed past the driver's side window. The light of the moon made the Kentucky bluegrass more of a green and black. The images of a triple-layer chocolate cake with mint icing started to tingle my taste buds. I'd made the dessert one other time, for the wife of the New York City mayor. She'd sent me her mother's recipe with a beautiful note asking me to make the cake for her mother's memorial. It was the end of the note that touched me. She gave me permission to duplicate the cake anytime I wanted to. That's when I called her up and thanked her, telling her I'd call it Mama's Mint Chocolate Love. She was delighted.

I circled Main Street a couple of times to check out the bakery and make sure everything looked safe before I parked in the alley. The lights buzzed on, and the kitchen came to life. I'm not sure how to explain how my creative mind worked, but I could see the lively kitchen as I filled orders, and all the customers in the bakery were ready to order their special dessert. Despite the recent vandalism, I couldn't help but feel safe in my bakery. It was my sanctuary.

I went through my usual routine of flipping the lights on, starting the coffeepots, taking out the frozen pastries that would line the glass counter once the sign on the door was flipped, and I put Reba's blue cake on the counter to thaw so I could pour that melted chocolate over it before I strategically placed the macarons.

The Small Talk Café dark roast coffee I was going to feature today had a rich smell that filled the room. The warm brew was the perfect choice to rush away the cold and frosty morning. As I sipped on my first steaming cup, I grabbed the ingredients to make the white chocolate mint frosting for Mama's Mint Chocolate Love.

There were two types of butter I baked with: softened to room temperature and very cold. Both had different purposes when it came to baking. In this particular recipe, I used the room temperature butter because it folded better with the heavy cream, peppermint extract, mini chocolate chips, and green food dye that made the icing such a nice green.

I'd only ever made it as a cake before, but today I decided to feature the recipe as cupcakes. It wasn't a smart business idea to create a cake right off the bat when I wasn't sure how the folks around here would like the taste. Offering Mama's Mint Chocolate Love in cupcake form was not only a perfect mini bite, but the color would go very nicely with the color scheme of the bakery window when I displayed them in a fancy cake holder dome.

My phone chirped a message and brought me out of my head. I pulled it out of my pocket. The good morning message from Carter made me smile. He wanted to make sure I was safe and that the bakery hadn't been vandalized again. I quickly texted back that it was fine, and I was busy making Reba's cake.

The next text I got from him was the photo he'd promised to send me of the half brick that'd been thrown through the display window. I glanced over to the floor where I'd found the brick, and it must've hit a nerve because my feelings from that morning rose up inside of me. With my fingers on my phone screen, I blew up the picture and took a good long look at the strange coloring of the brick. It was definitely a red brick that'd been whitewashed. Most of the houses in Rumford were Cape Cods with wood siding.

I made a good mental note of the photo and slipped my phone into my back pocket. Soon the bakery ovens were buzzing, and the bell over the door dinged with customers coming in for a quick donut to start their day. I even took a few orders for cakes to be picked up later in the week.

I couldn't help but wonder if this was what a typical morning would look like if my mind weren't somewhere else. I rubbed my hand over my back pocket, remembering the photo of the brick on my phone.

Chapter Nineteen

Charlotte was busy with baking the new orders and holding down the fort. Meanwhile, I finished Reba's cake just in time to deliver it to Perry's office, with the intention of snooping a smidgen.

At the four-way stop on Main Street in downtown, the Rumford National Bank was opposite what used to be the old medical building, where the local family doctor, pediatrician, dentist, and a couple of specialty doctors had their offices. After the new medical annex with an emergency room had been built on the outskirts of town, the old medical building became available. That's when the real estate office that Madison worked for relocated there, and Perry Dugan rented an office for his law firm.

I was driving the bakery van because I had more desserts to deliver to the Garden Club, and it made me feel better telling myself that I was really delivering a client's cake instead of snooping, just in case Carter asked. I'd been there a few times before with Madison, because she was the real estate agent for my house. This was where we'd done the closing. Plus, the bank was right there, and Bob Bellman, the loan officer from the Rumford First National Bank, could just walk over for the closing.

I didn't care how long ago the doctors had vacated the building. The horrible smell of fluoride and plastic bibs the dentist used was still in the air, or at least still in the walls. It brought back the terrible memories of Bitsy bringing me here to get all my cavities filled. That was another strike Bitsy had against me being a baker. No doubt I'd been pretty gifted at baking when I was young, but I was still a child and had eaten what I'd baked—and most often forgotten to brush my teeth afterward.

The real estate office took up the entire first floor. The second floor had Perry's office and an accountant's office. I climbed the stairs and held on to both sides of the cake box. It was three layers of yummy chocolate and very heavy. The last thing I needed was to drop this cake.

Perry's law office was through the first door on the right as soon as you got up the stairs, and the only sign was the small gold plate screwed onto the wall. It was simple. Lucky for me, the doorknob was the hook type, so I could simply use my elbow to push it down and open the door with my hip.

"Can I help you?" The face of the woman behind the counter lit up. That was my cue to throw on the charm.

"Hi," I smiled and walked over with the beautiful cake box held in front of me. It was worth the extra expense to purchase the cake boxes with the side windows so everyone could see what was inside. "I'm Sophia Cummings, the owner of the new bakery in town, For Goodness Cakes, and Mr. Dugan ordered a cake to be delivered today."

"I'll take it." She stood up and put her hands out over the desk. "Mr. Dugan had an early court appointment this morning, but I'll leave it on his desk."

"That's so sweet of you, but he paid a lot of money for this cake, and I'd feel a lot better if I could just stick it in his office. That way I'll know if anything happens to it, it'll be my fault." Taking the blame for something yet to happen was an infallible way of getting people on your side.

"Are you sure?" the lady asked. The phone rang. "I do have to get the phone. His office is three doors down on the left." She pointed and grabbed the phone.

"Perfect," I whispered, like I was giving her some privacy to answer the call. *Please, please, please let me find that lease agreement quickly,* I thought, mentally counting the doors as I walked past them.

The door was cracked open, and I used the toe of my shoe to push it open wider. It was a typical lawyer's office, or what I imagined one would look like. A wall of shelves held rows and rows of books. A minibar tempted me as a possible solution to my nerves. Then there were the desk and filing cabinet in the corner of the room.

After I carefully set the cake on the desk, I zeroed in on the cabinet. The drawers were labeled alphabetically on the outside. I ran my finger down the cabinet until I got to the

G's, looking for Grape Valley Winery. The drawer pulled out long, and the tabs of the folders clicked when I dragged my finger across the top of them.

"Good boy," I said, happy with Perry's straightforward filing system, and I grinned when my finger stopped on the folder tab with "Grape Valley Winery" typed on it. "Let's see this agreement."

The file had the typical lease agreement, but an amendment caught my attention.

I scanned the paper and got to the good stuff: "In the case of death, the lessee, Giles Dugan, has the first opportunity to purchase the land."

I read it again to make sure I understood what I was reading. If Ray Peel died, the Dugans got the chance to buy the land.

"Here's the motive," I gasped and grabbed my phone from my back pocket. "Carter is going to freak." I snapped a few photos of the file and immediately sent them to him. "Here is your proof that Madison didn't kill Ray," I said as I typed.

I could suddenly hear the shuffling and murmuring sounds of people coming down the hallway. I shoved the file back in place and shut the cabinet, leaving the file in it for Carter to retrieve. For a second, I wondered if I should take the cake back with me, but I left it there and scurried out of the office.

"You find it okay?" The receptionist asked me on my way out the door.

"All good," I said, waving over my shoulder and pushing open the door.

"Hey!" I ran into Madison at the end of the stairs. "What are you doing?" She looked past me and over my shoulder.

My phone rang, and I took it out of my pocket, thinking it was Carter. It wasn't. It was the phone number I had for the Fords.

"The Fords." I showed Madison the screen and hit the green button. "Mrs. Ford?"

"Who is this?" The crackle of an aged old lady's voice came through the phone.

"It's Sophia Cummings. You called me. Or are you calling me back?" I asked, a bit confused.

"Sophia." There was switch to a joyous tone. "I was scrolling through this fancy caller ID box, and I didn't recognize the number."

"You didn't get my message?" I asked.

"Honey, we don't know how to use all the new technology. Our phone hangs on our kitchen wall, and it's all I know how to use," she said, laughing. It brought back so many memories. There wasn't a time I'd gone to the bakery that Mrs. Ford wasn't smiling, giving away cookies and treats. Her laughter was just as much a part of the bakery as the wonderful smells their fabulous creations filled the air with.

"Mrs. Ford, I called because I found a journal at the bakery after I bought the building." I looked at Madison and crossed my fingers in the air. "It's filled with your recipes, and I wanted to know if I could use your Long Johns recipe. Of course, I'd give all the credit to you, but I just wanted to ask first."

"Honey, that journal is very old. I've perfected that donut since that journal was written. If you come by the house, I'll give you the new recipe, and you can use it all you want." Her words were music to my ears. "I'd love to see the community enjoy our treats again. You have my full permission to start making them again."

"That's wonderful. Can I stop by in about an hour? I have to drop something off at the Garden Club meeting, and then I'll be over." I nodded to Madison. She bounced on the balls of her feet and silently clapped her hands together.

Mrs. Ford gave me her address, which was out in the country, and we hung up.

"That's great news!" Madison cheered after I put my phone back in my pocket.

"That's not the only great news I've got." I grabbed her arm and dragged her into her office. "You aren't going to believe this." I pulled my phone out and clicked through my photos. "Close your door."

I wasn't about to take any chances of someone hearing me. Especially someone who was associated with the Dugans.

"What is it?" Madison looked at the photo. Her face scrunched up.

"It's a photo of the lease agreement between Ray Peel and Giles Dugan. It's the Dugans' motive for killing him."

I felt like I could take a nice deep breath, and all was going to be all right with the world.

"What?" She grabbed the phone out of my hands and zoomed in on the photo.

"It says that the Dugans get the chance to purchase the property if Ray dies. Ray wasn't going to renew the lease. He just so happens to get murdered hours before the lease agreement ran out? Coincidence?" I asked.

"Where did you get this?" she asked.

"Perry Dugan ordered a cake for Reba—I'm not yet quite sure why." I put my finger in the air. "I knew he was the lawyer on the agreement, so I figured that I'd do a little snooping when I dropped off the cake, and I came across this."

"This gives them way more motive than me." She grabbed me this time and hugged me. "Thank you, thank you, thank you!" She let go and gave me my phone back. "We've got to call Carter."

"I've already sent the photos to him." As though he had ESP, my phone chirped a text. "I thought I told you to stay away from this. On my way there now." I read the text aloud and laughed.

"That boy has got a lot to learn about you," Madison teased, and we hugged again.

"Does he ever." There was never a better time to get out of the building. "I've got to run those bakery treats over to Bitsy at the Garden Club meeting." I gave Madison a quick hug. "Are you going to hang around and see what happens?"

She nodded. "Of course I am. I have to hear Carter say I'm not a suspect."

"Let me know how it goes." I left the building and got into the bakery van. My gaze moved across the street to the Rumford First National Bank.

Using the voice command to call Carter, I spoke again into my phone, "I really wanted to see you, but I have to get some treats over to the library for the Garden Club." It was the perfect excuse not to explain to him how I'd gotten my hands on the lease or that I was thinking about going over to the bank to see if I could get some face time with Bill Bellman.

"You know what I'm going to ask you," He wasn't going to let me off the hook.

"How I got the photos?" I whined.

"Mm-hmm," he agreed on the other end of the phone.

"You're not going to like it." There was no sense in sugar-coating it. I was met with silence. "Okay. Fine. Perry Dugan ordered a birthday cake for Reba Gunther, and I was delivering it."

"And the file jumped into your hands?" he asked in a sarcastic voice.

"If you want to believe that and it makes you less angry at me, then yes." I tried to lighten the mood the best that I could.

"Tell me the truth. Even if I'm not going to like it." There was no playful tone in his voice.

"I just wanted to see what the lease agreement said

because I thought it was strange that the winery was still open even though they all knew Ray wasn't going to renew their lease," I said as I pulled into the library parking lot. There weren't any available parking spaces, so I edged up close to the curb to unload the pastries.

"It was on our list. You aren't giving me the time necessary to investigate," he said. "The guys in the department are starting to wonder if you're going to run against me for sheriff."

I laughed. He didn't think it was funny.

"Nah, your job is safe." I put the bakery van in park and waited for him to say something. "Carter?"

"Yeah. I'm here." He didn't sound like himself. "As in here at Perry's law office. Stay at the library or go back to the bakery. I'll call you back."

"Before you go, I have some good news." I couldn't wait to tell him. "Mrs. Ford called me back. and she asked me to come to her house and get the latest recipe for the Long Johns." My heart started to race. I couldn't believe my luck. "I'm going to be making and selling them."

"That's great, Sophia." He paused. "Maybe this lead you've uncovered will give us two things to celebrate. I need to go. I'll call you back." He clicked off.

Chapter Twenty

Since the Rumford First National Bank was across the street from Perry's office, I decided I was too close not to go in. Bill Bellman was the President, and we'd established a good working relationship. Maybe I could squeeze some information out of him about the rumor I'd heard that Cat Fraxman's parents had mortgaged their home and land to help the library fund.

If Carter had seen my van parked out in the rear parking lot, he'd have been sure to stop by and check on what I was doing. I could've made the excuse that I was taking care of some banking business, but one lie after another was going to jump up and bite me in the you-know-what, and I didn't want that to happen today. After all, I was about to get my hands on the Fords' Maple Long Johns recipe.

The inside of the bank was an open floor plan. The offices had glass walls, so you could see who was meeting with which officers. Bob Bellman was in his office alone.

When he heard the echo of my shoes walking toward him, he looked up and waved me in.

"Sophia." He stood up and put his hand out for me to shake. "How's the bakery? I apologize for not stopping by yet, but my wife said your treats are amazing."

"I'm so glad. I did see her at the Friends of the Library meeting." I gestured to the chair, indicating that I wanted to sit down.

"Please. It's a shame about the Fraxmans. I've tried to do everything I could to refinance or come up with a way to not put them in bankruptcy," he said.

"I'm sorry. Bankruptcy?" I asked a little confused.

"I thought you were stopping by to meet them." He ran his finger down the calendar on his desk. "I have a meeting with someone from the Friends of the Library." There was a horrified look on his face. He ran his hand across his jaw. "Oh, man. I'm sorry. Why are you here?"

"I wanted to know if I could get the address for the Fords," I lied. My mind felt like a tornado as I tried to focus on why I was there and not the bombshell he'd just dropped on me, which I believed would be a perfect motive to kill someone. "Bankruptcy?"

"The Fords are filing bankruptcy?" he asked and clicked around on his computer.

"No. You just said the Fraxmans." I blinked in bafflement.

"I'm sorry I said anything. Please forget I said that." He tapped away. "The Fords' address." He stopped typing.

"Oh." He drew back and tapped a little more. "It appears their accounts were only through the bakery, and that's the address they used. Apparently, they don't have an account with us anymore."

He grabbed a piece of paper and jotted something down. While he did, I quickly texted Carter.

I think Cat Fraxman killed Ray Peel. Hand to God, this information just fell into my lap while I'm at the bank, trying to get the Fords' address. Fraxmans took out second mortgage on good faith that Ray Peel was going to donate the money to pay them back.

Carter responded immediately: *I'm heading over to library now. Don't look into this. Let me do my job.*

"I'm sorry I couldn't help you." Bob stood up, indicating with an obvious gesture that I should leave. "I feel like I've said too much about the Fraxmans' personal life."

"I'm sorry, but I can't keep this from Sheriff Kincaid." I didn't want to lie to him, because Carter would definitely be coming here to ask questions. "I'm sure you understand that my friend, Madison, is the only suspect because she said something stupid to incriminate herself. But this is a big motive to kill someone. And I think it needs to be looked into."

"I never even thought about how this would involve Ray Peel, but I'm more than happy to cooperate with the law," he said, nodding. "I'm sorry I couldn't help with the Fords' address, but I am going to look into why they don't bank here."

"Thanks for your help anyway. I'm hoping to get in touch with them about making their famous Maple Long Johns and selling them at the bakery." Telling him part of the truth made me feel a little bit better.

I was dying to get out of there and over to the library.

"That would be incredible. I do have to say that I miss those the most." He sighed.

"I think everyone misses them." I shook his hand. "Thanks, again."

I'd always loved the fact the library was across town because when I was a child, it felt like Bitsy was taking me on a girls' day trip out of town, but truly it was only a few minutes from our house. It felt different because we had to actually drive there and not just park downtown and walk like we would for most of the shops that Bitsy needed to go to.

I beat Carter there and parked in the lot. I was a little relieved that there weren't too many cars. I'd hate for Cat to get arrested for murder in front of a lot of people.

"Welcome back." Cat stood up from behind the reference counter when I ran in the automatic sliding doors. "Are you here to discuss the menu again?" I detected a hint of sarcasm in her tone.

"No. Actually I came here because I wanted to ask you

about Ray Peel." There was no reason to pretend to be there for any other purpose. "I was at the bank today, talking to Bill. He apologized for not being able to stop by the bakery to try out my pastries. Of course, he said that he was looking forward to having some of For Goodness Cakes' desserts at the library ribbon-cutting ceremony. That's when we started to talk about Ray Peel and how it was a shame that the library wasn't going to have a loan."

By the look on her face and her reluctance to look directly at me, I could tell that she knew I'd found out about the loan her parents had taken out.

"He informed me that the loan the bank gave the library wasn't enough, but that your parents had come in and taken out a second mortgage on their property." I tapped my temple. "Now, I'm not a detective. As you know, I'm just a baker, but something didn't sit right with me, and I got to noodling with this idea." I paced back and forth in front of the reference desk. "What if Catherine Fraxman killed Ray Peel? Before, I didn't think you had much of a reason, other than him withdrawing his donation. Big deal, it's not like you were personally relying on his donation. I just figured you were so upset because of how passionate you are about the library."

I stopped pacing, snapped my finger, and then pointed it at her, knowing that if Bitsy was here, she'd smack my finger down because that just wasn't good Southern manners.

"That's not the reason you're upset. You're upset because now your parents are in danger of losing everything they've worked for all of their lives." I knew I'd hit the nail on the head because Cat started to cry.

"Is this true?" Carter had been standing by the door. He slowly walked into the library.

"Yes, it's true. I only asked them after Ray Peel had told me he'd donate the money. I asked him to donate the money up front, but he insisted he didn't have the money but he had a big business deal going through. He promised me he'd have it the night of the fund-raiser. That's when I went to my parents." Tears streamed down her face. "They were hesitant at first, but they know how much this library means to our town. To you. To me." Her chest heaved as the tears got bigger and faster. "I didn't kill Ray Peel, but I wish I had because now my parents are going to have to file for bankruptcy."

"I know sometimes we do things that are out of character. If you just tell the truth, I can talk to the judge and try to get you leniency." Carter talked to Cat in a calm voice.

"Yes. I was with Tammy Dugan, Reba Gunther, and Megyn at the vineyard offices," she blubbered, trying to catch her breath. "I ran into the offices to see if I could recoup any money from them. I was in desperate need."

"Into the office? You weren't in the vineyard with Ray?" Carter asked.

"No. I was in the parking lot with Ray. He was getting into his car to leave." She didn't quiver one bit as she gave her recount. "Tammy and Reba saw him. He even stopped Megyn and asked her a question while I was stewing inside."

"What did he ask her?" Carter wanted to know.

"I don't know. I wasn't listening. I was just trying to figure out how I was going to save my parents." Her chin dipped. Her shoulders began to shake up and down as the sobs poured out. "I didn't kill him. I never even thought about killing him. If anything, I was blaming myself for letting my parents get involved in this whole thing. His donation was going to pay off their second mortgage. That's how it was going to work."

"Did you have a contractual agreement?" Carter asked.

"No," she whispered, "but Tammy and Reba can vouch for me. We were inside the offices when the police cars came squealing into the parking lot, and that's when we realized something had happened. We didn't know it was Ray."

"If that's the case, that means Tammy and Reba didn't do it either. Of course, I'm going to have to check out your story." Carter had just blown all of my suspects out of the water.

"Yeah. Go on over and see Bob at the bank. He's been trying so hard to help me figure something out." Her voice trailed off. She jerked a tissue out of the box and dried her eyes with it.

Carter pointed to the door, indicating for us to leave.

"I'm sorry, Cat." I felt the need to apologize. "I should've asked you about it before I called Carter."

"It's okay, Sophia. I understand it looks bad, and if my best friend were in Madison's shoes, I'd be doing everything I could to help her out." It was kind of Cat to forgive me.

My heart was beating a whole lot faster in the parking lot, waiting for Carter to say something to me, than it was when we were questioning Cat.

"I'm sorry." I had to get it off my chest. "It really did make a whole lot of sense, and I did text you before I went in—"

"With your guns blazing, throwing out all sorts of questions and accusing her." He shook his head and guided me by the elbow over to the car. "That's not how we operate in the sheriff's department. When we want to bring someone in for questioning, we bring them in."

"Then why did you ask her questions?" I jerked away from him.

"I was following up on your questions to get to the bottom of it. Normally, I'd have asked her if she had an alibi, and then I'd go check it out. Not accuse her and point the finger at her, though it was a good motive," he said. "Now that that's over, do you think you could stop?"

I nodded.

"Good." He kissed the top of my head. "I'm going back to follow up on some leads and see if any of the evidence collected at the scene is back yet."

There was a stride in his walk that told me he was a little mad at me, and I knew better than to run after him. Besides, Cat wasn't the killer, but Madison was still the primary suspect, and I couldn't swallow that.

Chapter
Twenty-One

The address Mrs. Ford gave me wasn't exactly on the same road as the library, but near there. I'd decided to stop by the Fords' house first, then head to the library afterward. The Fords lived in a small brick ranch home that was right off a two-lane, curvy country road.

There was a chicken pen to the right of the house and a water cistern to the left. They were the typical good ol' country folk who knew how to cook. Not only did she make the finest donuts in Kentucky, she also had the best fried chicken.

Of course, she didn't sell it at the bakery, but she did bring it to all the repasts after someone died. Sadly, when someone did die, the first thing that popped into my head was the mouth-watering thought that I was going to get to eat some of her fried chicken.

"Who're you?" The young girl's words ran together. She stood with her hand over her eyes to shield them from the sun. She wore a pair of blue jeans, Converse tennis shoes, and a Rumford high school T-shirt. Her hair was in braided pigtails.

"I'm Sophia Cummings." I shut the car door. "I bet you're Patsy's daughter."

"Yep. How you know my mama?" This girl was definitely wary of me. She shifted her scrawny hips to one side and took her hand down from her face.

"Well," I said, pulling a bag of the Heart of Rumford cookies out of my purse and handing them to her. Reluctantly, she took them. "Your mother and I went to high school together."

"She looks a lot older than you." She ripped open the baggie and smelled the contents.

"Aw. You're just saying that because she's your mom." I looked over the girl's shoulder. "Your granny here?"

"What you want with my granny?" she asked.

It was apparent this girl was protective.

"She's expecting me. I bought her old bakery." I nodded toward the cookies. "I know I'm not as great a baker as your granny, but I sure do try."

"No one is as good as Granny Dixie." She took out a cookie and held it up in the sunlight. "It looks like you have a lot of holes in the middle."

"Try it. I think you'll like it." I encouraged her, hoping I could get past her to see Dixie.

She took a nibble before she took a bite, then stuck the whole thing in her mouth.

"Not bad." She shrugged and took out another one.

"She's back there." The girl's head turned slightly to the right as she gave me the side-eye. "She's working on her vegetable garden today."

"Thanks." I walked past her. "What's your name?"

"Sally Ann." She stuffed another cookie in her mouth.

"It was nice to meet you, Sally Ann. Please tell your mom hello for me." I stopped. "Say, come on down to the bakery and see me sometime."

I felt sorry for Sally Ann. Even though I knew the Fords were good people, I couldn't help but wonder if the rumor that they were raising Sally Ann, instead of her own mother taking care of the girl, was true. She was a bit gruff for a girl her age. Not that being a tomboy was uncommon in Rumford, but she looked like she could use a friend or two, or even a mentor. I also couldn't help but wonder if she was as talented as her granny.

When I walked behind the house, I saw Dixie Ford bent over in the garden. It wasn't the corn that'd already grown as tall as me, or the full pepper plants that caught my eye. It was the whitewashed red brick gardening shed.

"I was so happy to get your call," Dixie greeted me with that same smile that I remembered.

It was warm and welcoming. The way she'd treated people was a part of the bakery experience I remembered and how I wanted my customers to feel when they came into For Goodness Cakes.

"Hi." It was as though my mouth had dried and my mind went blank. "This shed." It was all I could say, especially when I took one more step toward the shed, and there was a red spray paint can propped up against the crumbling wall.

"It's a disaster. The bricks are falling off the backside, and we're trying to figure out if we want to just tear it down and build a new one or build onto it." She stuck her hoe in the ground and pulled off the green gardening gloves. "Are you still just as delighted as the day you signed the papers to buy the building?"

Sally Ann walked up, still eating the cookies.

"Yes." I shook my head in confusion. "But I'm not clear on why you wanted to sell."

"We retired." She slowly walked out of the garden.

I pulled my phone out of my back pocket and clicked through the messages to find the one that Carter had attached—the photo of the brick someone had thrown through the bakery window.

"Do you mind looking at this photo on my phone?" I held the photo out to her. "That's the brick that was thrown through the bakery window. There was a clear warning for me written in red spray paint."

"Are you saying that the brick in this photo is from my shed?" Dixie's brows furrowed.

"Yes. I am. If you didn't want me to open the bakery, why did you sell it to me?" I asked.

"I don't know what you're talking about, Sophia." Dixie was playing the good part about being confused.

"I'm sure Sheriff Kincaid can clear this up for us real quick." I hated to call him, but I could make out neither hide nor hair of what was going on, and if I had to get him out here to make her talk, then I would.

"Stop!" Sally Ann appeared in the back yard. "Don't call the law. Granny Dixie didn't do it. I did."

Dixie and I both looked at the girl. Her bottom lip started to quiver.

"I . . ." Her chest heaved up and down.

"What did you do?" Dixie gasped.

"I love your bakery and when this girl called and said she had your journal, I couldn't even think about letting her take away my only good memories of my mama and me." The girl started to cry. "Mama and I used to make the Long Johns that you want the recipe to, and if you take that memory away from me, then I've got nothing."

"Why didn't you say something?" Dixie hurried over to her granddaughter and curled her into her arms. "Honey, Sophia has the talent to make the Long Johns, and everyone in Rumford will be able to remember all the good memories when they bite down. She can't steal your memories. Your memories are in your head. No one can take those. Or how those make you feel in your heart."

"It wasn't the only thing I did." She looked up. "I broke into your house. I was looking for the journal, but I couldn't find it."

"You broke into my house?" I didn't know whether to hug and thank her or cry because I'd thought it was the killer who had broken in and thrown the brick through the bakery window.

"I'm sorry. I didn't know you were such a nice lady." Her fingers fidgeted. "I'm more than happy to come clean up the damage."

"Clean it up?" Dixie's eyes widened. "How're you gonna pay for it?"

My heart hurt for Sally Ann. ""Mrs. Ford, I know what Sally Ann did wasn't right, but I do think it came from a good heart. I'm sure we can work something out. I've already put my house back together. And the front window of the bakery was replaced. It's all good now. I'm just glad I know who did it." I gave Sally Ann a weak smile, and I saw the relief settle on her face. "I thought someone really wanted to hurt me."

"I'd never do that. And," Sally Ann said, shrugging, "your cookies are pretty good."

"Pretty good?" Dixie asked her granddaughter.

"Darn good." Sally Ann smiled as big as the sun that was hanging over our heads. "I'm truly sorry for all the trouble I caused. I'll do anything to make it up."

"Well, Sophia is going to come up with some sort of payment plan, and you're going to make good," Dixie warned the girl.

"Yes, ma'am. I will." She held up the Scout's honor gesture in the air. "I promise."

"Now, go on and get in the house. I'll deal with you in my own way." Dixie pointed toward the house. Sally Ann wasted no time in taking off in that direction. "I'm sorry. I had no idea."

"It's okay. I really am glad that it wasn't Ray Peel's killer who did it. That's one thing off my mind." I gnawed on my lip and wondered just how off base I was about Ray's murderer.

"I heard about that. Shame someone would go to such great lengths to hurt someone." She looked off into the distance. "Patsy, my girl. She doesn't mean to hurt Sally Ann, but she does. Floats in and out of that girl's life like a feather. Her doing all them bad things to you is partially my fault."

"No, it's not. You're doing a fine job with her." I guessed the rumors I'd heard were true. The Fords were raising Sally Ann.

"Mm-hm," she hummed. "I spent so many years with Patsy in the bakery kitchen, and with Sally Ann in the high chair, telling them that it was going to be theirs one day. I'd tell Sally Ann she was going to grow up and bake just like me and take over. Little did I realize Patsy wanted nothing to do with the bakery and blamed all her issues on me spending dusk to dawn there."

"I'm sorry you feel that way." I reached out and grabbed her hand. "It's simply not true. Your baking brought so many good memories to Rumford. You were a big reason I decided to be a baker. When I came into the bakery, it wasn't just about the delicious smells or the perfect combination of your pastries; it was the kind words and warm smile that you gave me that sealed the entire experience."

"You are too kind. I truly loved being a baker, but maybe

I can be here for Sally Ann like I wasn't for her mother." She squeezed my hand before she let go. "Come on in the house and I'll get us a glass of sweet iced tea while I go over the recipe with you."

"Are you sure you don't want to save that for Sally Ann?" I offered, knowing how important it was to her.

"No." She shook her head. "I gave Patsy everything, and I'm not going to do this with Sally Ann while she's under my roof. She needs love and guidance, not someone in the kitchen all day." Dixie's words sounded sweet, but I wasn't sure if she realized just how strong-headed that little girl was.

Regardless, I kept my mouth shut. I wasn't sure what I'd do, but in some way I'd give some honor to the Long Johns to Sally Ann's fond memories.

"So, you're telling me that it's the added salt to the maple icing that's the special ingredient?" I sat dumbfounded at their round and wobbly kitchen table as I looked at the piece of paper with her recipe in my hand. "Knock me over with a feather," I muttered. "Brilliant."

"This old bird had a few secrets up her sleeve that no big city or fancy pastry school can teach." She placed a glass of sweet tea in front of me. "Adding the salt to the frosting enhances the maple flavor and takes out that too-sweet just a bit. And when you mix up your dough, I suggest you whisk the cinnamon into the flour instead of the milk. Then add that mix to your yeast mix." She laughed. "It took me years to figure out why some of my Long Johns were lumpy and some weren't. It was that cinnamon added to the milk." She tapped the recipe paper. "This is damn-near perfect."

"I'd never even thought about adding salt," I admitted. I couldn't wait to get back to the bakery and start making a batch.

"I'm thrilled to have helped." She sat down and took a drink of her tea. "Now, what do you have in mind for that granddaughter of mine?"

"I might have a few things in mind." I polished off my glass of tea. "Can I get back to you about it?"

"You sure can, honey." The smile faltered. "You aren't leaving, are you?" she asked when I got up.

"I've got to go. But can I ask you a favor?" I asked. "I'd love it if you'd come down to the bakery and taste my treats. If something is missing or you think I could make it better, I'd love your advice."

"Are you sure?" she asked. "I'd never let another baker in my kitchen."

"I'm more than positive. You have some pretty big shoes that Rumford is expecting me to fill. That's a lot of stress." I tensed my jaw.

"I'd be more than delighted. Though I doubt I can help." She and I gave each other a quick hug.

I didn't bother telling Sally Ann goodbye. I could only imagine what Dixie was saying to the poor girl. I knew what she'd done wasn't the right way to go about things, but I empathized with the girl.

When I got into the car, I carefully laid the recipe in the passenger seat next to me. It was more precious than gold. I dragged my phone out and scrolled through the contacts.

"Is this a real phone call?" Bitsy answered teasingly.

"It is." I couldn't stop myself from smiling or tearing up. "I know I don't tell you this a lot, Mom,"—it was a rare occasion that I called her mom—"but I love you so much. Thank you for the amazing lifestyle you gave me as a child. I'm truly grateful."

"Are you drinking?" Bitsy asked on the other end of the phone, with a little skepticism in her voice.

"No." I sighed. "I'm on my way to the meeting."

I couldn't help but smile on my way to the Garden Club Meeting, but first I stopped by the bakery to pick up the Cherry Flip-Flops and tell Charlotte that all the people on our suspect list pretty much had alibis. We were back to square one.

Chapter
Twenty-Two

The Garden Club was in the meeting room in the back of the library. The new addition was really coming along, and it appeared the finishing touches were being set.

"Hi, Cat." I stopped by the reference desk. It was the first time I'd talked to her since I stood in this very spot accusing her of killing Ray Peel. "Any news with the bank?"

"No." She turned away from the filing cabinet and looked back at me. Her eyes dipped down on the edges. "We'll make it through. I've been taking a lot of photos of my parents' antiques and stuff to put on Craigslist. I know we aren't going to be able to recoup the half a million their property is worth, but it's a start to something."

"I'm really sorry." I looked toward the conference room when I heard some clapping. "I've got to get these into the Garden Club meeting." I lifted the lid. "Would you like one?"

"Are those Cherry Flip-Flops?" she asked.

"Yes. And I know how much you love them." I set the

container on the counter of the reference desk and took out a couple of Flip-Flops. "It's the least I can do."

"I'll see you in the meeting." Cat returned to the filing cabinet.

Snapping the lid back on the pastry box, I walked through the library and slipped into the conference room. Bitsy had just taken the microphone at the front of the room. The applause I'd heard must've been the Garden Club president introducing her.

Her eyes met mine, and then she looked at the front row, where Clarice Covington was sitting. I was thrilled Bitsy had decided to do the right thing and tell the Garden Club what she'd been up to.

In true Bitsy style, she put her own spin on it.

I tried not to burst out in laughter as I listened while I placed the Flip-Flops on the table in the back.

"I've always admired the beautiful flowers in nature. As you know, my daughter, Sophia Cummings," she said, drawing the attention to me as I waved, "was not into nature or flowers. We'd spend all of our mother and daughter time in the kitchen." I had to face the wall, so they wouldn't see my reaction to her lie. But she was going to save face as much as possible, and I was going to let her. "As most of you know, I hired a landscape architect to design my garden. When I decided to do the Garden Club's annual plant swap, I wanted to feature a Rumford treasure that's sorely overlooked. Clarice Covington is an amazing gardener, and her bed and breakfast is picture perfect. In light of all the bad publicity with the library, Clarice would like to host the flower swap event at the bed and breakfast." Bitsy started to clap.

"What do you mean 'in light of the bad publicity'?" Cat Fraxman asked. She had slipped in behind me and was standing in the back of the room. "If you take the plant swap away from the library, that'll be the first of many organizations that will follow your lead. Then my parents will have gone bankrupt for nothing!" She rushed out the door and slammed it shut behind her.

There was a collective gasp. It was the first time Cat had made it public that her parents had put up the loan.

"That's a showstopper," Lizbeth muttered next to me. "I got it all on camera too." She patted the Canon hanging around her neck.

"I feel so bad for her."

"It looks like she'd have good motive to kill Ray Peel too." Lizbeth started writing in her notebook. "Anything new with that? Or anything you want to tell me about the investigation of your house and now your bakery?"

"We were all wrong. Or should I say that you were wrong about someone sending me a very clear message?" I asked.

"Really?" She stopped writing and took a sudden interest in me. "I'm the first one to admit when I'm wrong, if it's going to give me a good scoop."

"This isn't going to be on the record," I warned.

"That's not fair." Her nose turned up.

"It is when it involves a minor and I'm not pressing charges." It was as simple as that.

"Fine." She rolled her eyes and stuck her notepad in the fanny pack she wore around her waist. "Off the record."

"It's no secret that Dixie Ford made the best Maple Long Johns. I found their recipe journal in the office when I bought the building. The recipe was in there, but it wasn't special." My brows furrowed.

"What do you mean by 'special'?" she asked.

"As a baker, I knew there was something different in her Long Johns. I spent countless hours trying to perfect them, and when I found the recipe, there wasn't anything unusual about it, but I didn't feel right using her recipe." I shrugged. "I called her and left a message with Patsy's daughter, Sally Ann, for them to call, and I even said that I found the recipe journal and wanted to make some of them, with her permission."

"If they left it, then isn't it fair game?" Lizbeth scooted closer. All the Garden Club women were gathering around the food and chattering.

"Technically, but not morally. Anyway," I said, taking a step back, "Sally Ann has very fond family memories about the time she spent in the kitchen, and felt that if I started to make their recipes, I'd take away her memories."

"So, the granddaughter did it?" Lizbeth's mouth dropped.

"Yeah. She broke into my house to try and find the recipe journal. When she didn't find that, she didn't want to ruin anything in the bakery because it was originally her family's, and to see it destroyed would hurt them." My eyes glanced over Lizbeth's right shoulder when Reba Gunther walked up to the food table. "I'm going to have her come do some things at the bakery. The good news is that I got the real recipe, and Dixie Ford is a genius."

"Are you giving me the scoop that you're going to be making and selling Fords' Maple Long Johns?" Lizbeth asked eagerly.

"You'll see." My brows rose, and I walked around Lizbeth to get to Reba.

She and Priscilla Cartwright had their heads stuck together and were in deep conversation, whispering about something.

"Hello, ladies." I didn't mind interrupting them. "Priscilla, I've been meaning to get over to the Back-en-Thyme. I'm doing a cake for a bridal shower, and I'd like to order some flowers for the bouquet that I'm placing on top of the cake. As a matter of fact, I've given the bride your business card because she doesn't have a florist."

"No florist and she's already having her shower?" Priscilla gave me a funny look.

"Her cousin was doing the flowers, and you know how that can go." The three of us nodded. We all knew how sticky those situations could get.

"I'll get her your information, and we can come up with something. I'll stop by the bakery," she said before excusing herself.

"I didn't know you and Priscilla were good friends," I said to Reba.

"She's been so kind over the past year." Reba's voice was low, to the point where I had to lean in to hear her.

"Back-en-Thyme does all the flowers for the winery. "Most of the time when she comes in, I'm there alone."

"That's nice that the two of you have gotten to know each other." I wanted to ask her about her birthday cake, but I didn't want to spoil the surprise, so I kept my lips tight.

She gave me a pinched smile.

"I guess it's no secret to you that Carter has pulled Perry down to the station for questioning." A sadness hung in Reba's eyes.

"No. I'm sorry. I hadn't heard." I wasn't about to tell her that I'd been snooping and found the reason for Carter to haul Perry to the station.

"I'm afraid it's all because of me." Her voice trailed off. "I probably shouldn't dump all my problems on you, but you've always been so kind."

I reached behind her for the last Flip-Flop on the tray.

"Here, you need this." I offered it to her.

"Yeah." She took it and closed her eyes after the first bite. "Everything you bake is amazing. It always makes me feel so much better."

"I use a dash of hugs." I winked, laughed, and reached out to touch her arm. "Why do you think that Perry talking to Carter is your problem?"

"Perry is the Grape Valley Winery lawyer. He does it all for free for his father and sister. He's so kind." Her tone sounded like her feelings for him were more than platonic. "There's a clause in the contract that states employees can't date."

"Does that include Ray Peel?" I asked and wondered if she was going to finally confess that she was dating Ray.

"I don't know. Who would've wanted to date him?" she asked me but continued with her story. "Perry and I are . . ." Her lips curled in, and she bit down like she was trying to stop from crying. "We are an item, and Ray told Giles. I was so scared I was going to lose my job. Giles says that workplace relationships make for a messy office, but Perry doesn't work at the winery. He only does the legal things."

"You and Perry?" I asked.

"Yes," she whispered, her eyes darting around the room. "The only thing is that now it looks like Perry had a motive to hurt Ray since Ray spilled the beans. But I would've quit before I broke up with Perry. Our age difference does play a part, but age is just a number. I feel alive and happy when I'm with him."

"I'm sure Carter will get it all figured out," I assured her. "Where was Perry at the time the coroner believes Ray was killed?"

"He'd come to the winery. While all the festivities were going on for the fund-raiser, we were going to have a little romantic time in the offices, but Tammy wouldn't leave, and Cat came in upset, so Perry hid in his father's office. That's when all the scuttle went down with Ray."

She'd just given me reason to take Perry off my list of suspects.

"Now I'm worried about whether Perry still wants to date me." She sniffled.

"There's no reason to keep you apart." I ran my hand down her arm. "You're free to date since the lease agreement is up."

"About that." Her brows pinched together in a frown. "There was a clause in the agreement that said Giles had the option to purchase the winery land if something happened to Ray."

"But you said that Tammy and Perry were in the winery offices when Ray was killed. What about Giles?" I asked.

"They didn't kill Ray. Giles was at home with his wife. The police have already cleared him," she said.

"Then what are you upset about?" I asked.

"If the Dugans do buy the winery land, then Giles won't take out the clause about no employees dating, and I'll have to quit my job." She put the last bite of the Flip-Flop in her mouth. "What if Perry and I break up anyway? Then I'll have left a good job for nothing. It's the age difference. What man wants to take care of a wrinkly old woman when he's still young and handsome?"

"Can I ask you again why you were seen with Ray?"

"Whoever killed Ray Peel, I could kill them," she spat. "Perry and I couldn't wait until the lease was up. Then we wouldn't have had to make choices about our relationship. We could date and enjoy each other."

"That meant you'd have to find a new job anyway. Maybe it's a good thing, and you can find another job. You're amazing at your job." Suddenly I had a brilliant thought. I snapped my finger. "I've got the perfect job for you."

"What?" she asked eagerly.

"Effie Glass down at the sheriff's department is retiring. They're looking for a replacement. You'd be perfect, and I hear it's great pay." It was the perfect solution.

Reba grabbed me, wrapping her arms around me.

"Sophia Cummings, you are heaven-sent." She squeezed me and hurried out the door.

While the women were debating the issue, I slipped out the door and ran right into Ella Capshaw.

"Sophia, I'm so thrilled to see you. I need to order a birthday cake for Grant. Something lavish." She pronounced these words with a grand gesture.

"I don't have any ordering pads on me, and I'd love for you to take a look at some of the cakes I've done for my New York City clients." I knew that when I mentioned the city, she'd have to see the designs. She was so egotistical. "Why don't you call Charlotte at the bakery and make an appointment? I couldn't possibly give you the attention needed for such an extravagant cake right here in the middle of the library."

"You are so professional. Thank you." Southern charm dripped off her like the pearls on her neck.

"By the way, I found out who almost ran you and Grant off the road on your way to the fund-raiser."

"Who?" she asked.

"There's a wine convention in town, and it was the lady in charge. Her name is Lanie Truvinski. She admitted she was going a little too fast for being unfamiliar with the roads and swerved a few times." It wasn't a great excuse for her excessive speed, but it was the truth.

"She's lucky she didn't kill someone. But at least we're all fine now." Ella clasped her hands together.

Cat Fraxman walked up. Her face was blotchy red.

"I'll give Charlotte a call." Ella waved bye and headed back into the meeting room where the Garden Club was coming to an end.

"What is it with you and your mother? Are y'all trying to destroy me?" Cat asked through her tears.

"What?" I asked. "I'm sorry if you feel this way. But it has to be brought up to the community that their beloved library expansion is only going to happen on a broken promise from Ray Peel that he was going to pay your family back for putting up the money. You did the only thing you could think of, out of passion." I patted my chest. "I get that. I did everything I could to buy the Fords' bakery. It's my passion. This is your passion." I sucked in a deep breath. "Maybe the community will be able to come up with something to help pay down the loan. We can do more fund-raisers after the ribbon cutting. What if we went around to local businesses and asked for donations? Something at the RCC?"

I was grabbing at straws. There must be something the community could do for the Fraxmans.

"I can't even think about this right now." Cat shook her head and sauntered back to the reference desk.

It was better to just walk away instead of trying to apologize. If I was in Cat's shoes, I'd be really upset too. She should have known better, but this community wasn't going to let her parents take the fall due to Ray Peel's ignorance.

Chapter Twenty-Three

"How could I have been so wrong about all those people?" I asked Duchess. She was sitting next to my feet while I stirred the Maple Long John ingredients in a medium saucepan so the milk wouldn't scald.

I'd already added the shortening, sugar, and salt.

"I truly thought one of them had killed Ray." There was something so unsettling about how I thought I could just figure out who killed Ray like I'd done before with Emile. It just proved I was no sleuth, and baking was my job.

I took the saucepan off the stove so it could cool to a lukewarm temperature. I reached up into a cabinet for a larger mixing bowl, ready to add in the water and yeast. I stirred more sugar into the yeast and whisked it all together.

"Everyone has an alibi." I whisked faster and faster because the mixture needed to become foamy, according to Dixie's recipe. Duchess looked up at me with her big blue eyes. Her squishy face made me smile. "At least we know that our house wasn't broken into because of Ray, so we just need to go on with our lives and let Carter do his job."

Now that her belly was full, Duchess ran off to the window seat and found a comfy spot to nap while I finished adding the eggs to the yeast, along with more milk, cinnamon, and flour. Kneading the dough was the perfect therapy for me to relax and get all the nonsense out of my head.

The dough had to rise for an hour before I could cut it into large rectangles. It was just enough time for me to get some comfy clothes on, put on makeup, and try to look decent for my dinner date with Carter.

After I'd gotten ready, I put the to-go containers that I'd picked up from Café Italia for our supper in one of my double ovens to start heating. Carter texted to say he was running a few minutes late, which I didn't mind since I wanted to get the maple glaze made for the Long Johns. I was eager to see just how it would turn out when I added salt to the maple glaze.

I used a small saucepan to add the butter, brown sugar, and milk before I brought it to a boil and simmered. I said a little prayer before I added the salt to the maple and powdered sugar. It was an odd combination, but I trusted Dixie Ford.

I used a hand mixer, just like her recipe called for. I closed my eyes and stuck my finger in the maple glaze and gently brought it up to my mouth so none would drip off.

"Mmm." My soul soared with the deliciousness. "I'll be," I whispered and stuck my finger in again, this time getting a little more to taste. "She was right. The salt takes out the too-sweet taste, and it's perfect."

It was one of those rare times that I wished I didn't have plans with Carter because I wanted to go to the bakery and just start cranking out the Maple Long Johns. That's how excited I was.

But I knew I couldn't do that. Now that I'd hung up my sleuthing cap for good, since all of my suspects weren't the killer and I'd found the culprit who'd broken into my house, I had plenty of time to be in the kitchen. And enjoying time with Carter was a number-one priority. I had just enough time to bake the Long Johns for seven minutes and get the glaze on them before Carter was at the door.

We headed outside to the lake behind my house, where I'd set up a little romantic table for us to enjoy a cocktail before we ate.

"This is a great night to sit out here." Carter uncorked the bottle of red wine, and I held the glasses.

"I've not taken full advantage of this house and this cute little pier, so I thought we could have supper out here tonight." I knew he was going to be so happy that I'd finally crossed off all the suspects on my list. It was going to be cause for celebration. "And I even ordered out from Café Italia. The food's in the oven, keeping warm."

"Sophia Cummings, just when I get a little upset with you, you go and do something so sweet I can't even recall what it was that I was upset about." He took his glass from me, and we clinked them together.

After a couple of sips, we each settled into the Adirondack chairs that Madison had given me as a housewarming gift. They were the perfect size for the little pier that jutted out into the small lake behind my house. I'd even found a small table to put between them, where Carter and I could set our wine glasses.

The lake was still. The last of the sun's rays exploded across the water in vibrant yellows and oranges. The chirps of the crickets grew louder and louder as the sun went down. Soon it would be dark.

"I have to tell you, this is a little celebratory supper." I pulled my feet up into the chair and sat sideways on my hip to face him. "I figured out who broke into my house and threw the brick into the bakery."

"You did?" he asked flatly and gave me a *yeah right* look.

"Yes. Dixie Ford's granddaughter," I said.

Carter sat still in awe, shaking his head, as I told him about it.

"I never saw that coming." He pulled his phone out of his pocket. "I've got to call the station and let them know, so they can stop going around looking for that type of brick." He hit a button and put it up to his ear. "Are you sure you don't want to press charges?" he asked.

"Positive." I sucked in a deep breath of the cool spring air and turned myself back around in the chair to face the lake.

I finally felt calm, sitting there taking in the sights and sounds of my amazing property. A feeling of gratitude covered my soul and warmed my insides like a quilt. Never in a million years would I have imagined living in Rumford would make me this happy.

Finding out who Ray's killer was would've helped, though.

"I brought Perry into the department today," Carter said when he got off the phone.

"Really?" I asked, as if I didn't know. I felt it was better to let him tell me about it. I didn't know that outcome, and I wanted to. "About the lease agreement?"

"The Dugans do have the option to buy the property now that Ray's dead, but all their alibis check out." He ran his hand through his hair. "This case is just a dead end, and the mayor is breathing down my neck to get it solved."

"I'm confident something will turn up." I took another sip of wine. "Did you know that Perry and Reba are an item?"

"Yep. You thought it was Reba and Ray." He laughed.

"Yep. Forbidden love and all." I finished off my glass. "Sounded like a good motive for murder to me."

"You already knew I talked to Perry?" He shook his head. "Of course you did."

"I saw Reba at the garden club meeting. She spilled the beans about their relationship. I just can't believe that they had all these stipulations in the employee contract and the lease agreement."

"The department doesn't want us to date other officers if we can help it." He reached over to pick up the wine bottle and pour us some more. "That's why you can't take over Effie's job."

"Speaking of Effie, did Reba come down and apply?" I asked.

"She did, and you'll be happy to know that she's got an interview in a couple of days." He stood up and held out his hand. "I'm starving. Let's go eat."

"Sounds good." I took the opportunity to hold his hand. We walked back to the house, side by side.

"I do have to say that I'm surprised none of your suspects panned out." Carter stood in front of the screen pantry door, looking at the chalkboard. "You had Tammy because of her son's tuition."

"Plus, she said that she would take care of Ray if her father wasn't going to." I took the lasagna for two out of the oven and turned it off. "You can mark her off since she, Reba, and Tammy were in the offices at the time of death."

The parmesan, mozzarella, and garlic aroma floated up from the dish, making my taste buds water. The cabinet door squeaked when I opened it to retrieve two dinner plates.

"You can scratch all of them off. And Perry while you're at it." I used a spatula to cut the lasagna and scoop some onto each plate. A long foil bag with two buttered breadsticks remained in the to-go bag.

"I feel bad for Catherine Fraxman." He drew a chalk line through her name. "I can't believe that Ray Peel left her parents with all that debt."

"And that's the key to your killer." I took both plates over to the bar. "All of the people that I thought were suspects had one thing in common. They were all promised something from Ray Peel, and he didn't follow through."

"I've looked through all his contacts. My men have combed his house. We've practically torn apart the winery. There's no hard evidence except the forensics that prove he was hit in the head with an object."

"You've looked into the Café Italia?" I was more thinking out loud than really asking.

"Everything." He opened the pantry door and got another bottle of wine from the small wine rack. "I guess we can cross off Lanie Truvinski."

"Yep." I set our wine glasses in front of our plates and took a seat on one of the stools.

Carter poured each of us a very generous glass of wine. It wasn't turning out to be the romantic and celebratory night that I'd assumed we were going to have. Instead, we sat in silence, taking mindless bites of our food. Both of us stared at the chalkboard with the crossed-out names.

* * *

"Duchess," I said as I looked at her standing at the front door after Carter left. I bent down and picked her up. "It appears we are safe, and we don't have to worry about anyone breaking in."

The past couple of nights it'd been hard to sleep because I was a little on edge that someone was truly trying to send me a message about my snooping. I was looking forward to a solid night sleep now that I knew better.

My cell phone chirped as I was turning down the bed and making a place for Duchess. It was a text from Madison. She said that she'd gotten a late-night call from Perry Dugan, and he wanted to see her in his office first thing in the morning. She told him that she had a breakfast date with me. She didn't, but she didn't want to go to his office alone. He told her I could come with her, but I couldn't attend the meeting. I texted her back, asking if she knew what this was about. She thought it could be her big break. Since the lease agreement had given the Dugans the option to purchase the property, she thought they might want to use her services.

The last thing she texted was to meet her at eight AM at Perry's office. Of course, I agreed. I was curious to see what he wanted.

Chapter
Twenty-Four

"Good morning," I sang out to Duchess when I realized we'd slept all the way until the alarm had gone off.

She purred and stretched her front legs out in front of her, spreading her paws right before she raked the bedspread.

I gave her a couple of good rubs down her back before I got up and quickly texted Charlotte to make sure everything at the bakery was okay. It was her day to open early. I felt bad because she'd been doing a lot more openings ever since I'd stuck my nose into Ray Peel's murder. Not that she hadn't egged me on.

Charlotte said everything was good and that we'd already gotten a couple of orders from people who'd been to the wine convention. Apparently, Lanie Truvinski had raved about my pastries, although participants had to take her word for it since none of my sweets were at the event.

I didn't want to spill the beans about the Long Johns. I

wanted to surprise her. The thought that I was going to get to eat one this morning along with my coffee made me rush off to shower and get dressed.

* * *

"These are so good." I slowly chewed and savored every bite. Duchess meowed with her head hung over her bowl of kibble. "Trust me, my food is much better than yours today."

After I'd eaten two, I had to force myself to put the rest in a container so I could take them to the bakery when I was finished with Madison this morning.

"I'm going to have to start running again," I said to Duchess, who was now full and happy, licking her paws before she rubbed them along the back of her ears. "Especially now that I know how to make these." I held the container up, but she didn't look like she cared in the least little bit.

I was careful to put the Long Johns in the passenger seat next to me so I could keep a hand on them and they wouldn't be flung onto the floorboard if I had to make a sudden stop. Thankfully, the Long Johns and I made it to Madison's office building safe and sound.

"There you are." Madison flung my car door open and tapped her watch.

"I'm early." I grabbed the container of Long Johns and opened it.

"Are those what I think they are?" Her eyes widened at the possibility.

"Uh-huh." I ho-hummed. "Go on. Eat one. I know you want to," I teased and held up the container.

She took it and I got out of the car. Her eyes darted around the inside of the container, doing what most of us did when we were children. She was looking for the one with the most maple frosting on top.

"I can't believe you got the recipe." She took one and licked her lips. "I can't wait to eat this."

While she devoured the donut, I filled her in on what had happened with Sally Ann and Dixie Ford.

"You won't believe it, but y'all were right about Patsy leaving her daughter with the Fords. Not only that, but you know my house break-in and the brick through the bakery window?" I asked her, but I wasn't sure she heard me because her eyes were closed, and there was a look of satisfaction on her face. She chewed and moaned. Moaned and chewed.

"I wonder where Patsy is?" I didn't dare ask Dixie that question yesterday. I felt like it was a touchy subject.

"I heard she'd run off with some guy she met down at the bar. But right now, I don't care. My mind is blown." She licked her fingers clean. "I'm not missing one single crumb of this."

"You're gross. I can always give you more." I put the lid back on the container and put it in the car before I hit the key fob to lock the doors. "Are you ready for a new car?" I asked. That was Madison's motivation for trying to score a big real estate deal.

"Yes." She bounced on her toes. "I'm guessing that's what this is all about."

"For your sake, I hope it is true. Plus, I have Lanie Truvinski's contact information, and she's got all the info on the clients who could possibly want to own a winery." I patted her on the back.

"Let's go find out." We started to walk up to the building but stopped when we noticed another car pulling into the lot.

"That's Catherine Fraxman's car," I pointed out. "I wonder what she's doing here?"

"I hope it's not about a foreclosure on her parents' house. Those things can take so long to sell." Madison and I both waved at Cat when she got out. We waited for her to join us.

"What's up?" I asked nonchalantly.

"Are you two here for the will reading?" She looked between Madison and me.

"Will reading?" My brows shot up.

"Perry called me and told me that I needed to be here because Ray Peel had mentioned me in his will. Perry was his lawyer." Every word out of her mouth filled me with curiosity.

"He texted me that he needed to see me at eight this morning, but nothing about a will." Madison pointed to me. "I didn't want to come by myself, so I asked Sophia to join me."

"A will reading?" I couldn't stop saying it. Why on earth would Ray Peel put Madison in his will? Or Cat, for that matter.

"Ladies." Perry Dugan greeted us at the door. His arm was extended as he held it wide open. "Come on in."

The three of us walked in. He gave me a weird look.

"I'm just here to support Madison." I shrugged and walked behind all three of them up the steps to his office.

"I'm going to have to ask you to wait in the lobby while I read the will." He didn't let me get any further than next to one of the plastic chairs that faced the receptionist I'd met earlier. "Do you mind taking the ladies back to conference room one?" he asked the receptionist.

She nodded and waved them to follow her. I heard her ask if they'd like a glass of water or a cup of coffee.

"I wanted to thank you for the cake. Reba loved it." There was a gentle tone in his voice that I'd never heard from him. Actually caring and loving. "I also know that Reba told you about us. As much as I keep telling her age doesn't matter, she seems to think it does. When she went in to apply for Effie Glass's job, Effie is like a mind reader. She asked if there was something on Reba's mind, and Reba felt like she could tell Effie about us. Effie really gave her some good advice." He reached out and touched my arm. "If you hadn't talked to Reba, she wouldn't have gone to see Effie and might've even broken up with me."

"Nah." I tried to lighten the situation. "The cake would've reeled her right back in." I winked.

"All joking aside, thank you." He dug a business card out of the front pocket of his trousers. "If you ever need any legal services, the first time is free on me."

I took the card and smiled. He headed down the hall, and when the door to the conference room clicked, I sat in the chair. After about thirty minutes, the group all emerged laughing and looking shocked.

"You aren't going to believe it, Sophia," Cat said, her eyes tearing up. "Ray Peel owned the old Benton estate, and he put it in his will to sell, using Madison as the real estate agent. The money from the sale of the estate is going to be used to pay my parents back for the loan."

"Perry said that Ray had come in a few days before he was murdered and put that in his will. He said he did it because he didn't have the cash to make the donation he'd promised Cat. By adding it to his will, he knew it was legal and would allow him to do good by Cat." Madison was all smiles.

"Why didn't he tell Cat?" I looked at Perry. "He just let her be upset at the fund-raiser."

"He was just the type of person who did business that way. He was very private. I didn't even know that he'd bought the property." Perry shrugged. "And we were best friends."

"What about the winery?" I asked.

"My dad and Tammy are going to use my dad's savings to come up with the money. I told them I'd help them only if they took out that clause Reba told you about." He shook his head. "But Reba insists she doesn't want to continue to work there, and she'd love to take over Effie Glass's job."

"Effie Glass is retiring?" Madison's lips turned down. "She's so sweet. When they had me in lockup a few days ago, she brought me a tea and one of your cookies."

"Maybe I can get her to volunteer in the new library space. She's always knitting, and the knitting club is planning on meeting there once the renovation is finished," Cat suggested. A great idea.

"I do know that she's coming to the ribbon-cutting ceremony, because she asked Reba to work the phones at the sheriff's department while she goes," Perry said, and we all laughed.

"I'll ask her then." Cat nodded and then turned to Madison. "Can we go right down to your office and get the real estate paperwork started?"

"Sounds like a plan. I'll let Bill Bellman at the bank know this can be used as collateral for your parents' loan until the sale. All the proceeds will pay off the loan once the sale closes." Perry rocked back on his heels. "Congratulations. It appears that Ray Peel has made good on something around here, to leave a better legacy."

Madison and Cat thanked Perry profusely before we left his office and walked downstairs to Madison's office.

"This is where I'm leaving you." I stood by the entrance.

"We are going to the estate to take some photos in about an hour. Please come," Cat begged. "I really want you to be there. You've been such a big supporter of the library since you've been home, and I was terribly awful to you after the Garden Club meeting. Maybe we can all go to a late breakfast or brunch afterward."

"You can take a day off. After all, you deserve to celebrate with us now that you've found the real recipe to the Fords' Maple Long Johns." I could tell there was no sense in arguing.

"Okay. I'll meet you two at the estate in about an hour." I looked at my watch. "One hour." I held up my finger so they knew not to be a second late.

* * *

Perry was trotting down the steps as I left the building.

"Perry, I do have a question. When Carter and I did some digging into Ray's life, there was never a deed for the estate." I wondered how we missed it.

"He had bought the house under one of his many limited liability companies. In fact, your boyfriend subpoenaed the will. I'm taking it to him now." He shook the file in his hand. "Now that I feel like I've done right by my best friend, I want him to rest in peace. I know Carter will find out who did this to him."

"Yeah. He will," I agreed.

We headed in opposite directions to our cars. When I got in, I pulled my phone out of my pocket and sent a quick text to Charlotte, asking if she was okay if I didn't come in until the afternoon. She could take off once I got there. She was delighted to be in charge of the kitchen, so it wasn't a problem.

There was no reason to head back into town, so I steered the car toward the old Bernstein estate. I'd always heard about it, but I hadn't seen it up close. It was one of those places that, when I was a child, seemed to be mysterious, like the scary house on the street, where you wondered what was going on inside. You could only imagine the gossip about that place.

No one ever talked about it, but we all knew that Mr. Bernstein had lived alone on the one hundred and ten acres of land. I could walk around and look at it while I waited for Madison and Cat. Besides, if I got hungry, I had my Long Johns with me.

Chapter Twenty-Five

I still couldn't believe that Ray had left his entire estate and money to the library. Even though Bitsy said that Ray Peel's mama was a huge reader and he'd spent more time at the library as a child than I had, I didn't remember him that way.

The estate had one main house along with a very secluded cabin near one of the lakes. It would be a perfect getaway.

Suddenly a brilliant idea popped into my head. I dragged my phone out of my pocket and quickly dialed Clarice Covington.

"Hi, Clarice. It's Sophia Cummings." I put the car in park and looked out the front windshield. It appeared that I had beaten Cat and Madison there. I looked at the clock on the dash and realized I was about a half hour early. They were probably finishing setting up the ribbon-cutting ceremony that was finally going to take place the following morning. What a relief Cat had to feel, being able use the property as collateral for the loan her parents took out.

They would no longer have to worry about going into bankruptcy. "I've got something to tell you."

Since the will had just been read this morning, I knew the news wasn't out yet.

"Does your property back up to the old Benton Estate?"

"It does. Why?"

"Ray Peel actually owned the Benson property. He left it to Cat in his will. She's hired Madison as the real estate agent." I got out of the car and walked up to the property. "He didn't live here, but I thought it would be a great place for you to expand the bed and breakfast."

"This sure is a turn of events," Clarice said.

"Apparently, he'd planned to give the library the money; it was just his assets that were about to be tied up." I jiggled the door handle, and it opened. "I'm not sure how much work the inside is going to need, but if you are interested, I know that Madison will be here soon, and you might want to drive over and take a look."

"I'll think about it." She didn't sound as excited as I thought she would.

"It's the perfect opportunity."

"Any news on his murder?" she asked. "Bitsy told me about your Operation Merlot."

"No. It appears that all my suspects had alibis. Now that Madison has been cleared, I guess I'm just leaving it up to Carter." I let out a sigh. Operation Merlot was no more.

"It's best you leave it up to the sheriff. Thank you for

calling. I'll think about the property and get back to you," she said.

"You can just give Madison a call if you decide you want to look at the property. Like I said, I'm not sure how much work it needs or how much Cat's going to ask for it. I immediately thought of you when I realized it was next to your property." I stepped into the house and was taken aback when I noticed the table lamp in the middle of the entryway was on. "I'll let you go."

I clicked off the phone and stuck it in my back pocket.

"What on earth? Was he living here?" I couldn't help but notice that the place was spic and span. Much cleaner than Perry had even alluded to. If I recalled correctly, Perry had said that the house hadn't been lived in since Ray had bought it.

Maybe I should've waited to call Clarice. Who knew how much Cat was going to ask? I'd probably overstepped my bounds.

No harm, no foul, I thought to myself when I let myself in the house. There was nothing that needed to be done to the place. The three-inch crown molding was a dark oak that appeared to be in great condition. The entrances to each room had decorative openings, not like the square doors you'd see in houses today. Even the hardwood floors were polished and shiny.

I made my way through each room and finally ended up in the kitchen. My heart stopped when my eyes took in the twelve-burner gas stove and double ovens. I didn't know who had ever cooked in this kitchen, but I could literally imagine the warm smell of cinnamon, nutmeg, and sugar that floated out of the oven.

When I'd first come into the house, I'd noticed there was a set of stairs that led to the second level. There was another set of stairs in the kitchen, and I wondered where they led.

My imagination got the best of me as I took each stair, but I stopped midway up and looked out the small round window. In the distance, the lake and small cabin looked serene. Why on earth hadn't Ray Peel lived here?

As I climbed the rest of the way, I took my phone out. I wasn't sure who I was going to call first, Madison or Carter. I couldn't wait to tell Madison that she was going to get that new car after all. This property was going to bring her plenty more than just money for a new car. Carter wasn't going to be coming out here, and Madison was, so I decided to let it be a surprise when she arrived, and dialed Carter's number.

"Dang." There was no cell service on my phone. I held the phone over my head and walked down the hallway, looking up a few times to see if I'd gotten reception.

There were at least six bedrooms: three on each side of the big staircase I'd seen when I first walked in, and a couple of bathrooms that were the size of bedrooms on each end of the hallway. What I took to be a door to a closet was actually a door to another set of stairs.

A third floor. This was a bonus. I was filled with excitement as I climbed the steps to a small loft that appeared to be an office. "I don't think they had Mac computers back in the day," I said to myself when I noticed the fairly new computer on the desk in front of the window.

There was a chaise lounge in the corner, with a rumpled-up cover draped on the end.

"There you are," I said to the gun that was sitting on the table next to a lounger; it had Ray's name personally etched on its wood handle. Apparently, Carter was wrong. Ray hadn't kept it strapped on his ankle at all times. I snickered and couldn't wait to tell Carter where the gun was.

I wasn't about to touch it either. Not that there was any sort of crime here, but if we'd all found out this was Ray's place, maybe the killer had known too. There could be evidence here. Clearly, in the past few days I'd proven myself not to be any sort of a credible sleuth. Still, that didn't stop me from looking around.

As I went to look out the window, I bumped the edge of the desk in front of it, and the computer screen came to life. There was a set user by the name of Ray Peel. I hit the "Enter" button, and a password screen flashed.

"Password," I whispered and decided to have my hand at it. "Why on earth did you have an office here, Ray?" I asked in the silence of the office.

I typed in the typical things like Ray_Peel, Raypeel, RayPeel. The screen jiggled, letting me know that I wasn't at all correct.

"Fine." I looked at my phone again and thought I should definitely call Carter. Maybe there was something here that he could pull for the investigation. After all, my list was null and void. As much as I wanted to hang up that sleuth hat, the fact was I'd not helped Madison.

I walked around the room with the phone in the air and couldn't get a single bar. If Clarice did purchase this land, she'd have no problem selling cell phone companies a spot on her land for a tower. Another source of income for her, and a reason she should purchase it.

Instead of trying to get a bar for service, I set my phone down on the desk. I had a few more minutes until Madison and Cat were coming by, and it wasn't going to hurt to look through the desk. The whole idea that Ray Peel had been living and working here was fascinating to me.

There was only one file in the drawer. I pulled it out and placed it on the desk, opening it. A piece of paper floated out and landed on the floor next to the chair. I bent down to get it. The sun darted through the window like a spotlight and made something shimmer on the floor.

Like a cat, I crawled out of the chair on my hands and knees and over the floor to find out what was sparkling.

"Strange." I sat back on the heels of my feet and held the earring up in the air. "Where have I seen this before?" I rotated it to see every angle. Images of Lanie Truvinski popped into my head, but it wasn't her lobe where I'd seen this earring. Then I thought about Tammy Dugan. It hadn't been her. My thoughts drifted to Reba; I would've remembered her wearing it, because of her super-short hair. I didn't think she even had pierced ears. *Think.* I shook the earring.

Café Italia popped into my head.

"The password." I pushed up off my toes, and with the earring in hand, I sat back down in the chair and carefully typed in CaféItalia. "Voilà!" I put the earring on the file.

A couple of beeps came from the computer, and a message screen appeared. Did Ray Peel have an iPhone? I couldn't remember what brand of phone Carter had told me Ray had, but I did remember he'd said that Ray didn't have any messages on his phone and that there weren't any unusual numbers on the cell log he'd gotten back from the subpoena.

If he didn't have text messages, then why were there some here? I looked at the messages and started to scroll through them. "Lizbeth," I gasped when I saw a text from her and remembered the earring that she'd been wearing the day I'd gone to the Rumford newspaper offices. She had been looking for the match to the exact one I'd just found. *But I thought you said you took it out of your ear when you talked on the phone,* I thought, recalling her desperately searching for it that day.

I clicked on the message bubble with her name on it.

You owe me the money. The text was from Lizbeth.

Having invited you into my bed was payment enough. Ray Peel's response made me sick to my stomach.

I'm going to go public with this. Lizbeth's response to him made me wonder what Ray owed her money for and why he'd responded to her about their obvious intimacy.

You do and I'll ruin your little newspaper and your career. I think I'll go ahead and let people know just how you do business. As I read Ray's comeback to her, I couldn't help but think Lizbeth had a motive to kill Ray.

Whatever it was that he owed her, could she have she wanted it so badly that she killed him? I kept that question in my head as I read through the rest of the messages.

I'll destroy you before I let you do that. You made me a promise.

What was the promise? I asked myself.

"*Oh, honey. Mighty men have tried to take me down. I dare you. Promises are meant to be broken.* I read the text from Ray out loud and could clearly imagine him saying it.

Pay me or else. This was a direct threat from Lizbeth.

Is that a threat? Ha-ha, Ray asked and appeared to be mocking her.

Just see what happens if you don't pay me. I read the last text from Lizbeth and looked down at the earring. "What on earth were you doing with Ray Peel?" I said aloud, and I held the earring back up to the window to get another look at it.

The cock of a gun caught my attention, and I jerked around.

"I've been looking for that."

I stared at the end of a handgun that was in the grip of Lizbeth Mockby.

"Why don't you just hand me the earring, and we'll talk about it," she said.

"Why don't you put the gun away?" I stood up with my hands in the air and with the earring dangling from the thumb and finger of my right hand. I glanced over at the table next to the lounger. The gun that'd been there was gone.

"I can't do that now that you've found my earring and read through the text messages." She held her free hand out in the gimme gesture. I dropped the earring in her palm, and she immediately shoved her hand into her pocket. "I really did like you. And the day you came to the office, I knew you were going to be trouble. I just never figured you'd beat me here."

I gulped and really wished I'd been able to make the phone call to Carter so he knew where I was. Knowing that Madison and Cat would be here soon didn't make me feel any better. I'd be dead by then, and Lizbeth would be long gone.

She stuck the gun in my ribs and said through gritted teeth, "Turn around and erase the messages. All of them."

"I'm not sure I know how," I lied, but I didn't really have much to lose. "Carter has Ray's phone. He probably already has your messages."

"I took care of the phone. I erased all the messages after I hit Ray. I didn't figure on this computer. I've been search- ing for my earring and just realized that I was wearing it the last time I was here." For a split second she looked toward the chaise lounge and frowned. "I truly thought we were going to be a great couple."

"I didn't even know you were a couple," I whispered and winced when she shoved the gun deeper into my ribs.

"Delete the messages," she insisted.

"Fine." I did know how to erase them, but if I acted like I didn't, then maybe it would buy me time. "Since you're going to kill me anyway, tell me: Why on earth would you kill Ray Peel?"

"He wasn't very good at keeping his promises." There was a crack in her voice. I could tell that she was very emotional, and I played on that.

"Just like a man," I said, agreeing with her just to get more time to think through what was going on. I clicked a few buttons to pretend like I didn't know what I was doing. "I didn't even know he lived here."

"I didn't either until the other day. He said that he was transitioning his office from the winery to this location for his new franchise adventure." Lizbeth seemed to know a lot more about Ray than I'd thought.

"Were you and Ray an item?" I asked, taking my time clicking down all the messages.

My eye caught one from Reba. It was exactly what she said she'd asked him about getting Giles to lift the employee dating rule.

"I found out that he was going to sell the property. He'd asked me to do a feature on the grand opening of Café Italia, and I told him I would be more than happy to do it if he put an ad in the paper. Ads are what keep the paper up and running." She was so dedicated to her job, just like she'd been in high school.

She stood over my shoulder and didn't jab me when she saw me hitting the "Delete" button.

"I hate computers," she spat.

"I'm not sure—what does all of this have to do with Ray Peel?" I went ahead and deleted Reba's message, knowing it'd go into the trash icon for Carter to find, just in case I did make it out of here alive and needed proof that Reba wasn't lying.

"He said he was going to take out a full-page ad and that would take care of my production cost for a couple of weeks, buying me a little time to help bring in more ads. Just like I got you to take out an ad for the bakery. He said that he wanted to see and approve the photos I'd taken at the grand opening. That's when I found out about him working out of this office."

"Did he not like your pictures?" I still didn't understand.

"Oh, he liked them. All of them. He also said he liked me, and he had this big spread of wine and cheese up here," she said.

I could see her reflection from the screen of the computer monitor. She turned her head and looked back at the lounge.

"Are you telling me that Ray Peel forced himself on you? Because if he did, then Carter will see this as self-defense." It was a long shot, but it was an excuse to get me out of here. At this point, I was willing to do just about anything.

"No. He said all the right things, and we did become intimate." The gun against my ribs started to jiggle around as she tried to steady her shaking hand. "I couldn't wait to get back to the office the next day to get his ad and the grand opening photos put in. I'd gotten a lot of great feedback, and he said that it brought in a lot of business. It was when I asked him to pay that he scoffed at me. He made fun of me and said that his payment was our intimate night together."

"I'm so sorry." It was Ray's usual song and dance. He was very nice and charming to get what he wanted, and then when it was time to collect, he tore people down.

"I didn't care about the one-night stand," she seethed. "It was his lack of respect for the newspaper. He just thought he could throw his words around town to people. When I was at the grand opening, he told this one girl with blonde hair how excited he was that she'd chosen the winery for the location of the convention she was hosting. He also told Reba that he'd take care of the lease issue with Giles Dugan." Her jaw tensed and her lips quivered. "At the fund-raiser, I was taking photos for Cat Fraxman. I overheard him tell her that he wasn't going to give her the money. He also told the blonde that he wasn't going to let her have her wine convention there, and then he told Reba that he did take care of the lease issue because he wasn't going to let them use the winery anymore."

When I finally got to her messages on the computer, she stopped and leaned over my shoulder. The entire thread was about him not paying for the ad and even a couple of threats about how he wasn't going to get away with this. She'd written that somehow, some way, she was going to make him pay.

"Erase it," she demanded.

"At what point did you decide to kill him?" I asked and scrolled down to the bottom of the thread.

"After the blonde slapped him, I knew I had to confront him. The text messages weren't enough. I followed him through the vineyard. He was nasty and said that I was following him because I wanted him. I told him I didn't want a liar and that he couldn't make promises to people and then just throw them away." She paused. She took a deep breath and looked at the computer.

I dragged the arrow icon on the computer over the trash icon and was ready to hit delete. When that seemed to pacify her, she continued.

"I told him that I was going to put an exposé in the paper and interview all the people he'd made veiled promises to and then gone back on. I told him how he was going to be exposed for how he ruined people's lives just to get ahead. I even threatened to dig into his background because I heard from the blonde how he'd made promises all his life to her and never held up his end of the deal. He said that he was the wealthiest man in the town and that no one would believe me because my 'little waste of paper' would be out of business soon enough. He said that no one read the paper anyways. They were googling and getting information online." She put her hand to her heart. "I stood there watching his lips move. I heard a few words here and there, but I was calculating a plan to destroy him."

I hit the "Delete" button and turned around to face her. She took a step back and held the gun out in front of her.

274

"So how did you kill him?" I had to know.

"I agreed with him. It took everything in my power to act like I believed another lie he was telling me. I said, 'You know what Ray? You're right. I'm going to do one last story, and it's going to be on the closing of the winery and how you're going off on this big franchise adventure.'" She drew a hand in the air like it was a Broadway marquee. "'Small-town Boy Makes Big-Time Moves.' He liked that. He suggested I get a picture of him by some of the vines we were standing near. He turned around and walked over to pose. When he turned around, I'd already drawn my camera up over my head to hit him as hard as I could. I knew if I got him to the ground, I'd hit him again and again until he was dead." Her voice faded, and she looked down at the camera hanging around her neck. She gently stroked it. "Little did I realize this fellow could take down Ray Peel in one hit." She smiled.

"That's why he had a look of shock on his face," I whispered.

"Now that there's truly no evidence in the computer and no one knows you're here, it's time I take care of you. I'm not a big fan of blood, so I think I'll use my weapon of choice." She slipped the gun in the waistband of her jeans. It was like she was in slow motion as she walked and drew that camera up in the air. "I hope you only have to have one whack too." There was a sick upbeat tone to her voice.

"You don't have to do this." I put my hand up. "I would never tell anyone. I think Ray got what he deserved. I'll buy a year of ads in the paper," I begged, squeezing my eyes shut.

When I realized she wasn't going to listen to me I jumped out of the chair and lunged forward in the hope that I'd be able to either push her out of the way or dodge the bullet to save myself. She gasped and grabbed my arm, and her nails ripped into my skin.

My goal was to stay out of the morgue drawer. My adrenaline took away the pain and any rational thoughts I had. I jerked my leg up, giving her a good swift kick to the knee, sending her to the ground.

"Stop right there, Lizbeth." The cock of a gun and Carter's voice sent a sudden surge of relief through me. I opened my eyes. "I know what happened. I got the messages from Ray Peel's cell phone carrier."

Lizbeth let go of the camera, and it thudded against her chest. Carter jerked the gun from her waistband.

"I'm not sorry I killed him." There wasn't any trace of remorse in her voice. If Carter hadn't shown up, I'm sure she would have killed me too. She was willing to do what she needed to do to keep the *Rumford Journal* alive and well.

Carter quickly cuffed her and read her rights. I could hear sirens approaching. It was over.

* * *

"All because of the newspaper." I stood in the foyer telling Madison, Clarice, and Cat what'd happened.

"If I'd walked in this house ten minutes earlier, I might've stopped her." Clarice looked at me.

"What do you mean?" I asked.

"After I talked to you on the phone, I got to thinking that it wouldn't hurt to drive over and look at the place. I saw that your car was here, and I recognized Lizbeth's because she has done some stories on the bed and breakfast in return for me putting an ad in the paper, so I figured she was here to do a story on the property." She shook her head. "I decided to go and get a look at that cabin near the lake. When I got back, all this was going on."

"So, are you thinking about buying the property?" Madison asked Clarice. "I'm representing the seller, and we'd love to entertain an offer."

Cat readily agreed. "Plus, all of the sale will go toward the loan on the new addition to the library. I'm willing to give you a good deal."

"I think we can make a deal," Clarice agreed.

Madison clapped her hands together and smiled widely.

"I guess this is kind of my revenge on Ray after he said I was only good for the less-fortunate clients." She laughed and put her arm around my shoulder. "Let's get you home."

"That sounds like a great idea," I said, nodding.

Chapter
Twenty-Six

The day had finally arrived, and Rumford was buzzing with excitement. The Garden Club had new banners with a photo of the library made for the lampposts along Main Street. The mayor even declared it Library Day and was going to give Cat a key to the city at the ceremony.

The two-story extension made the library the tallest and newest building in our small town. It was the living roof that was the most spectacular.

"Mother Nature was good to us today." Cat had on a very pretty A-line, flower-print dress and black flats. "Can you believe it's finally here?"

"I think it's pretty amazing." I looked around at the rooftop getaway. There were trees, bluegrass, and even moss that had the most beautiful green tones. The pops of red, yellow, white, purple, and orange flowers made the living, green-space areas of the roof stand out.

"These are amazing." I'd recreated different book covers on cookies and cupcakes for the occasion.

"I did a whole section for the children's addition." I pointed over to another display. "I could've done a lot more fancy desserts, but I knew there were going to be so many kids here with their families, and I really wanted the families to feel welcome. This is the heartbeat of the town, and if they ever need a safe place, you've created it right here."

Cat hugged me. Her face beamed with pride, as it should have.

"I can't thank you enough. When I asked you to cater the desserts, I never imagined how all this was going to come together." She wiped a tear that'd fallen down her cheek.

"This isn't a time for tears. It's a time for smiles and celebrations," I assured her. "Tell me, how are your parents?"

"After Clarice Covington signed over the check to buy the estate, I could see relief on my dad's face that he wasn't going to have to come out of retirement so he could put food on the table again." She pinched her lips together. "Who knew Ray Peel had a kind heart after all?"

"I still can't believe that it was Lizbeth Mockby who did it," Madison said, walking up to us.

Charlotte, Bitsy, Clarice, and Carter trailed behind her.

"Y'all are a little early." I looked at them.

"No," Cat said, "they are right on time."

A waitress from the food catering company Cat had hired walked up with a tray of champagne, as if right on cue. Carter took the liberty of helping himself to a flute off the tray and handing each of us our own drink.

"I'm not going to lie. When I'd heard you'd come back to

town months ago, I was curious how this was all going to play out." He stared straight into my soul. "I never thought you'd stick your nose into Emile's death and certainly wouldn't have thought you'd do it again with Ray Peel." He sighed. "No matter how much I begged you to stop, you couldn't do it. Your heart is so big when it comes to your family and friends that sometimes it just takes over your thoughts. And if it weren't for your curiosity about looking at his computer and finding his text messages, I'm not sure I'd ever have found out that Lizbeth Mockby was the killer." He held his glass into the air. "To Sophia. We are all glad you found your way home."

With tears in my eyes, I held my glass up and made eye contact with each one of my friends. They all held a special place in my heart. I was excited to see exactly where my relationship with Carter was headed.

"Sophia!" Sally Ann Ford ran toward me.

If it weren't for her voice, I'd never have recognized the little girl I'd seen a few days ago. Today her hair was out of the pigtails and hung straight down her back. Instead of the dirty jeans and Converse shoes, she had on a pair of black and red striped leggings and a school T-shirt to match.

"Sally Ann," I said, smiling and giving her a hug, "I'm beyond thrilled you're here. I wasn't sure if you'd come or not."

"When you called my granny and told her you had a surprise for me, I had to come. I was bursting with excitement. What do you have for me?"

"Sally Ann!" Dixie Ford gasped and put her hands on the girl's shoulders. "That's rude. I'm sorry, Sophia," Dixie said. "As you can see, we've been working on her becoming a little lady. We've got a lot of work to do."

"She's fine." I laughed remembering how hard it was to be her age. "Do I have time to give her something?" I asked Cat. I didn't want to be in the middle of doing that when people started to arrive for the ribbon cutting.

"You're fine." She turned her attention to Sally Ann. "I do hope you come and take advantage of the services we're going to have for preteens and teens."

"I hope so too. Granny and I talked about it." She looked at Dixie for assurance.

"We did. And I'm excited that the knitting club is able to meet here and do community projects." Dixie was finding her retirement groove, and that made me happy.

"We can go together," Effie Glass chimed in out of nowhere. "Now that Reba is going to take my job at the sheriff's department, I'm retiring."

"You come with me," I whispered in Sally Ann's ear while the women talked about retirement.

She followed me over to the pushcart I'd bought. I thought it would be cute to push it through the library while everyone walked around looking at the new addition and all the changes Cat had been working so hard on in the older part of the library.

Sally Ann was eager, and the smile on her face showed her excitement.

"I want you to know that I completely forgive you for my house and the bakery window. I didn't come up with any sort of punishment." I wasn't going to let her completely off the hook. "Granted, you could've handled it a little better, and I'm hoping when something like this comes up in the future, you'll think twice before you do anything." I pulled out a plate from a compartment on the side of the cart. One Maple Long John rested on it. "I made the recipe, and I have to say that these hold many dear memories for me too. So," I said, waving the plate in her face so she'd take it, "if you don't mind, I'd like to rename them Maple Memories."

She took a bite and then another, rapidly nodding her head.

"Did I hear you say Maple Memories?" Dixie asked walking up. Sally Ann held what was left of her donut up to Dixie's lips.

"You've created such a great memory for every person I know with this donut. It wasn't right for me to use your recipe without giving it an appropriate name." I watched as satisfaction spread across her face.

There was no greater compliment than that.

Peanut Butter and Jam Sandwiches

Ingredients

½ c. unsalted butter, softened
½ c. light brown sugar
¼ c. granulated sugar
½ c. creamy peanut butter
1 whole egg
¾ tsp. vanilla extract
1⅓ c. all-purpose flour
pinch of salt
¾ tsp. baking soda
¼ c. sugar for rolling

Ingredients for the Buttercream

3 T. unsalted butter, softened
¼ c. creamy peanut butter
1 c. powdered sugar
3 tsp. heavy cream
strawberry jelly

Directions

1. Preheat oven to 350°F.
2. In a stand mixer with the paddle attachment, cream butter and both sugars until light and fluffy, about 3 minutes.
3. Add in peanut butter and mix for 1–2 minutes.

4. Add in egg and vanilla. Mix until combined and clump-free.
5. Combine flour, salt, and baking soda in a small bowl.
6. Add the dry ingredients to the batter in two parts, with the stand mixer on the lowest speed. Mix for a little less than a minute. Do not overmix.
7. Portion dough into 12–16 cookies (depending on how big you would like them).
8. Add sugar to a small bowl.
9. Roll each cookie in the sugar and place on a silicone baking mat on top of a baking sheet.
10. Bake cookies for 10 minutes, until lightly golden brown and firm on the edges.
11. Remove from the oven and let set for 3–4 minutes.
12. Transfer to cooling rack to cool completely.
13. Once cool. frost half of the cookies with the peanut butter buttercream.
14. Spread jelly on the other half of the cookies.
15. Sandwich a jelly cookie and a peanut butter cookie together.

Buttercream

1. Cream butter and peanut butter in a stand mixer with the paddle attachment until smooth and creamy, 2–3 minutes.
2. Alternately add powdered sugar and heavy cream. Add more heavy cream if the frosting is too thick to spread.
3. Set aside until ready to frost the cookies.

Nanner Mini Pie

Yields: 24 mini pies

Ingredients

1 roll prebought refrigerated sugar cookies
1 box banana cream pudding, prepared according to
    package directions and chilled
1 banana
whipped cream for topping

Directions

1. Preheat oven to 350°F. Grease a 24-cup mini muffin tin. Divide sugar cookie dough into 24 even pieces, and roll each piece into a ball. Place dough in prepared muffin tin cups.
2. Bake dough until golden brown.
3. Remove from oven, and use the bottom of a shot glass to make depressions in each cup. Cool about 10 minutes.
4. Carefully remove cookie cups from muffin tin.
5. Put cookie cups on a cooling rack and cool completely.
6. Spoon a teaspoon of chilled pudding into the center of each cookie cup.
7. Slice banana and place on top of pudding. Top with a dollop of whipped cream.

Mud Puddles

Ingredients

Cookie Cups
½ cup margarine or butter, room temperature
½ cup peanut butter
½ cup sugar
½ cup brown sugar
1 egg
1¼ c. flour (I used all whole wheat)
¾ tsp baking soda
½ tsp salt

Filling
2 c. semisweet chocolate chips
1 can sweetened condensed milk

Directions
1. Preheat oven to 350° F and grease a mini muffin pan.
2. With a mixer, cream together butter, peanut butter, and sugars.
3. Beat in egg.
4. Add flour, baking soda, and salt, and beat until combined.

5. Drop teaspoons of dough into mini muffin pans.

6. Bake for 9–10 minutes until the center is set. Remove from the oven, and use a small, round object to make an indent in the center while still warm.

7. Let cool for 20–30 minutes before removing from pan.

8. In a medium pot, combine chocolate chips and condensed milk over medium-low heat, and stir until melted and smooth. Fill cookie shells and set aside to set for about 20 minutes.

9. Store at room temperature.

Cherry Flip-Flops

Ingredients

1 box puff pastry dough, thawed according to package
instructions
1 can cherry pie filling
1 egg white, lightly beaten

For the Vanilla Glaze

1½ c. powdered sugar
2 T. milk
1 tsp. vanilla extract

Directions

1. Preheat oven to 375°F.
2. Unwrap both packages of puff pastry, and cut into 8
   squares (4 from each dough).
3. Place a tablespoon of cherry pie filling in the center of
   each square. Brush the edges of the squares with the
   egg white and fold over to enclose the pie filling.
4. Bake on an ungreased baking sheet for 20 to 25 minutes, or until puff pastry is golden brown.
5. Let cool on a wire rack.

To make vanilla glaze

1. Combine the powdered sugar, milk, and vanilla extract in a bowl, and whisk until smooth.
2. Pour in a frosting bag or zip close bag, then snip off the tip or corner to pipe on the cooled turnovers.
3. Enjoy!

Peachy Surprise Bites

Ingredients

Peach Filling

2 peaches with skin removed, finely chopped
1 T. sugar
⅓ c. water

Pie Crust

2½ c. all-purpose flour
½ tsp. salt
16 T. cold butter
6 tablespoons cold water

Directions

1. In a small sauce pan combine peaches, sugar, and water and cook on medium heat stirring occasionally until the water begins to reduce and becomes more like a syrup.
2. Remove from heat, set aside, and let cool for 30 minutes.
3. To make the piecrust, combine flour and salt.
4. Cut butter into thin slices and add to flour. Combine flour and butter with a pastry cutter or two knives until flour is crumbly.

5. Add in cold water and mix until all the flour has been incorporated.
6. Roll into 2-inch balls.
7. Flatten balls with hands.
8. Place a few chunks of cold peaches into the center of the round. (You can substitute any fruit.)
9. Bring all of the sides together, and pinch shut.
10. Place on a parchment-lined cookie sheet.
11. Cut a small X on the top of the peach bite.
12. Once you have formed all of your peach bites, freeze bites for 1 hour.
13. To bake, preheat oven to 350°F.
14. Before baking, baste each bite with egg wash and sprinkle with sugar.
15. Bake at 350° for 15 minutes or until golden brown.

Mint Chocolate Chip Frosting

Ingredients

1 c. (2 sticks or 230 g) unsalted butter, softened to room temperature

3–4 cups (360–480 g) powdered (confectioners) sugar

2 T (30 ml) heavy cream

¼ tsp. peppermint extract (or more, see recipe instructions)

2 drops green food dye

pinch of salt, as needed

⅔ cup (120 g) mini chocolate chips

Directions

1. Beat softened butter on medium speed with an electric mixer. Beat for about 30–60 seconds until smooth and creamy.
2. Add 3 c. of powdered sugar, cream, peppermint extract, and food coloring.
3. Increase to high speed and beat for 3 minutes.
4. Add more powdered sugar if frosting is too thin or more cream if mixture is too thick.
5. Add salt if the frosting is too sweet.
6. You may also add more food coloring or more peppermint extract.
7. Stir in the chocolate chips.

Maple Memories
(Formerly the Ford's Bakery famous Maple Long Johns)

Ingredients

1½ c. milk
⅓ c. shortening (I used butter-flavored Crisco)
4 T. granulated sugar
2 tsp. salt
¼ c. lukewarm water
2 envelopes yeast
2 large eggs, beaten
5 c. flour (might need a bit more)
2 tsp. cinnamon

Maple Icing

⅓ c. butter
1 c. packed brown sugar
¼ c. milk
1½ c. powdered sugar
2 tsp. mapleine (found by the flavor extracts and
    seasonings) or maple extract
⅛ tsp. salt

Directions for the dough

1. In a medium saucepan, scald milk.
2. Add shortening, 3 T. granulated sugar, and salt. Stir to combine, and set aside to cool to lukewarm.
3. In a large mixer bowl, add the lukewarm water and the yeast. (Remember, the water should be just lukewarm; too hot and it will kill the yeast)
4. Add the remaining 1 T. sugar to the yeast and water, and whisk to combine.
5. Let sit for about 5 minutes until it starts to bubble and become foamy.
6. After the yeast is foamy and the milk mixture is lukewarm, add the eggs to the yeast, and stir to combine; then add the milk mixture to the yeast mixture.
7. Whisk the cinnamon into the flour and gradually add to the yeast mixture. You may need to add more. You want the dough slightly sticky, but not too sticky.
8. Knead for 3–5 minutes.
9. Spray another large bowl with nonstick spray. Place dough in the bowl and let rise for an hour or until double in size.
10. Punch down and roll out into a large rectangle about 1 inch thick.
11. Cut into rectangles to make 12 bars, then place on a greased baking sheet.
12. Let rise for about 30 minutes.
13. While bars are rising, preheat the oven to 425°F.

14. Bake the bars for 7–8 minutes or until light golden brown.
15. Cool slightly before icing.
16. Make the icing while the bars are rising.

Directions for the Icing

1. In a small saucepan, mix butter, brown sugar, and milk.
2. Bring to boil on medium heat, and simmer 3 minutes.
3. Remove from heat and cool for 15 minutes.
4. Add the mapleine, salt, and powdered sugar, and blend well with a hand mixer.
5. Add a little more powdered sugar if needed.
6. Spread on cooled maple bars and enjoy!